GRAVE SECRETS

GRAVE
SECRETS

a novel

CATHERINE SOETE

Mill City Press

Mill City Press, Inc.
322 First Avenue N, 5th floor
Minneapolis, MN 55401
612.455.2293
www.millcitypublishing.com

This book is a work of fiction. Aside from factual references to historic persons
and events, the characters, places, and incidents in this novel are either fictitious
or fictitiously depicted.

ISBN-13: 978-1-62652-879-6
LCCN: 2014912074

Cover Design by Alan Pranke
Typeset by Colleen Rollins

Printed in the United States of America

ACKNOWLEDGMENTS

Grave Secrets is a crime novel set in the fictional town of Bethany, Iowa, in 1973—a year best remembered for the long-running political scandal known as Watergate.

I am grateful for the Watergate timeline made available online by the Washington Post Company, as well as for the chronological details recounted by Keith W. Olson in his book, *Watergate*, published in 2003 by the University of Kansas Press.

Many thanks go to friends and relatives who took the time to read various drafts of *Grave Secrets* and offer comments and encouragement: Mary Bowers, Shirley Fister, Missy McKernan, Margaret Odorizzi, Deborah Ostrowski, John Ostrowski, Peg Ryan, Barb Soete, and Rita Soete. Additional thanks are owed to Deborah Ostrowski for researching questions about popular culture in the early '70s.

Matthew Lakin offered valuable information about automobiles, and Keith Chisamore answered my questions about drugs, drowning, and emergency assistance before the days of 9-1-1 and EMTs. I am also grateful to Dianna Graveman and Robert Schmidt for their copy editing assistance.

Through the ups and downs of writing, discarding, revising, and polishing drafts of *Grave Secrets*, my partner, Amy Fister, was there without fail. Her unwavering support, encouragement, and love are gifts beyond measure. To whom else could I possibly dedicate this book?

To Amy,
Always

CHAPTER 1

The faded barn stood with its broad doors wide open, just like any other Iowa barn on a mid-June morning. Unlike any other, this one had yellow tape draped from jamb to jamb.

Stationed right outside the cordoned entrance were an ambulance and patrol car, their shiny, patriotic colors a bit loud for the rustic landscape.

Carol Hagan knew she'd end up back at the crime scene, but she headed first for the cream-colored clapboard farmhouse at the top of the gravel driveway, where a second police cruiser was parked.

The signs of a recent move were obvious: flattened packing boxes stacked near a rusty ashbin, clean but uncurtained windows, tall weeds still triumphant in the flower beds.

She parked the car and ascended the steps to the wide, covered front porch.

"Good morning!" said a voice from inside as the front door opened before Carol could knock.

She jumped back with a start.

"Hi, I'm Carol Hagan with the *Daily Bugle*. Sorry to bother you, but I need to talk to Sergeant Padgett about the skeleton. Is he here?"

"He's over there," the woman said, pointing toward the barn with a box cutter. "Help yourself."

Carol returned to her dusty '71 Maverick and took a Pentax 500 from the trunk. Photography wasn't her forte, but reporting for a newspaper the size of the *Bugle* required knowing how to aim and shoot a 35-millimeter. She kept a wide-angle lens on the camera to capture the usual subjects—auto accidents and house fires.

At a distance of about twenty yards, she took three quick shots of the barn, capturing the Cadillac ambulance and the Dodge Polara cop car in the foreground.

When she reached the barn's entrance, she lowered the tape and stepped over it, calling out to identify herself.

"I didn't think it'd be long before you'd be out here," a man's voice said from above. "We can't keep Lois Lane away from the scene of any crime."

Anyone else, she'd have been annoyed, but Jack Padgett's teasing was tolerable. Among Bethany's uniformly tight-lipped cops, Padgett was a friendly exception.

"Maybe I wouldn't have to be slogging around the back forty right before deadline if a certain investigating officer had turned in his report properly," Carol parried as she climbed the hayloft steps.

"Watch who you accuse of impropriety. I turned in what I had."

"Then it must have been nothing, because that's what I found in the log. If Donna hadn't given me a heads-up, I wouldn't have known anything about this. She said if you didn't have the write-up out here, Chief Bryce must have taken it. Why would he do that?"

Padgett frowned. He had put the report in the log when he got back to the station around five yesterday afternoon, two hours after the shift change. It was his only write-up of the day.

"Beats me. I can give you the info now, though. They're just about ready to transport the remains to Fort Madison to determine the cause of death and start the process of identifying the body," Padgett said, gesturing toward two men who were preparing to lift the bones into a body bag.

Keeping a healthy distance between herself and the skeleton, the reporter scrawled notes in a pathetic version of shorthand as the sergeant filled her in.

The farm's new owner, Miss Joan Sizemore, had spotted a tarpaulin under a shelf in the loft at approximately 2:15 p.m. on Tuesday, June 19. After pulling back the top portion of the tarp and seeing the human hair and skull, Miss Sizemore immediately returned to the farmhouse and called the police. Padgett arrived at 2:35 p.m., took a statement from the property owner, cordoned off the scene, and conducted a brief investigation. Then he notified the Lee County sheriff and the medical examiner, both in Fort Madison. They had agreed that this morning would be soon enough to collect the remains.

The victim was an adult male, about six feet tall, with brown hair. The lower part of his skull was caved in. The ragged remains of clothing suggested that death had occurred in warm weather. The victim had been wearing khakis, a cotton shirt, T-shirt, briefs, socks, and a pair of brown oxfords. There was no wallet or jewelry. After their joint investigation, Padgett and Officer Matt Wilson concluded that the homicide had occurred elsewhere and the body probably had been moved to the loft by two men.

"Someone acting alone couldn't have gotten a body this size up the steps, and there wasn't room for more than two to maneuver the dead weight," Padgett said.

"Any idea how long he's been here?"

"Judging from the state of the remains, plus the fact this place has been vacant for two years, I'd say it's been about that long," Padgett said.

"Donna said nobody local's been reported missing, is that right?"

He nodded.

Carol looked at her sparse notes, wondering what else to ask. "Any idea where he was killed?"

"Probably someplace outdoors. Me and Wilson looked through the house and all the outbuildings," he said, pushing his brimmed cap back to reveal thick, curly black hair wet with sweat. "Miss Sizemore told us she cleaned the house thoroughly before moving in and saw nothing unusual. We didn't find anything that resembled a weapon or see any signs of blood in the outbuildings.

"If you want my guess, I think the killers used a car, maybe a truck, to transfer the body to the most forsaken place they could find to hide it. If that's the case, their plan worked pretty well. The trail is freezing."

The ambulance driver and the ME's assistant lifted the black vinyl bag of bones off the loft's plank floor and carried the unwieldy package down the stairs and out to the ambulance. Carol recorded the sunlit portion of their morbid activities with her Pentax.

"Thanks, guys," she said with a wave. "I'll come back by the station later this afternoon and talk to the chief."

She checked her watch as she walked away from the crime

scene. Ten after eleven. No time to drive back to the newsroom. She'd have to call the story in.

CHAPTER 2

"Thanks for letting me use your phone," Carol said, replacing the receiver in its cradle on the wall of the farmhouse kitchen, whose floor was littered with open boxes and wadded newspapers. "You must have been shocked when you saw the skeleton up there."

"Now, *that's* what I would call an understatement," Joan Sizemore said. "Things had gone so smoothly my first twenty-four hours here. I was hoping Governor Ray's 'Welcome to Iowa' would last at least another forty-eight."

Monday night, after carrying in the last box from the U-Haul trailer, Joan had relaxed with a hot bath and an icy Scotch and water, and then fell blissfully asleep to the buzz of cicadas.

She turned in the rented trailer Tuesday morning, planning to spend the rest of the day unpacking, sorting, and storing. But the urge to take a closer look at her property proved too strong.

In early February, when Joan had driven up from St. Louis to inspect the Sizemore homestead, the weather had been freezing, the land frozen. Then, when spring arrived, an epic flood came with it. Only now, in mid-June, was the land finally firm underfoot. The sweet-smelling farmyard grass, more untamed than her uncle had ever tolerated, lured her outside as it had when she was a child. She took a break from unpacking to take a good look around.

Stepping into the old barn, Joan felt nostalgic for the childhood summers spent with her Uncle Ed and Aunt Kate. In those days, the building had hummed with the sounds of animals and machinery. Now it was silent.

One of her favorite places as a girl had been the loft, where she would seek out the cats that slept in the hay bales, resting up for a night of mousing.

For the first time in twenty years, Joan climbed the loft steps again. This time, there were no cats, and the only remainder of hay was a fusty smell hanging over the emptiness. The loft was darker than down below but light enough to see the shelf along one wall where her uncle used to store machine parts and odd items he wasn't ready to discard.

She swung open the large wooden window and briefly surveyed her property from above, then turned back toward the empty loft. The dust-laden rays of afternoon sun pointed directly to a long shape under the shelf. She walked toward it with an intuitive dread and pulled back just enough of the tarp to catch a glimpse of brown hair on a fleshless, human skull.

Goose bumps raised the hair on her arms as she shivered in revulsion. Without another look, she ran down the loft steps and back to the house to call the police.

"Maybe Sergeant Padgett was only trying to make me feel better," Joan said to Carol, "but he said he thinks the abandoned barn was just a lucky pick by fugitives looking for an isolated place to dump a body. I guess your paper will play this up, won't it?" she asked, already sure of the answer.

Carol nodded. "As a rule, unexplained human skeletons are news. Besides, Sergeant Padgett can't be so sure, this soon, that the victim isn't from around here. You've got to follow the evidence." Then she laughed. "Listen to the expert. Counting this one, I've covered one homicide in my time as a reporter."

"How long is that?"

"If you don't include my stint on the *Columbia Missourian*, all of a month. This is my first reporting job that pays."

The reference to the daily newspaper published by the journalism school at the University of Missouri made Joan feel a little more comfortable with this stranger in her home. Hearing that Carol was a recently transplanted St. Louisan, Joan visibly relaxed.

"I'll need a follow-up for tomorrow's paper," Carol said, noticing the shift. "Is there anything you can tell me about who lived here before you?"

"There's little to tell. My aunt and uncle bought the place right after they got married. When they died four years ago, their son Michael inherited it, but he hasn't lived here since he was a kid. He went to college in Des Moines and moved to California when he graduated."

"This house has been sitting vacant since your aunt and uncle died?"

"Some newlyweds rented it for a while, but they left a couple of years ago. Michael said a local handyman kept an eye on things after that."

"Have you told your cousin about finding the skeleton?"

Joan hesitated, then shook her head. "I didn't even think to. Michael hasn't been around here in so long. A local real estate agent and title company handled the paperwork for the purchase. We did everything by phone and mail. He wouldn't know anything about this."

"Well, he could give you the name and number of the handyman. Maybe he noticed something. Can you call your cousin?"

Joan glanced at the wall clock tilted against a ceramic canister on the counter. It was almost ten in California.

"I can try, but he's probably on the road. His real estate business takes him up and down the coast."

Joan dialed the number and waited in silence while the phone rang eight times. "No answer," she said as she put the receiver back. "I think I might have better luck this evening."

"Would you mind if I check later to see if you were able to reach him?"

"Sure. Call me around nine. My number's right there," she said, pointing to a plastic label on the front of the wall phone. "Haven't memorized it yet."

As Carol jotted the number in her notebook, Joan admired the bright white Kenmore range the Sears deliveryman had installed earlier that morning.

"I've got an idea," she said. "If you don't have any plans, why don't you come back later when I try Michael again? It would be more fun to try out my new oven cooking for two."

So far, Carol's social life in the little town of Bethany hadn't gotten beyond late-night burgers and conversation with Tim Terrell, part-time reporter for KKYX radio, after city council or school board meetings.

When there were no meetings on her schedule, Carol's evenings "out" consisted of walks in the neighborhood that surrounded her furnished apartment on Harrison Street. Besides cheap rent, the main advantage of living on the once-grand street was that it intersected with Riverview, a tree-lined boulevard atop the bluffs of the Mississippi River. Riverview was where many of Bethany's more affluent residents lived in large old stone homes with French doors that opened onto backyard terraces overlooking the river and neighboring Illinois.

After a walk and dinner, Carol usually spent her evenings reading, keeping the radio tuned to Cardinals' baseball games.

"I don't have any plans for tonight. Dinner sounds great."

"Good. Come back at seven thirty. I'll try Michael a little before six, his time, and see if I can catch him at home."

CHAPTER 3

On the drive back to the *Bugle*, Carol wondered how she
would report on an old, cold homicide. It wasn't the
type of story they typically assigned in J-school.

Without an identified victim, possible suspects, or a trail of
evidence to follow, it was unlikely the sheriff's office, the state
patrol, or the Department of Criminal Investigation in Des
Moines would devote any manpower to the cause. The Bethany
police and the county medical examiner probably would be her
only official sources of information.

When she got to the newsroom, she would pick the brains
of her managing editor, Charlie Vogler, and Bob Hartman, the
paper's state editor, to see if they recalled anything sinister from
the farm family's past that the newly arrived niece didn't know—or
wasn't telling.

She'd check the *Bugle*'s morgue, where clippings from past
editions were stored, to see if old news articles about the Sizemores
suggested homicidal motives.

Sergeant Padgett's assertion that no one had gone missing in recent years was something she would need to confirm.

Noting the distance between farmhouses along Route 2, Carol was pretty sure that unless fireworks were involved no neighbor could ever see what occurred on another neighbor's property. Still, there was a chance that maybe someone had noticed something out of the ordinary at the Sizemore farm. She decided she would call all the homes on Route 2.

By late afternoon, Lee County's medical examiner probably would have completed the autopsy and be able to tell her what had killed the man in the barn. At least she would know that much before leaving the newsroom for the day.

Her last stop before heading home would be the police station. With luck, Chief Larry Bryce would be in his office and willing to talk to her.

Carol pulled alongside the hooded parking meter that reserved her spot in front of the two-story, red brick *Bugle* building and greeted a handful of picketers with a smile and a wave. Skilled linotypists all, the men could have found work at any big city newspaper in the country. But here in Bethany, all they could do was pace the sidewalk with signs, their real jobs now obsolete.

Since late winter, the *Bugle*'s newsroom and advertising staffs had been typing their copy on word processing equipment, eliminating the need for the nimble-fingered tradesmen to set type by hand. While it was bad news for the linotypists' union, the newspaper's investment in automation had been a "pro" on Carol's list when deciding whether to start her reporting career in a town of only 12,490.

Arriving at the *Bugle*'s second floor, Carol stopped in the photo lab, a cramped work space between the news and advertising departments. Kenny, the part-time photographer and darkroom technician, would punch in after Carol was gone for the day, so she put the roll of film on his desk along with a note asking him to make four-by-six prints of all the shots from the farm and leave them on her desk.

When she entered the newsroom, Charlie Vogler and Bob Hartman were reading the day's edition at their desks. The page one article above the fold was headlined, "Skeletal Remains Found in Barn on Rte. 2." Charlie had run the story with her byline, just as she'd dictated it to him over the phone.

"What did you find out, Carol, ol' girl?" Charlie said with a good-natured grin. "Do we have a good story cookin', or what?"

"Until I talk to the ME, all I've got for sure for tomorrow are some shots of the Sizemore barn cordoned off and the body bag being carried out, plus more of the homeowner's story about how she found the skeleton. I want to check a few things here and then I'll call Fort Madison.

"Can either of you remember anything about the Sizemores that could connect them to a victim of homicide?" she asked the two men, almost certain neither would answer "yes" to such a question about upstanding townsfolk.

Bob Hartman scratched the right edge of his brow as though riffling through a mental filing cabinet.

"You know, the only thing noteworthy I can remember about the Sizemores is that they died within a few days of each other," he said. "Kate Sizemore died first, and then Ed, which isn't really unusual. The old man often goes right after his wife dies. Both of them had bad tickers."

"What about the son, Michael? What's the story with him?" Carol asked.

Bob furrowed deeper, trying to remember something helpful.

"Michael Sizemore's been gone since long before I got here in '60," inserted Charlie, a fiftyish native of Chicago who had been trying to adapt himself to the rural Midwest for thirteen years. "What, Bob, didn't he leave right after high school?"

"That's right. Went to Drake, up in Des Moines. He'd come back to visit his parents every now and then, and for their funerals, of course. He's lived out in California for quite a few years," Bob said.

"It sure doesn't look like the skeleton came from the Sizemores' closet," Charlie said, happily clapping his hands for having gotten off the predictable line before Bob.

His two editors groaned in unison.

After both men agreed with Sergeant Padgett's assertion that none of Bethany's residents had disappeared, Carol headed for the morgue to look through the alphabetized envelopes in their narrow file drawers.

There wasn't much in the *Bugle*'s files about the family of three who had lived on Route 2. In Catherine Dixson Sizemore's flat little envelope, her death notice stated that she had died of heart disease on February 23, 1969, at the age of sixty-seven. Edgar Lee Sizemore's notice said he had died of a heart attack on March 4, 1969, at the age of seventy-one. The only clippings in their son Michael's envelope were his parents' death notices and the rewrite of a press release from Drake University announcing his graduation in May 1952, with a BS in business administration.

When Carol reentered the newsroom about one thirty, sports editor Tom Matthews was pecking at his computer keyboard with two index fingers, writing his column for the next day.

Ron Davidson, the wire editor, was reading the paper, feet up on his desk.

"Thanks for picking up the hospital notes for me, Ron," she said. "Could your heart stand the excitement?"

"No problem," Ron said with a slight smile and a shrug. "We missed you at lunch."

Once the presses started rolling at eleven thirty each morning, Carol usually went to lunch with Ron and Tom at the Brass Kettle Café, a block and a half east on Main. Their lunchtime conversations typically meandered through the news of the day, including the latest from the Senate Watergate hearings, which had begun on May 18, the Friday before Carol had arrived in Bethany; and highlights, if any, of the previous day's Cardinals' game.

When she had first arrived at the *Bugle*, taking long lunches had seemed like loafing on the job. But guilt dissipated when Carol got into the routine of work days that sometimes spanned fifteen hours.

Charlie wanted her to write two or three human interest profiles or feature stories a week, cover proceedings in police court and small claims court, and report on evening meetings of the Bethany School Board, city council, and the county planning and zoning commission. On mornings after one of those meetings, Carol usually got to the office by six thirty to write the story before collecting news from the police and fire departments, City Hall, and Bethany Memorial Hospital.

"What happened out there?" Ron Davidson asked her, folding up the newspaper and swinging the large feet that supported his tall frame back to the floor.

"If I go along with Sergeant Padgett's guess that the skeleton doesn't belong to someone who lived in Bethany, then I'm thinking the victim was killed here or not far from here," Carol said. "It was warm weather. The killers weren't going to hang out in the heat with a corpse for too long.

"Do you remember seeing anything on the wires about a missing person or escaped convicts a couple of years ago?"

"At thirty-five, I'm far too old to rely on memory for unsolved mysteries," Ron said. "For that, I have my own private 'morgue.'"

He opened the left bottom drawer of his desk and pulled out four manila envelopes, dated for each year he had been at the *Bugle*. Each envelope contained several pages of folded wire copy, tinged the faded yellow of aged newsprint.

"The seed corn of future novels?" Carol asked, trying to raise an eyebrow but breaking into laughter instead.

The shy editor just shook his head and smiled.

"I've got to make some phone calls now and then go see Chief Bryce," Carol said. "Let me borrow these overnight. I'll see if I can find anything that might be connected to the Sizemore barn skeleton."

"Watch out, Hagan!" said the sports editor, who had been listening from his desk on the other side of the room. "You're gonna make the rest of us look bad if you go gittin' all ambitious."

"Stay out of this, Matthews," Carol said, wadding up a piece of copy paper and hitting him with it square in the back. "Nobody comes between me and a good story!"

CHAPTER 4

Simba jumped on a kitchen chair and rubbed his furry head against Carol's hand, begging for attention. This new housemate, an orange tabby, was an unintended consequence of the reporter's quest for a feature story at an animal shelter.

He watched her with a predator's focus as Carol opened a can of tuna. She watched him with a trace of envy, hoping her dinner at Joan Sizemore's would serve up something substantial for tomorrow's follow-up on the skeleton.

"Blunt force trauma to the head" had been the ME's pronouncement on the cause of death, and that would be her lead. After that, Carol had nothing. No identification of the victim had been made, nor did the authorities think one would be made soon. Almost everything else the medical examiner had told her she had already gotten from Jack Padgett. The skeleton belonged to a male, between forty and sixty years of age, five foot eleven, brown hair. His dental x-rays would be sent to the DCI in Des Moines, in search of a match with a missing person.

Carol's calls to the residents of Route 2 had turned up no clues, hints, or helpful suggestions as to who the victim might be, where he might have come from, why he was killed, or how his body landed in the Sizemore barn.

The neighbors all had known Ed and Kate Sizemore, were sympathetic when they died, went to their funerals, and then went on about their lives.

The young husband and wife who had briefly rented the farmhouse had kept to themselves. They moved away almost before anyone noticed they were there, after which the house sat vacant.

One neighbor volunteered that it was a shame the Sizemore boy never seemed to appreciate farm life.

Chief Bryce had been cordial when she stopped by his office. Before she could ask him about it, he apologized for absentmindedly locking Padgett's report in his office the day before.

"The wife tells me I'm getting forgetful, Carol. I usually deny it, but I guess she's right," Bryce had said. "My specs were on my desk, so I brought the report in here to read and then forgot to return it to the logbook when I went out. Sorry for the inconvenience. Padgett said he filled you in out there this morning. What you have in today's paper is as much as we know."

Carol asked if he had any theories about the who, what, why, or how of the skeletal remains.

"Nothing I want to speculate about on the record," he had said. "The trail is obviously cold from an investigative standpoint. I think you can just quote me as saying, 'We'll let the Department of Criminal Investigation in Des Moines do its work, and then we'll go from there. If they can give us an ID, we'll be happy to work with the concerned jurisdictions, as much as we can, to learn what happened.'"

As usual, his comments were noncommittal. Carol couldn't figure out whether the chief was an utterly bland man or just unwilling to give Charlie Vogler's paper any more information than he had to.

"Don't you think it's strange, Chief, that somebody would go to all the trouble to hoist a body up to a hayloft rather than just bury it somewhere in the woods?"

"Ask me if I think it's strange that people beat one another over the head in the first place. Sure, it's strange. But people who do that sort of thing are a different breed altogether."

"But how can you catch them if you don't try to imagine what they're thinking?" she said, coaxing him to speculate.

He didn't bite. "Listen, Carol, I don't *want* to know what they're thinking. I'd just as soon not deal with the criminal element at all. My job is to keep the peace among law-abiding citizens, not track down killers. If I'd wanted to do that, I'd have joined the FBI," he said with a complacent smile. "Don't worry. Sergeant Padgett or I will be sure to fill you in on anything we learn."

She thanked him and headed for home.

It was six o'clock. Joan had told her to come for dinner at seven thirty. She would freshen up and then take a look at Ron's old wire copy.

Before stepping into the shower, Carol fastened a barrette to hold back her shoulder-length hair and inspected her appearance in the mirror on the bathroom door. Her lean figure was the result of a love of tennis and a habit of walking, not any trace of abstinence. She didn't think of herself as pretty, but she'd heard enough from others about her brunette hair and dark brown eyes that she didn't spend time worrying about her looks.

CHAPTER 5

Strewn on Carol's bed were the contents of Ron's "1971" envelope.

Of ten articles, only three had Iowa connections. One was a story about the apparent ritual mutilation of three horses in Storm Lake, a town in northwest Iowa. Another was about a woman from Des Moines, who had committed suicide in a hotel in Santa Fe, New Mexico. The third was a profile of a disabled World War II veteran from Fort Madison, whose family was urging the Army to award him a Purple Heart. None of the stories seemed connected to the bones found in the barn.

Maybe in his daily rummaging through the streams of copy that clattered off the AP and UPI wires, Ron had overlooked a missing person who was now much worse than missing. Or perhaps, Carol mused, he had failed to notice the news of gallivanting criminals in summer of '71 who ultimately killed one of their own in southeast Iowa.

Carol's expectation of finding any clue in envelopes "1970," "1972," or "1973" fell far below her hopes for "1971." She would look through those envelopes on the other side of dinner. First, though, she wanted to learn if Michael Sizemore had any idea why his barn was chosen as a grave site.

CHAPTER 6

Joan was cutting tomatoes for a salad when she heard Carol Hagan's automobile tires crunching the gravel driveway. Even though the occasion wasn't exactly her idea of festive, she was happy to be occupied with the here and now of putting a meal on the table. She feared that if her mind wandered back to yesterday's grisly scene in the barn, less than a hundred yards from where she now stood at the kitchen sink, a dark mood might overtake her.

For that, she could have stayed in St. Louis.

"Hello again," Carol said when Joan answered the door. "I hope Chablis will go with dinner." She extended a brown bag containing a chilled bottle of white wine from the state liquor store, the only place in Bethany where one could buy packaged liquor.

"Thanks. It will go perfectly," Joan said, taking the package. "You must have seen the menu."

Joan led the reporter into a kitchen brimming with the mingled aromas of roasting chicken, celery, onions, and potatoes.

"It's delicious in here," Carol said.

"Home cooking once again transforms a humble abode!" Joan said, dramatically spreading her arms to encompass the plain farmhouse kitchen with its pale yellow walls and black-and-white-checked linoleum floor. Cardboard boxes, which earlier had filled the middle of the room, now stood neatly stacked against the camelback staircase that led to the second floor.

An uncurtained casement window above the sink gave a view of the faded red barn, an untended lawn, a few crab apple trees and a manmade pond. Ed Sizemore had devoted most of his modest farm to corn and soybeans, but he had reserved an area between the house and barn as a playground for his son, neighbor kids, and city cousins.

"I'm having a little J&B on the rocks. What would you like?"

"Chablis is good for me," Carol said. "If you point me in the direction of a corkscrew and wineglass, I can pour my own."

While Joan continued preparing the salad, Carol sipped wine and reported on the medical examiner's statement and the rest of the day's inquiries.

Though she didn't say so, Joan felt relieved that neither the neighbors nor the reporter's co-workers had anything negative to say about her aunt and uncle.

"The chicken's got about fifteen more minutes. I'll give my cousin a call. It's close to six out there; he might be home."

"Don't forget to ask about the handyman," Carol said, taking a notebook from her purse.

Joan stood at the wall phone, listening to another phone ring eighteen hundred miles away in Los Angeles. Then she smiled and nodded at her guest.

"Michael, it's Joan. I'm so glad I caught you at home. Do you have a couple of minutes? I need to tell you about something that's happened here."

She described the events of the last thirty hours in an even voice, without drama or exaggeration. Then she listened.

"Don't feel bad about it, Michael. How could you have known?" She listened again and said, "But you had someone looking out for the place."

Joan took the notebook and pen that Carol offered her, jotted down a name and number, and wrapped up the call. "Yes, I'll let you know as soon as we find out anything. Thanks, Michael. Enjoy your evening."

She turned to the reporter with a shake of her head.

"He's as mystified as me. He said he had thought about coming back here to check on everything before I closed on the place. Now he feels terrible he didn't, but neither of us thought it was necessary. Everything was left in good shape when the renters moved out."

Carol looked at the name Joan had jotted in the notebook.

"Dan Taylor?"

"Michael said he hired the guy through an employment office. He's never met him in person. Do you think he might know anything about this?"

"I don't know," she said, putting the notebook back in her purse. "I'll call him first thing tomorrow and find out."

The wine was doing its work. Carol stopped worrying about the skeleton follow-up and simply enjoyed the break from her routine of solo dinners.

"So, what in the world had you move a hundred eighty miles upriver from St. Louis?" she asked.

Joan laughed. Usually reserved with strangers, she surprised herself with a willingness to open up about her recent past. Maybe it was because she was sitting in a familiar kitchen that, while not yet entirely *her*, was entirely hers.

"Did you ever get to a spot in your life when you just knew you had to make a change, no matter what anybody else said?" Joan asked.

"Yep." Carol nodded emphatically and recounted the spring of her second year as an English teacher. Contracts for the next school year were on the table and the job market was tight. It seemed foolhardy to quit, but she knew her only options were to find a new career or jump off the Eads Bridge.

Joan gave a smile of recognition. "My husband, Dave, and I divorced last summer after eight years of marriage," Joan said. "To hear my friends tell it, that was all the change I'd need for the rest of my life. I took back my maiden name, went on dates when I wanted to, and luxuriated in independence."

"But being single in St. Louis wasn't enough?"

Joan shook her head. "Maybe it was being single *and* turning thirty-two that did me in. Right after my birthday, between Christmas and New Year's, I had the bright idea to buy this farm from my cousin. All of a sudden, one Sunday afternoon, I was calling California practically begging Michael to sell it to me."

"I hate to seem nosy, but it *is* my occupation to ask questions," Carol said. "How could you afford to buy this house, plus acres of Iowa farmland?"

"My mother's family wasn't wealthy by any stretch," Joan said, "but my grandfather turned out to be an amazingly sharp investor in his retirement years. He set up a trust fund and managed it for me until my twenty-first birthday.

"Grandpa Ted worried that my parents were older when I was born. He wanted to make sure I would have something for a 'rainy day.' He was close. It was a *snowy* day last January when I got Michael's okay to buy this place.

"I figured as long as there was a post office in Bethany, I would be able to keep my editing job at Crawford Medical Publishing and still have time to work at writing a novel," Joan said.

Rising from the table to get a wineglass, Joan asked Carol about herself.

The reporter gave a *Cliff's Notes* version of her family. Besides her mother, she had an older brother and two older sisters who lived in St. Louis with their spouses and kids. Her father, a sergeant for the St. Louis Police Department, had died of cancer when she was ten.

"Well, now it's my turn to ask. What made *you* decide to move to this little river town?" Joan said.

"That was easy. The *Bethany Daily Bugle* offered me a job and the *New York Times* didn't."

"You like it here?" Joan asked.

"Let's say I think I made the right choice for now. I'm learning how to do the job, my skin is getting thicker every day, and I don't think it'll take long for me to find something bigger and better."

CHAPTER 7

In the early morning darkness, the man slouched in an
Adirondack chair and waited for sunlight and signs of
movement from within the stone house. A cigarette dangled
from the fingers of his right hand, which rested on the chair's
broad armrest. He closed his eyes.

* * *

*Walking into the Hawkeye Café in Ottumwa, Iowa, he felt hungry,
tired, and ready for a break.*

*He had spent the last five hours sitting in his car, parked across
the street and down a little ways from the home of Mr. and Mrs. Eric
Holmstead. Finally, he had focused his Nikon's telephoto lens and
documented the moment when Mr. Luke Wright walked out the front
door of the Holmstead residence, and Virginia Holmstead, in a fancy,
flimsy dressing gown, waved goodbye to her lover.*

*Now he could reward himself with a meal and a brief rest before
driving back to Des Moines.*

The young woman in the foyer of the café smiled and took a menu off the pile.

"Just one today, sir?"

He nodded and scanned the main dining area, partially blocked by an ornate mahogany grille in back of the hostess stand. He started to follow the hostess to a two-top by the window, then suddenly stopped and returned to the foyer.

The young woman came back to him with a puzzled look.

"Please seat me over there," he said, pointing to a booth on the far side of the room.

"Of course."

Instead of letting the girl lead the way, he walked alongside her, using her body to shield himself from the view of others patrons.

Seated in the booth, he immediately opened the menu she placed in front of him.

"A waitress will be right with you."

He took a ball cap from his jacket pocket and pulled it down so the brim shielded his eyes. He raised the menu in front of his face and peered over the top of it toward the opposite side of the dining area, where a man and woman sat at a table for two against the wall.

Unfortunately, his eyes had not fooled him. The woman with the lustrous black chignon clasped in a tortoise shell barrette was his wife. He did not recognize the man seated with her.

From his vantage point, across the room and to the side, he was able to watch the couple unnoticed—her in profile and the man straight on.

He no longer had an appetite. The ham sandwich and coffee he ordered would merely justify his surveillance.

His beautiful wife was showering the stranger with the full force of her radiance. From across the table, they gazed at each other, her right hand entwined with his left. There were no papers, no portfolios, no swatches of material on the table. She had no business with this man.

* * *

He opened his eyes, tossed the glowing cigarette onto the flagstones in front of the Adirondack chair, and crushed it under the sole of his shoe.

CHAPTER 8

"Is Dan Taylor there?"

"Sure is. Who's this?"

Carol identified herself and apologized for the early morning call.

"I understand you used to work as a handyman out at the Sizemore farm, Mr. Taylor. Do you know anything about the skeleton found out there a couple of days ago?"

"I read about it in the paper yesterday. I figured somebody would either be calling me or coming for me," he said with a short laugh.

"What do you mean?" Carol asked, knowing what he meant but wanting him to talk.

"Well, I took care of the place for about two years, you know, for Mr. Sizemore. Going out to mow the grass and check on the pipes in the winter, things like that there, when the house was vacant. But I tell you, I've never seen a living soul out there. Never even went into the barn. I was dumbfounded to read about a body layin' up in that loft, all the while I was out there cuttin' grass."

"I want to make sure I'm getting this right, Mr. Taylor," she said, scribbling in her notebook. "You worked at the farm regularly for two years, but you never went into the barn?"

"No need to. All Mr. Sizemore wanted me to do was check on the house and keep the grass mowed. Used my own mower."

"How did you happen to get the job, may I ask?"

"Through the employment office. He just wanted somebody to check on the place every other week and do whatever needed doing. I'd call him afterwards and give a report on what I did. Then he'd send me a check for my work and any expenses for gas and such."

"When did you stop working for Mr. Sizemore?"

"Back in April. He'd sold the property and told me he wouldn't need me any more. Sent me my last check at the end of April. He seemed like a straight-arrow guy. You think he had anything to do with this?"

Carol assured him she didn't know and thanked him for his time.

She looked at the notes she had taken since yesterday morning. Other than the cause of death, she had nothing of substance for today's article. The faded stories in the three manila envelopes she had looked through after returning from dinner had offered no clues.

All she would have after leading with the COD were a few comments from Joan, the innocuous quote from the chief of police, and the statement from the handyman. Her brilliant conclusion would be that, apparently, nobody knew anything about anything or anyone related to the victim.

It was seven thirty. Charlie walked into the newsroom in his usual upbeat mood.

"What's cookin', good lookin'?"

"Not enough to starve on, Charlie. I've got the cause of death, Joan Sizemore's account of how she found the body, a noncommittal quote from the police chief, and a total lack of awareness on the part of the neighbors. Dan Taylor, the handyman, just told me he never saw anyone out there. Never even went into the barn. I'll write a short article and cuts for some of these photos," she said, fanning four of the prints Kenny had left on her desk. "Which ones do you want?"

Charlie looked over the photos.

"Let's take these two," he said, pointing to a wide shot of the barn and yard with the ambulance and patrol car, and a closer one of the body bag being loaded into the ambulance with Sergeant Jack Padgett and Officer Matt Wilson in the foreground.

"Chief Bryce didn't give you anything good?"

"No. I think he's already convinced that the barn was picked at random by fleeing criminals who needed a hiding place. He wants the DCI, FBI, or somebody else to take it off his hands."

"Well, go with what you've got, and check at the police station later to see if Jack Padgett's come up with anything else."

CHAPTER 9

E xcept for an occasional overnight companion, Bethany's
city manager, Jeff Ryan, lived alone in his house on the
river side of Riverview Boulevard.

This morning, carrying a cup of strong black coffee, Ryan
walked through the French doors of the formal dining room and
out onto the terrace that was his refuge.

He had read the article in the *Bugle* late last night when he
got back into town. It startled him to see in print what had been a
secret for two years. He had known the body would be discovered
someday. He had hoped it would be someday when he no longer
lived in Bethany.

After several beers, he had slept fitfully. Now he had to gather
his thoughts and get over to City Hall.

"Good morning, Mr. City Manager!"

Ryan spun around, sloshing coffee on the right sleeve of
his starched white shirt, well-shined wingtips, and the terrace's
flagstone surface.

"What the hell are you doing here?" Ryan snapped. "I thought you went back under your rock!"

"Jeff, my boy, that's no way to treat a guest. I've been sitting here since before dawn waiting for you. You could be polite and offer me a cup of coffee."

"I'll offer you nothing, you bastard. You promised you'd stay away. Get off my property!"

"Listen, my friend," the man said with venomous politeness. "That promise came with a condition. One that you evidently didn't grasp. You didn't take care of what I asked you to take care of."

"What are you talking about? We did exactly what you asked. It's been two years, and nobody has any idea what happened."

A chilling sneer crawled across the man's face as he waved a copy of yesterday's *Bugle* at the city manager.

"Jason and I can handle this," Ryan said with a calm voice that masked his terror.

"Oh, that's rare. I really love how you've handled it so far. Do you think I wanted to come back to this jerkwater town to clean up after you and your idiot sidekick?"

Ryan desperately regretted, for the thousandth time, that he and Jason Eberle had become ensnared in this madman's hell.

"You've got to believe me. There's nothing for you to do here. It's been so long, for Christ's sake. The police aren't going to be able to find out anything."

"You do have a point there. The police you hire don't know their asses from holes in the ground. But what about the bitch reporter? What do you plan to do about her?"

Ryan barely knew the new city editor, but he had seen a parade of her predecessors.

"Believe me, she's no problem. First, the managing editor at the *Bethany Daily Bugle* doesn't go in for investigations. Second, there's nothing more to report."

The intruder picked up his discarded cigarette butt from one of the flagstones and walked to the edge of the terrace, as though considering his options. He flicked the butt high into the air, over the bluffs of the Mississippi.

"Okay, City Manager Ryan. I'll give you one more chance to get this right. Make sure the keystone cops stay stupid and the reporter stays out of our business. But remember, I'll be watching closely. You screw this up again, and *you*, my friend, are screwed."

He turned abruptly and walked through the terrace's wrought-iron gate carrying the newspaper, leaving the city manager holding a half cup of tepid coffee and wearing a stained white shirt.

CHAPTER 10

Mayor Jason Eberle only appeared to be working on the stack of correspondence his secretary, Marjorie, had placed on the large oak desk in his office.

To the right of the stack was a copy of yesterday's *Bugle.* The mayor had read the article on the front page several times, but his eyes kept returning to it. "Skeletal Remains Found in Barn on Rte. 2."

He felt sick to his stomach. Small beads of perspiration covered his forehead and upper lip even though he had just wiped his face a minute before with his pocket handkerchief. He feared he might be having a heart attack.

Since seeing the story on the front page, Eberle's equilibrium had been rudely disrupted.

Two years ago, when everything had gone off kilter, he knew he had to get himself straightened out. He and Anne had taken a Mediterranean cruise. He had come back a renewed man, throwing himself into his work like never before. When he was in town, he was at City Hall every morning by nine. He was prepared for every city council meeting. There wasn't a Kiwanis pancake breakfast, Lions Club barbecue, or Rotary luncheon he didn't attend. His constituents counted on him to be first in line at every blood drive. He was ready to cut a ribbon or present a key to the city any day of the week.

Eberle's love for the job was not lost on Bethany's voters. Some even said they thought he should be mayor for life.

A light tap on his office door shook him from his reverie.

"Mayor, there's someone here who says he's been out of town a long time and would like to see you," his secretary said. "Mr. Eugene Montgomery?"

Eberle was up and out from behind his desk faster than Marjorie had ever seen him move. Before he could reach the door, a lean man of medium height was walking past her and into the office.

"Good morning, Mr. Mayor!" the visitor said with excessive cordiality, thrusting out his hand.

Eberle ignored the hand. Without a word, he sidestepped Montgomery and firmly closed the door in his secretary's face.

"What are you doing here?" he hissed. "You've got no right to come barging in here. You've got no right to be back in this town."

The man waved his copy of the *Bugle* at Eberle. "Oh, that's where you are so wrong," he said, matching the mayor's low, hostile tone. "This very much gives me the right to be here."

"How did you find out about this?" Eberle asked.

"Don't worry about that, my friend. I have plenty of sources. Do you think I'd actually wait for you and your pal to tell me anything I need to know?"

Jason Eberle now believed he really was on the verge of a heart attack. Sweat rolled down his neck, over his shoulders, and into the fibers of his cotton undershirt. His forehead and upper lip were again shiny with moisture. His stomach was roiling the remains of his breakfast.

Trying to compose himself, Eberle turned his back on Montgomery and walked to the area of his office where a tan leather sofa and two matching leather armchairs surrounded a bird's-eye maple coffee table. This was where he loved to meet with his city manager and various department heads or with visitors to City Hall. He always felt so munificent when he invited someone to sit with him in this cozy den and offered them coffee and Danish or icy soft drinks and his wife's homemade cookies, served by his secretary.

Now, Eberle felt the extreme opposite of munificence. He was an animal trapped. Montgomery was blocking access to the mayor's desk and the chair from which he, Jason Eberle, proudly reigned.

He didn't know if he felt more enraged or frightened by this madman who had insinuated his way into their business and then left them to deal with the result of his insanity. Regardless of the prevailing feeling, Eberle knew his reputation, his freedom—maybe even his life—depended on his ability to express the rage. Turning to face Montgomery, he planted himself.

"You bastard. You think you can come back into my town, my office, my life, and threaten me by wagging a newspaper in my face?" He spat out the words with hushed intensity, mindful of his secretary on the other side of the door. "You have no idea who you're dealing with. If you want to bully somebody, you'd better look somewhere else, because I've kept your ass out of a stinking prison cell!"

At last, Jason Eberle felt fully in command, spewing his contempt for the man who threatened to destroy his life.

His guest stood straight and calm, watching the moving

mouth. He had the strength to grab Eberle's neck and twist it until the mayor fell like a limp puppet. But that wasn't what he had come for.

"Oh, my goodness, Jason," he said in a friendly tone. "Let's calm down, my friend. The only reason I came here was to let *you* know that *I* know we've got some unfinished business. I only want to make sure it gets finished. Just like you do, I'm sure. I've already had a little chat with your city manager. He and I are in complete agreement. The cops have to be kept in the dark, and the newspaper has to keep its nose out of this."

Eberle felt stomach acid boiling into his esophagus. Nothing would stop Montgomery until he got his way. Even after that, Eberle could never be sure this madman wouldn't come back for something else. He was a cold-blooded killer, for God's sake.

"Trust me," the man said in a soothing voice. "I mean you and your pal Jeff no harm. I just want you to finish the job I asked you to do two years ago. Maybe you tried your best then. I'll give you the benefit of the doubt. But now we've learned your best wasn't good enough. Jeff has promised me that you and he can work out a plan. So I tell you what. Take another crack at it. I'll observe for now. Then, when this is all over with, maybe we can still be friends."

Taut with fear, Eberle knew he needed to match Montgomery's dispassionate tone. He had no idea what to do. He had spent the last two years *not* dealing with what had happened. He certainly had no plan. All he wanted was to be free of this vile man's presence.

"Listen, Jeff and I will find a way to handle this," Eberle said. "Tell me where I can reach you. I'll let you know as soon as it's taken care of."

"Thanks anyway, Jason," he said with a wet, slippery smile. "My sources will keep me informed. All you and Jeff need to do is finish up the loose ends. I'll know when that happens."

The visitor took his copy of the *Bugle* with him as he turned and walked out of the office.

CHAPTER 11

"Hi, hon. You comin' or goin'?"

The waitress smiled as she set a glass of water and a stainless steel knife, fork, and spoon rolled up tightly in a white paper napkin in front of Jeff Ryan. He was seated in a booth toward the back of Tucker's Café, just outside Batavia, on Highway 34, a few miles east of Ottumwa. This was a customary stop for him as he traveled between Bethany and Des Moines.

"Going," he lied. "I've got a meeting in the capital this evening. Just wanted to do a little work, have some lunch, and leave myself plenty of time to get there."

"You look tired, hon. You should stay over in Des Moines and get a good night's sleep."

"I'll be okay."

It was odd for Ryan to be on the road this time of day, and he was trying to act like it was perfectly normal. He had had to get out of Bethany. He had to get some place where he could think without interruption. He had to come up with a plan that would work, and that Jason would accept.

The waitress set a sweating bottle of Budweiser and an empty glass on the table.

"You want the usual, hon?"

Ryan smiled and nodded. "That'd be great, Mona."

He pulled a leather portfolio from his briefcase and set it beside the glass, signaling he had work to do and no interest in conversation. She walked away with a nod, taking her cue from the good-looking regular from Bethany.

He opened the portfolio, wrote today's date, June 21, 1973, at the top of the page, and then stared at the blankness.

What was he supposed to do? He and the mayor had never even had a conversation about what had happened that day, much less planned what to do about it if their actions were discovered.

It angered him that Jason was so sure they could live the rest of their lives as innocent bystanders who just got caught in the wrong place at the wrong time. Despite all the mayor had taught him, the city manager now would have to insist the older man follow his lead. It wouldn't be easy. Jason would stubbornly claim they could keep their secret hidden beneath charm and influence.

Jason's problem was his cocksure notion that he was invulnerable to serious trouble. He could tick off the evidence. He had fought and survived the world's war against Hitler; he had escaped his father's sullen life of scarcity; he had married his high-school sweetheart; and, he had built the life of a successful businessman, relying on a genial disposition and an ingenious knack for deal making.

Ryan was sure Jason's charisma wouldn't be enough this time. Eugene Montgomery was invulnerable to charisma.

"Here you go, hon," the waitress said, setting a white ceramic plate bearing a cheeseburger and French fries on the far edge of the tabletop, away from the open portfolio. "At least take time to enjoy your beer."

"Thanks, Mona."

The lunchtime regulars started strolling in, ball-capped men in their forties and fifties, wearing Carhartt coveralls or Lee jeans with T-shirts that exposed souvenir tattoos from their days as GIs.

Ryan watched them take their usual places at the counter or at Formica-topped tables in the center of the room, picking up conversations right where they left them yesterday.

He longed to be that unburdened. How wonderful to have the freedom to walk around your town, chat with your neighbors, farm your land, and feel safe in the knowledge that nobody had anything on you.

They are blessed, he thought. No matter how much money they owe the bank, no matter how much it costs them to fill their pickups with gas, no matter how much they worry about their kids' college tuition, they are blessed.

Ryan turned back to his lined sheet of paper, still blank except for the date.

"Who?" he wrote on a line.

Who besides himself, Jason, and Montgomery could possibly know anything about what happened that day two years ago?

He had left City Hall at 2:15, telling his secretary he had some errands to run and that he wouldn't be back for the rest of the day. He drove home and waited for Jason to pick him up at 2:45.

Together the men headed out to the Sizemore farm for a meeting they knew wouldn't be pleasant and hoped to get through it as quickly as possible.

He was *almost* positive no one saw them going to or coming from the farm.

Driving down the quarter mile of flat, gravel road back to Route 2 in Jason's Lincoln about five o'clock that afternoon, Ryan had sat motionless, trying not to aggravate a throbbing headache and an angry stomach. Despite his distress, he stayed on guard, watching for passersby on Johnson Street Road, and did not see a single car or truck. Once on Main Street, the mayor's car blended easily into the back and forth traffic.

He had invited Jason into his house so they could talk about what had happened and figure out what to do. The mayor waved him off, saying he and his wife had dinner plans and he needed to stop by the carwash before going home.

"We'll talk tomorrow," Jason said.

They didn't. It wasn't the right time for the mayor.

For several days afterward, Ryan had worried nonstop. He watched in amazement as Jason carried out his mayoral duties, never revealing the slightest concern.

A few days later, Jason announced that he and his wife were taking a Mediterranean cruise and he was leaving his able city manager to mind the store.

"I almost don't have the heart to charge you for a cold cheeseburger," the waitress said, placing the check by Ryan's untouched food. "But I'm gonna anyway, or Mr. T will dock me," she said with a wink and a gravelly laugh.

"Don't worry about it, Mona," Ryan said, realizing it had

been a mistake to expect quiet and privacy at Tucker's. "Your smile is warming it up right now."

He pushed the portfolio aside, pulled the plate of food toward him, and took a bite of the cheeseburger.

Satisfied, the waitress walked off with a wave.

CHAPTER 12

A dark blue Ford LTD was parked on the side lot of Tucker's Café, allowing a clear view of the in-and-out traffic at the front.

The driver lowered the car windows, turned off the ignition, and listened to the pleasant hum of farm machinery in the background. He didn't know how long this little stop was going to take. That was okay, though; waiting was part of his job.

The local folks who came here for lunch, he noticed, were mostly farmers driving pickups. They would eat quickly and get back to work. Jeff Ryan was another story. A long lunch for him was just another perk on the taxpayer's nickel.

The charlatans who made up Ryan's circle thought they were smarter than the "general public." That's what had made it so easy to sell himself as a small-time grifter grabbing a little slice of American pie. He smiled, recalling his artful intrusion into a world of greed and chicanery.

* * *

"Mr. Eugene Montgomery is here for your one thirty, Mr. Whitlock," the secretary said from the office doorway.

Impeccably polite, Fred Whitlock, the arrogant tycoon and highway commissioner rose from the chair behind his desk.

"Hmm . . . did we have an appointment?" Whitlock asked, tilting his head to hint that he knew they did not have an appointment.

He put a smile on his face and reached out his hand. "I apologize for the confusion, Fred. We don't really have an appointment, but I told your secretary that we do and that you must have forgotten to tell her about it. Please forgive the little fib. I knew you would want to see me."

Whitlock tugged on his shirtsleeves, exposing monogrammed, sterling silver cufflinks that bounced balls of sun off the office walls, and shook the offered hand. "Well, now that you're here, what is it you wanted to see me about, Mr. Montgomery?"

Without waiting to be asked, he seated himself in the brown leather and chrome Wassily chair in front of Whitlock's busy desk stacked with file folders.

"Please call me Eugene. I know we're going to become good friends," he said, amused by Whitlock's look of bewilderment.

Dealing with underlings at the office, on construction sites, or in clubs and hotels, Fred Whitlock was quite comfortable. Little people knew their place. They didn't expect anything beyond polite consideration and, if appropriate, a generous tip.

Dealing with equals, Whitlock also was at ease. Oh, he didn't really see other men as his equals, but some came close enough. Enough money, social position, political influence, or some combination of the above, allowed them access to his amiable charm.

Dealing with men like him, on the other hand, wasn't easy for Fred Whitlock. The "Eugene Montgomerys" of the world, with overreaching *expectations and button cuffs, reminded Whitlock of how he might have turned out if it hadn't been for lucky breaks. To Fred Whitlock, men like him were, at best, an embarrassment. At worst, trouble.*

"I know you're very busy, Fred, so I'll come right to the point. Recently, I've learned that you've been sharing some nice business opportunities with friends in Iowa and California."

Fred Whitlock leaned back in his chair, put a hand up to his chin and nodded, a little too casually.

"I want to be one of your friends, Fred," he said with a genial, open smile.

"I imagine a lot of people do," Whitlock said.

His smile became a straight line.

"I'm not a lot of people, Fred. There's only one of me, and I want in on some of the deals you've been peddling."

Whitlock placed a set of manicured fingernails on the edge of his desk. "Listen, Mr. Montgomery, I'm not exactly sure what brought you here. I'm a businessman who owns a successful construction company. My real estate investments are highly speculative. One has to be able to afford the risks. Believe me, we don't have people walking in off the street to invest their life savings."

His politeness faded. He placed his unmanicured fingernails on the opposite edge of Whitlock's desk and leaned forward.

"Listen to me, Fred. You don't have to be 'exactly sure' about what brought me here. All you have to know is that I know enough about the nature of your high-risk, speculative investments to ruin you. If you want to talk about risk, let's talk about Fairport, Montpelier, and Buffalo; or Robins, or Urbandale. Let's talk about how quickly I can call Ben Williams over at the Register and set up a little interview session."

The color drained from Whitlock's face. "What kind of an investment are you looking for, Mr. Montgomery?" *he asked.*

"First, you've got to call me Eugene," he said, smiling again. "Second, I want you to introduce me to some of your friends at Foley's Restaurant *and Lounge. I want to sort of ease into the conversation. You know, hear what's on the market. Don't worry; I can pay the entry fee. I just want to get in the game."*

Whitlock allowed himself a little smile of relief, obviously imagining he had figured something out.

"Sure, I understand, Eugene. Do you want me to call you a couple of days in advance?"

"No. You won't have to bother. I'll see you at Foley's."

He stood up, reached across the desk for a gentleman's shake, and walked toward the door. "Thanks for your time, Fred."

* * *

The driver of the LTD watched through the open car window as Jeff Ryan came out of Tucker's Café with a black leather briefcase in his left hand and walked toward his red 1972 Buick Regal. Ryan put the briefcase on the passenger side, got behind the wheel, and drove east on 34.

Seconds later, the LTD pulled out of the parking lot and headed in the same direction.

CHAPTER 13

Mayor Eberle emerged from his office for the first time since his unwelcome visitor had left.

"Marj, you seen Jeff?"

"No. I haven't seen him *or* heard from him. Is everything okay?"

"Sure, everything's fine," the mayor said, approximating a smile.

"Want me to try him at home?"

"Don't bother; I'll get a hold of him. Just call my wife and tell her I'm having dinner with Jeff and won't be home till after the council meeting."

Eberle's day had started out rough, and Eugene Montgomery's visit had made it worse. After dinner, he would have to preside over the city council meeting and act like everything was normal. Where the heck was Jeff? He hadn't talked with him since last Sunday afternoon, right before the city manager left for the urban planners' conference in Omaha.

Unable to concentrate in his office, Eberle decided to drive over to Jeff's house.

When no one answered the front door, he went through the wrought-iron gate that led to the terrace and entered the dining room through the unlocked French doors. He called out to make sure Jeff wasn't there, then freely wandered through the familiar house looking for clues to his friend's whereabouts.

On the counter by the sink sat an unplugged percolator, an unwashed coffee cup, and several empty Budweiser bottles, a sure sign Jeff was back from his trip.

In the living room, on the oval cherry wood and glass coffee table, was a copy of yesterday's *Bugle* and a stack of unopened mail.

The bedroom was in uncommon disarray. The bed was unmade. A partially unpacked suitcase was sitting open on a chair. A fresh white shirt with what looked like a coffee stain on the right cuff was hanging on the closet doorknob.

Eberle walked back to the kitchen, took a bottle of Budweiser from the refrigerator, and returned to the living room to wait.

Once again, the newspaper headline caught his eye. "Damn it!" he said. "For God's sake, what were we supposed to do?"

The mayor took a long swallow from the bottle and sat down on the sofa. He and Jeff had to talk. They had to figure out a way to get Montgomery off their backs. Trouble was, Jeff would make a big deal of this. Their plan had to be simple. They just had to keep it low key.

He mentally rehearsed some ad-libs for the upcoming council meeting. . . .*Heck, this sort of thing can happen when escaped cons or fugitives have a falling out. Desperate men have no regard for law-abiding citizens and their property. It was simply an unfortunate turn of events at the old home of good people. It doesn't in any way reflect badly on the people of Bethany. We'll probably never really know what happened out there.*

Eberle grew restless. He returned to the kitchen for another Bud. He knew he shouldn't be drinking in the middle of the afternoon, but hell, he needed to stay calm. This would be the first public event since the news came out. Surely somebody would ask them about it. He and Jeff had to hit the same notes.

He took another pull on his beer and glanced around the room. On an end table by the sofa was a familiar framed photograph of Jeff, himself, and the governor, taken on the first tee of the Walnut Woods Country Club in Des Moines three years earlier. The men, dressed in bright polo shirts and chinos, were casually leaning on their two irons and smiling happily at the camera. Jason had a photo exactly like this in his office, except for the inscription. This one said, "Jeff, keep up the good work in Bethany! All the best, Bob."

Eberle smiled. Jeff was his boy. They would see this through together.

Eberle and Jeff Ryan had met in 1963, when the younger man was an assistant to the city manager of Des Moines. The lean, handsome thirty-year-old was intelligent and personable. Interested in politics, but not a politician.

Eberle had wanted the city council to hire Jeff as city manager immediately, but there were two problems. Bethany already had a city manager, and Jeff had just accepted a job as the finance manager for the city of Davenport. In 1964, though, after Eberle had won his second term in a landslide, he knew he could sway the city council any which way he wanted. He cajoled the councilmen, taking each of them to lunch and making the case for dismissing the current city manager, Ned Graves.

Bethany needed new blood, fresh ideas, youthful leadership, Eberle had asserted. Ned was tired and complacent. He only did what he had to do. He was getting harder to work with, and that sapped Eberle's time and energy. The mayor needed a true partner, a thinker and planner, to work behind the scenes while he worked out front with the people.

Once he had convinced enough councilmen that Ned Graves had to go, Eberle contacted Jeff Ryan and asked him to apply for the job in Bethany. The younger man didn't hesitate. To be a city manager at age thirty-one, even in a small town, would be the fulfillment of his ambition.

With Ryan's resume in hand, the mayor had gone to the Bethany City Council with a velvet-gloved ultimatum. Dismiss Ned Graves. Assuage his wounded pride by offering a generous severance package and laudatory letters of reference. Then, hire Ryan at a twenty percent higher salary plus a liberal travel budget.

"Bethany needs his talent, his drive, his energy," he had pitched. "I can work with Jeff Ryan. We'll work as a team with the state commissions and the feds. The people will love him."

Sold!

It had worked out pretty much the way Eberle thought it would. Jeff and he had become close friends, as fathers and sons often become friends when the son reaches adulthood. In some ways, though, especially on the road, they were running buddies. Eberle enjoyed traveling with his good-looking bachelor companion. Together, they could always charm their way into the company of a single woman or two in a bar or club.

The mayor wasn't interested in sleeping with any of the women on the road. He was always faithful to Anne. But Anne was at home. On the road, he loved the game: flirting, flattering, buying drinks, smoking cigars, slapping backs, telling stories, flashing a fat money clip.

He needed the road. Where else could he so freely display his *joie de vivre*? It made him feel good.

Suddenly, Eberle shook his head, as though rousing himself from an accidental nap. What was he doing? Why was he sitting alone in Jeff's house on a Thursday afternoon drinking beer?

"Jeeeez," he said, picking up a pillow from the sofa and spinning it fiercely onto a navy blue chair by the fireplace.

It wasn't that Jason Eberle couldn't face the brutal truth. It was just that, in his adult life, he had rarely been pressed to do so. He wasn't afraid to face his shortcomings. He was just confident that his assets surpassed them.

Business, marriage, politics, friendships, reputation. The entire course of his life since coming home from the war, whole and healthy, had been untarnished and uncomplicated.

Until two years ago.

Until *four* years ago.

Jason closed his eyes. In an instant, every detail of that night replayed itself as though he were living it again.

* * *

The buzz from the beer and Scotch sustained their conversation at perfect pitch all the way through dinner at Foley's Restaurant & Lounge. He and Jeff played off each other like brothers, recounting their best road stories, while Fred Whitlock confided the trials and triumphs of building a construction business from nothing.

"You know, gentlemen," Whitlock said, nodding at both of them through the haze of after-dinner Montecristos, "I think this is the beginning

of a great relationship. Let's head up to your room at the Savery, Jason. I've got some plans to tell you about that I don't share with everyone."

It was a short walk from Foley's to the Des Moines Savery Hotel on Locust. The old Georgian-style hotel was one of the finest in the city, a place fit for presidents. He wouldn't think of staying anywhere else when he was in town. This trip, he and Jeff had rooms on the tenth floor.

They had already shed their suit coats, loosened their ties, and removed their shoes when Whitlock knocked on the hotel room door.

The contractor and state highway commissioner walked in with a black leather case, which he had retrieved from his car. Inside were flasks of Chivas Regal and Rémy Martin XO, a set of small tumblers, and four Macanudo Portofino cigars, their white cylindrical holders slipped through velvet loops on the interior of the case.

"Shall we continue our conversation, gentlemen?" Whitlock asked, releasing the flasks from the leather straps that secured them and placing three glasses on a side table.

Whitlock poured two cognacs, then a Chivas for himself, handed out the panatellas, and invited them to be seated in two well-worn Victorian armchairs. Whitlock remained standing, snipping the tip off his cigar with a silver-plated cutter and igniting it with a matching lighter. Puffing the brown tip into red ash, he bowed his six-foot frame toward the men.

"Jason, Jeff, as I said earlier, I think the three of us have just begun a very good and, potentially, very profitable relationship.

"I want to share with you a business opportunity that a colleague and I have developed. Before I do so, though, I need your assurance that the conversation stays in this room, regardless of whether or not you decide to participate with us. Can I have your promise?"

He and Jeff looked at each other, caught off guard by the immediacy and directness of the highway commissioner's request but beguiled by the prospect of a business venture with this man. What else could they do but promise?

Assured, Whitlock loosely described the strategy he and a California associate had developed.

"It surely must be obvious to you both that my position on the highway commission gives me access to a great deal of information about various pieces of land in Iowa, right?" Whitlock asked with a wink.

The two friends glanced at each other again and nodded.

"My partner, on the other hand, has associates in California who know of certain tracts of land out there that are going to greatly appreciate in value as time goes on. We've determined that, by working together, we can package very attractive deals for a handpicked group of California and Iowa investors."

"How do we fit into the picture?" he asked, gesturing toward his city manager.

"We are looking for partners of a certain caliber. One, they must be men who can be trusted, and two, they must have the liquidity to take immediate action when golden opportunities present themselves. Like I said, this may not be something you're interested in, but I wanted to offer it to you because you strike me as the kind of men we need."

Whitlock tilted his glass of Chivas in their direction before taking a sip.

Jeff stood up. "What would we have to do?"

"For right now, all I need to know is that you're interested. My associate, Michael Sizemore, will be coming to Des Moines in the next week or so. I'll call you and arrange for the four of us to get together.

"It is elegantly simple," Whitlock said, slowly blowing cigar smoke up and away.

* * *

Eberle shuddered and opened his eyes. It hadn't turned out elegantly or simply. He and Jeff had slipped up. But they could figure this out. They would untangle themselves from the snare.

CHAPTER 14

H er leads for city council stories usually came easily. All
Carol had to do was decide which of the council's actions
was likely to have the biggest impact on the most people
and write a crisp opening sentence or two that said how, why, and
when citizens would feel the effects of the decision.

By that rule of thumb, tomorrow's article would begin, "If you
were awaiting action by the city council last night, prepare to wait
some more. City Manager Jeff Ryan's unexpected absence put all
decisions on hold for the next two weeks."

Gaveling the council session to order at 7:00 p.m., Mayor Jason
Eberle had announced to the twenty or so citizens in attendance
that Ryan was absent due to a scheduling snafu at an urban
planners' conference in Omaha. The city manager's presentation
had been scheduled for Thursday instead of Wednesday, and Ryan
felt obliged to stay over in Nebraska an extra day.

Bethany's councilmen declined to take action on anything,
saying that every item on the agenda required more information
and direction from the city manager.

Acting as though it was what he had wanted to do all along, the mayor announced he would devote the entire meeting to citizens' comments and requests.

When everyone who wanted to complain about dim softball field lights, early Sunday morning lawn mowers, late trash collections, and missing stop signs was heard, Mayor Eberle's motion for adjournment was promptly seconded. The meeting concluded at 9:30 p.m. with another bang of the gavel.

Carol had approached the mayor while he was still seated in the high-backed swivel chair at the center of the long table where the city council gathered. She had noticed during the meeting that he seemed preoccupied and wondered if it was due to Jeff Ryan's absence or something else. Like everyone in Bethany, Carol was accustomed to Eberle's jovial manner and tonight she wondered about his less-than-upbeat mood.

She maintained a cordially noncommittal relationship with the mayor, following the dictum of Dr. Eric Mallory, her Newswriting 101 professor and advisor, not to get friendly with news sources, especially politicians. Carol had taken her professor's lesson to heart.

Mayor Eberle's primary roles in Bethany's government were official spokesperson and good will ambassador. On the occasions Carol stopped at his office door, looking for a quote or two about some project or upcoming event, the mayor always seemed pleased to see her and even more pleased to direct her to the city manager or one of Bethany's department heads for details.

Carol hadn't seen Eberle since the skeleton had shown up, so she took the opportunity after the council meeting to ask him about it.

"You just never know, do you, Carol?" he said, shaking his head thoughtfully. "I guess this sort of thing can happen anywhere, but it sure is a shock to have it happen here. From what the police say, the criminals were just looking for a spot isolated enough to hide their crime and high-tail it out of here." He shook his head again. "We may never know what happened out there."

"So you're confident there's no local connection?" she asked.

"Well, based on what Chief Bryce tells me, I am. Nobody local's missing. If I were a betting man, I'd put my money on fugitives, maybe escaped prisoners from somewhere out west. Who knows?"

"'Who knows?' is right," Carol said out loud as she arrived at her car, now bathed in a pool of fluorescent light on the City Hall parking lot.

"Coming to HoJo's, Carol?" Tim Terrell of KKYX yelled from across the lot. "I'm starving!"

"Not tonight, Tim. Eat some fries for me!"

This was one of those times when being a reporter didn't seem like such a good idea. She had nothing worthy of a page-one city council story and, even though he hadn't said it in so many words, Charlie seemed disappointed today that she didn't have a better follow-up on the skeleton. She had ruminated all day, trying to justify the lack of information. Nobody in town was coming forward about a missing person or a killer. People were curious, but in a detached sort of way.

"Write it for what it's worth" was every editor's mandate. At this point, the skeleton story wasn't worth a damn. When the DCI in Des Moines identified the body, there would be something to write about. Until then, there was no story.

Carol drove off the Fourth Street parking lot onto Main and headed east toward Front Street, which ran parallel to railroad tracks and the river.

Stopping at a red light on Main, she honked and waved at Tim who was strolling into Howard Johnson's.

It probably would have done her good to join him for a burger, but if she had she would've had to stop feeling sorry for herself and be sociable, which she didn't feel like doing. She turned left on a green arrow and headed up the river. Several blocks north, Front Street would take on the high-toned name of Riverview Boulevard.

It was more direct to take Second Street home, but Carol preferred to drive along the river, turn west at Harrison, and drive just a little ways back to her apartment.

Except for teenagers who were allowed to take their parents' cars out for a cruise or adults who worked late, most of Bethany was getting ready for bed by ten, so traffic on this summer night was light. In her rearview mirror, Carol noticed a dark car behind her driven by a lone man. The sedan kept pace at a short distance for several blocks. As she approached Harrison, she flicked on her left turn signal as she always did, even when no one was behind her. This time, though, she didn't turn. The dark car remained on her tail. Two blocks later, she again put on her turn signal and slowed. The car behind did the same. She kept going straight on Riverview. So did the other car.

She was approaching Bethany Park, popular because of its scenic views of the Mississippi River. Teenagers congregated here on summer nights, not to view the Mississippi, but to hang out with friends, smoke, and drink soda or bootlegged beer. Through open car doors, she heard Paul McCartney and Wings singing "My Love," on synchronized radios.

Without signaling, Carol turned left into the second park entrance and drove to a spot on the parking lot close by a group of teenage boys and girls who were sitting on the hoods of cars while they teased back and forth. From this vantage point, she watched the dark sedan continue northward on Riverview.

Carol fished a tube of lipstick out of her purse. She turned on the overhead light in her car and studiedly applied the makeup. Her pantomime would satisfy the teens' curiosity, she figured, if they bothered to notice her.

News of the brutal murders of women in California a couple of years before had motivated Carol to join the better-safe-than-sorry school of single women. She usually felt silly after making some evasive maneuver that turned out to be unnecessary, but she preferred to live with a little embarrassment than to not live at all.

After a few minutes, with no sign of the sedan, Carol turned her Maverick southbound and headed home.

CHAPTER 15

Jason Eberle was seething, doubly so for having had to keep his anger in check all evening.

Thirty minutes after banging the gavel to end the city council meeting, he called his wife and told her not to wait up, then headed for Jeff Ryan's.

His city manager hadn't even shown him the courtesy of calling to say he wasn't coming to the council meeting. Embarrassed by Ryan's unexplained absence, the mayor had felt compelled to lie.

When he pulled in front of the house on Riverview Drive, Eberle knew that this time Jeff was home.

"Where the hell were you?" he shouted, stepping into the foyer without being invited. "I've been waiting all day for a phone call or something, and then you don't show up at the meeting! I looked like a jackass! I had to lie about you still being in Omaha! What in God's name's goin' on with you?"

The ruddy mayor turned redder as he seared his good friend with the hot temper he rarely displayed.

Ryan stood, head down, and waited for Eberle to finish. His starched white shirt, normally still crisp at the end of the day, was limp and wrinkled, the sleeves rolled up and the top buttons open, revealing a white T-shirt beneath.

"Come in, Jason. We've got to talk." He turned his back on the mayor and led him into the living room.

Eberle followed, cooler now that he had vented the steam inside and confident that he had the upper hand with his protégé. He would demand an explanation, accept Jeff Ryan's apology, and quickly get things back on an even keel. The men sat face to face, Ryan in one of the blue velvet easy chairs by the fireplace, his boss on the taupe suede sofa he had occupied earlier today while waiting for the prodigal son to return.

"I've got to get out of here," Ryan said without hesitation. "I'm submitting my resignation tomorrow. I'll be gone by the end of the month."

The mayor squinted as though suddenly blinded by a bright light. He shook his head. "Whoa, boy! You're going *waaay* too fast for road conditions! Did they put something in your beer up in Omaha?"

In spite of himself, Jeff Ryan smiled wanly. This was typical of his boss.

Whenever Jeff's viewpoint veered too far from his own, the mayor considered it a temporary aberration, brought on by alcohol or some other mind-altering drug.

"Jason, listen to me," Ryan said, taking a deep breath. "Montgomery's back. He tried to kill me this afternoon. Ran me off 34 on the way back from Batavia."

"I know Montgomery's back!" Eberle said, newly annoyed. "He had the gall to come to my office this morning. But what in heck were you doing in Batavia?"

Ryan described how he had gone to Tucker's to find some privacy and come up with a plan, after having been startled by Montgomery on the terrace this morning. When Tucker's didn't provide the necessary inspiration, he had headed back east on Highway 34 toward Bethany and had stopped at a small tavern in Lockridge, where he slowly drank his way through the afternoon.

"Around five, I got a cup of coffee to take with me on the road, planning to get back here in time for the council meeting. I was right outside Mount Pleasant when this LTD came roaring down on me. At first, I thought it was just some guy in a big hurry. I moved over to give him room to pass, but he deliberately swerved his car next to mine and forced me down the embankment. I was barely able to keep my car under control."

"Did you actually see his face?" Eberle asked, wanting to attribute the incident to an alcohol-induced illusion.

"No, I *couldn't* see his face clearly, Jason. I was too busy trying to keep the goddamned car on four wheels. But I know it was a rental car, and the guy had Montgomery's build. We know he's in the area. Who else do you think would be interested in trying to kill me?"

"But how did he even know you were out there? Nobody else knew," Eberle said, taking another jab.

"I don't know how he knew. But he *knew*."

CHAPTER 16

Before Mayor Eberle left his friend's house, he insisted on Jeff's promise that there would be no submitting of any resignation the next day, or the day after that.

Eberle wasn't given to sentimentality. Yet when Jeff had threatened to leave Bethany, the mayor felt like he'd been punched in the gut. Jeff was more than a trusted colleague and traveling companion. He was his closest friend.

"These are orders from the boss," Eberle had said in the reassuring manner he had perfected in thirteen years as mayor. "Take some Alka-Seltzer and get a good night's sleep. Don't come in till noon tomorrow. If anybody asks about the meeting in Omaha, tell them they mixed up the date for your presentation and you had to stay over an extra day. You and me will huddle in the afternoon, like we're catching up on city business. Don't worry. We've got more on that sonuvabitch than he has on us. We'll figure out something."

"I've been trying all day to figure out how to get out of this, Jason, and I don't see a way," Ryan had said.

"Listen, together, we can do this. If you go off half-cocked, who knows what Montgomery will do? We've got to stick together."

Now, sitting in his car in front of the city manager's house, the mayor felt too defeated to maintain his pretense. Like a schoolboy, he wished he could go back to that evening at Foley's and undo the decision that had started this mess. Wearily, he closed his eyes.

* * *

"Hey, Jeffrey, is that your third or your sixth? We haven't even ordered dinner yet!" he said, grinning at his friend.

"Since when did you start counting?" Michael Sizemore asked, laughing at him from across the table. "Are you afraid Jeff's going to drink up all the profits?" The three of them, seated with Fred Whitlock in Foley's Restaurant & Lounge, had hit it off instantly and segued easily from business to pleasure.

Sizemore was a Bethany native, and smart as a whip. As the four men sipped their cocktails, Sizemore described how, in 1952, he had packed up his ambition, along with his business degree from Drake, and moved to Los Angeles. Over time, he started panning the gold from the California real estate industry, all the while staying in touch with Fred Whitlock, his friend and mentor back in Des Moines.

The idea for Sizemore and Whitlock's partnership had sprouted from the Iowa farm fields soon after the older man was named to the state highway commission in 1968.

Using his connections with well-placed Angelinos, Michael Sizemore explained, he was able to identify opportunities for influential Iowans to invest in California property. In exchange, Fred Whitlock provided Sizemore and his clients with inside information about plans for land development in Iowa.

As Whitlock and Sizemore sat at the smoky table in Foley's and described their business arrangement, he and Jeff raised questions about the legality of the cross-country dealings.

Sizemore and Whitlock listened intently, and seemed pleased to respond.

"Shall I address their concerns," Whitlock asked, "or do you want to, Michael?"

Sizemore nodded deferentially to the highway commissioner, and Whitlock launched into a smooth apologia.

"Gentlemen, I'll explain how Michael and I see the situation. And, remember, you're perfectly free to participate with us or not, with no loss of regard on our part. The only condition is that you keep it confidential, right?" he said.

Jeff and he both nodded, eager to be persuaded.

"First, there are huge dividends to be earned by anyone who makes smart investments in property, right?" Whitlock asked. "The question is, 'What allows someone to make a smart investment?'"

Whitlock didn't wait for an answer.

"Good information, obviously," he said. "And, from our viewpoint, when you exclude honest, individual investors, such as men like yourselves, from the loop, the only ones who reap the benefits of development are the big corporations and the big wheels who will always be first in line for the really good information.

"In our view," Whitlock continued, "there's no reason why men like you, who devote yourselves to public service and ask for nothing in return except a modest salary, can't derive some benefit from your positions. Michael and I say, 'If somebody's going to make money off this country's development, why shouldn't it be the men who are working so damn hard to make development possible in the first place?'"

Whitlock picked up his glass with a flourish, tipped it toward them, and took a drink.

Michael Sizemore jumped in.

"Fred, let's not forget this is something you and I have thought about for a long while. Our friends need a chance to digest this and come to their own conclusions." Sizemore paused and looked at them thoughtfully. "I will just add one thing to what Fred has said, though. There are several respected men like yourselves, in various parts of the state, who have thought this over, just as you're doing now. And they've come on board with us. Of course, we respect their confidentiality, just as we do yours, so we can't name names. I think you'd be impressed, though, by some of our other partners."

This apparent afterthought was music to his ears. He was a man who loved deal making. He loved getting an edge in the game. Yet, he also believed himself to be a moral and ethical man. At least a mostly moral and usually ethical man.

"You're telling us, Michael, that other municipal officials around Iowa are taking you up on the invitation to invest in property with you?" he asked.

Sizemore smiled, apparently pleased.

"That's what I'm telling you, Jason."

* * *

Jason Eberle opened his eyes to the lonely glow of streetlights. Everyone on Riverview was tucked in for the night, including Jeff Ryan. It was time for him to get to bed, too. But first he had to do something to try and satisfy the demon.

CHAPTER 17

Chief Larry Bryce answered his phone at 11:45, awakened on the cusp of blissful sleep.

"Bryce here. Who's this?"

"Chief, it's me, Jason. You in bed already?"

"What do you mean, 'already'? It's almost midnight. What's going on?"

"Didn't realize it was that late. Sorry. I've been doing some thinking and wanted to ask you something. After the council meeting tonight, Carol Hagan, the *Bugle* reporter, asked me about the skeleton at the Sizemore place. I told her what you told me, but I think she's still trying to squeeze something out of it."

"Not much to squeeze."

"Well, that's my point, Chief. I'm concerned, what with her being new around here, she may try to make something of this that ain't worth the paper it's printed on. And in the meantime, the town's going to get a black eye every time the skeleton gets mentioned. If the story keeps running, the wire services may pick it up, and then Bethany gets known as some kind of crime town. Nobody wants that."

"Of course not, but unless I missed something, the first amendment is still in force. What do you want me to do about it?"

Jason Eberle laid out his request to the chief. "Give a call to Charlie Vogler in the morning. Appeal to his desire to be in the loop. Tell him you want to give any new information on the skeleton directly to him, *personally*, the minute it comes in from the DCI, the sheriff, the state patrol, or anybody else."

By now, Larry Bryce was fully awake and understood what the mayor was asking him to do. He just didn't understand why. As the chief of police, he was more eager than anyone to maintain Bethany's reputation as one of the safest, most crime-free towns in Iowa. But as far as he could tell, the story of the decomposed corpse had run its course.

Folks in Bethany didn't get riled up about much of anything that didn't affect them personally. Their families, jobs, crops, weather, the price of food, gas, and taxes were their main concerns. Other things might engage them, interest them, or whet their curiosity, but life's pressing problems always quickly pushed aside the extras.

"I think you're making this more important than it is," Bryce said.

"Maybe I am, Chief, but remember, I've been around here a while and I know what's good for Bethany. Just trust me on this one."

Bryce did trust Eberle. Few knew the men's friendship went back to their days in the U.S. Army's 80th Infantry. Before they shipped out to Europe, they were comrades in arms. After fighting side by side in the battle to close the Argentan-Falaise gap in August of '44, they were blood brothers.

Discharged as a corporal, Larry Bryce returned to his hometown of Omaha, where his grandfather had been a deputy sheriff for Douglas County and his father was the assistant police chief for the city. Even though the job held no visceral interest for Bryce, he chose police work for his career. The father helped the son steadily advance on the force. With guidance, Larry Bryce was able to put together a decent law enforcement resume.

In 1960, when the Omaha police officer learned his old friend Jason Eberle had been elected mayor of Bethany, Iowa, he applied for the position of Bethany's police chief.

In personality or aptitude, there wasn't much that recommended Bryce to be a top cop. Uncurious and averse to heavy lifting, he wanted no challenges. A respectable salary, the perks of authority, and the prestige of a uniform were the limits of his ambition.

On paper, though, he appeared more than adequate. Bryce's resume, reinforced by the new mayor's thoughtfully understated recommendation, was enough to win the council's unanimous approval.

Eberle got his wartime buddy a secure post *and* secured a friend at police headquarters for any and all future times when such a friend would be helpful.

As it happened, Bryce wasn't half bad as chief. Crime was low, the residents usually stayed on good behavior, and the small police force managed to do its job without scandal.

"You don't have to worry about me, Jason," Bryce said. "I understand what you want me to do, and I'll do it. I'm just not sure Charlie Vogler will trust me to give him the information. He knows darn good and well that no love's lost between me and him, or his paper."

The mayor chuckled.

"That is exactly why you'll have Charlie eating out of your hand! He knows you avoid him. His ego is starving for the police chief to pay attention to him. When you call, he'll think you are finally giving him some respect. He'll be delighted to cooperate."

CHAPTER 18

The phone was ringing when Charlie Vogler walked into the newsroom Friday morning. Wondering why Carol wasn't already at her keyboard writing the city council story, he picked up the phone. Maybe this was her calling.

He was surprised to hear Larry Bryce's voice.

True to his word, Bryce made the pitch to Charlie just as Eberle had requested and wrapped it up quickly.

"I understand," Charlie said. "And, thanks for the call. Let me know if anything comes through on this. Talk to you later, Chief."

Carol walked into the newsroom just as her boss was ending the conversation.

"You'll never guess who that was," he said, strolling toward Carol's desk.

"Unless there's someone else you call 'Chief,' I'm betting it was Larry Bryce. What did he want?"

Charlie was uncertain about Bryce's motives. Although he hadn't sounded huffy on the phone, Charlie thought perhaps Carol had said or done something to send the chief into a little snit.

"Have you talked to Bryce lately about the skeleton at the Sizemores'?" he asked.

"Not since the other day in his office. I told you, he's waiting for the DCI or somebody to come up with something. He said he'd be sure to tell me if he learned anything."

"Well, he just called to say he wants to tell *me* if he learns anything. Something about wanting to keep me directly in the loop."

"Do you think Chief Bryce is about to get some information from Des Moines about the identity of the body?" she said.

"Nah. He didn't sound like he was expecting anything. To tell you the truth, I think our skeleton story is DOA, anyway," Charlie said, returning to his desk.

"Last night's council meeting can join the ranks of the dead, as well," she said. "The mayor announced that Jeff Ryan was delayed at a conference in Omaha. The councilmen didn't want to do anything without his advice, so they spent the whole meeting listening to complaints and requests. I think all it deserves is a box on page one explaining why no actions were taken. What do you think?"

"I've got a better idea. Why don't we run a page-one story on how the chief of police wants to include me in the 'loop'? Now that's the real news of the day."

CHAPTER 19

On the walk to the Brass Kettle with Ron Davidson and Tom Matthews, Carol brooded over the chief's early morning call to Charlie.

With nothing new to report, she hadn't planned to write anything more about the skeleton until there was some official word. So what was up with Bryce suddenly deciding to bypass her? Had she offended him somehow? She didn't think so. Unless he was offended by her being young and female.

"Good win over the Expos yesterday," Tom said, trying to draw Carol into the conversation.

Tom Mathews, self-taught sports writer and columnist, was forty-one and single and lived with his mother in a bungalow on West Cedar Street.

His workday beat varied with the seasons, ranging from the senior high's football field, to the basketball court, to the baseball diamond. An RCA console TV in his mother's living room was his window to the games he would never see in person. The *Daily Bugle* was the platform from which he vented his passion for competitive sports.

"Yeah. I just heard the last inning," Carol said offhandedly, entering the restaurant filled with the familiar aroma of grilled cheese sandwiches and fried onions.

The three took their usual booth and their *pro forma* glances at menus.

"What's up, Carol? Charlie give you a hard time about the nonexistent city council meeting story?" Ron asked. "If anybody should be complaining, it's me. I was the one who had to find a decent wire story to fit the hole on page one."

"Well, then, you finally earned the big bucks they pay you," Tom inserted, eager to lighten the mood.

Carol's inclination was to rant about how Bryce had dared to interfere in the newspaper's business, but she didn't want to seem naïve. Professors at Mizzou preached journalistic principles, but did those principles really carry any weight outside the classrooms of Walter Williams Hall?

After ordering tuna salad on toast and a Coke, Carol plunged in.

"Larry Bryce called the newsroom this morning and told Charlie he wants to give any new information on the skeleton directly to him."

"You do something to get Bryce's goat?" Ron asked, squeezing lemon into his iced tea.

"Not that I know of. When I talked to the chief Wednesday, he said he'd tell me anything he found out. I haven't even seen him since then, so I don't know how I could have offended him."

"From what I know of Bryce's thin skin," Tom said, "it doesn't have to be anything much. If you looked at him cross-eyed on Wednesday, he could be out to get you on Thursday. I'd let it pass."

Ron nodded his agreement. "Didn't you say you asked him how he planned to pursue the investigation? He's very sensitive about the image of his department. He's probably afraid you'll show up his men by actually trying to find out what happened at that farm."

Carol appreciated their efforts to reassure her. At the same time, she sensed this was something other than the chief slapping her wrist. What had made him call now, out of the blue, and say he wanted to give information to Charlie? Even more puzzling, why would Charlie so nonchalantly take orders from a public official, especially at a time when the whole country was getting a civics lesson in the necessity of a free press?

Thanks to the work of two reporters, last summer's "third-rate burglary" at the Democratic Party's campaign headquarters in the Watergate Hotel had ballooned from a local crime story in the Metro section of the *Washington Post* into a national drama playing out on the floor of a Senate hearing room.

The reporters had been assigned to follow up on the Watergate break-in. And, boy, did they ever. The bylines of Bob Woodward and Carl Bernstein had become fixtures on the *Washington Post*'s front page.

Carol and the other J-school students who stayed on campus for intersession courses last summer had read their way through the deluge of Watergate articles in the newspapers that landed every day at the door of the school's library.

This summer, millions of Americans were watching TV screens in the middle of the day, riveted by the political scandal still unfolding.

"I appreciate your trying to make me feel better, guys," Carol said. "But what if something fishy is going on, and I'm missing it? Maybe there's somebody else I should be talking to who knows something about the skeleton. Maybe this is the chief's way to try to put me off the track."

"Are you thinking this could be our little town's very own 'Watergate'?" Ron said with a wink.

Carol laughed, admiring the wire editor's intuition.

"Speaking of our little town, I'm hitting the road for St. Louis as soon as the paper's out tomorrow," she said. "Maybe I'll figure it all out on the way home."

CHAPTER 20

By noon on Saturday, Carol was on her way to St. Louis. She didn't look forward to the long drive down U.S. 61, but time on the road bought welcome time in her hometown.

If she kept her foot on the gas all the way, it would take about two and a half hours to get to her mother's apartment in Richmond Heights, a St. Louis suburb just west of the city limits. Mrs. Hagan had sold the family home, on the north side of the city, soon after the youngest of her four children had left for college.

Although Carol didn't spend much time at the apartment on these one-night visits, she knew her mother still enjoyed having her home. On Sunday mornings, after a couple of vigorous tennis matches with a former teammate from her high school's varsity squad, Carol would catch up on family news over French toast and bacon in her mother's kitchen.

Carol pushed the Maverick to eighty and breezed past the signs announcing upcoming exits for Hannibal, Missouri, the long-ago home of Samuel Clemons, aka Mark Twain—a fact the town's businesses didn't allow even the speediest passersby to ignore.

Billboards promoting all things related to Tom Sawyer, Huck Finn, and Becky Thatcher were splashed with afternoon sunlight. The signs promised restaurant food as good as home-cooked, fun-filled gift shops, fascinating tours of Twain's favorite places, and even a chance to whitewash a picket fence.

If a filmmaker wanted to capture the simplicity of mid-America, Carol mused, he might focus on this stretch of U.S. 61 between Bethany and Hannibal. But, how much of this touted innocence is real, and how much is, itself, whitewash?

Her thoughts bounced back to Larry Bryce's phone call to her boss. Charlie wanted to portray the police chief's communication as some quirky courtesy. Carol didn't see it that way. Questions about the chief's real motives distracted her like an errant lash under an eyelid.

* * *

Her mother was at the front door, talking in the formal way she always did with official-looking strangers. Maybe they were door-to-door salesmen. No. She could tell from her mother's serious tone they were more important than salesmen.

"Come in, please. Take a seat in the living room. Andrew just went upstairs a few minutes ago. I'll tell him you're here."

The men, dressed in light-colored suits and ties, removed their fedoras as they walked from the hallway into the living room, lit only by rays of morning sun slanting through sheer curtains. They sat down on the sofa, as her mother had directed them.

She saw them from her position at the dining room table where she was folding laundry. They smiled and said hello to her, but she said nothing back, embarrassed that company had come into their home when the family's wash was spread all over the table.

In a few minutes, her father came downstairs, dressed in light blue cord pants, a white T-shirt, and the navy blue canvas shoes he always wore at home in the summertime. He extended his right hand to both men and asked how they were.

"Sweetie, you can finish that later," he said to her gently when he saw her in the dining room. "Go upstairs for a while, okay?"

Rather than walking through the living room and passing by the strange men to get to the stairs, she walked through the kitchen where her mother was washing breakfast dishes and looking worried.

"Who are they, Mom?"

"They're friends of Daddy's from the police department."

"What do they want? Why didn't they talk to him at work? He was just there."

"Never you mind, Carol. There's nothing to worry about. Go on upstairs 'til they leave."

She went up the stairs, then turned around and sat down on the top step. She couldn't make out the conversation, so she slid down several steps on her seat until the low-register rumblings turned into words.

"Jake and I haven't talked about it," she heard her father say.

"You know he could be in serious trouble, don't you, Andy?"

"I can't see why. He hasn't done anything wrong."

A second voice responded. "If you and Jake haven't talked about what happened, Sergeant Hagan, how can you be so sure he hasn't done anything wrong?"

Her father's voice hardened ever so slightly, the way it sometimes did when her brother talked back to him and got under his skin.

"I know because he's a good cop," her father said, not trying to hide his impatience.

"We really hope that's so," the first voice said. "But I have to tell you,

Andy, if you do know anything, or find out anything from here on out, you're obligated to let us know. Money's missing, and the circuit attorney's office is going to find out where it went."

"That's fine," her father said. "That's their job. But it has nothing to do with Jake."

"You've never been involved in this kind of thing, Sergeant Hagan. I'd sure hate for you to get caught in a whipsaw."

"Don't worry about me. I just hope somebody on the force is as concerned about Jake."

She could hear the shuffling of the men getting ready to leave. She quickly and quietly backed her way up to the top step, swung her legs sideways onto the same step and pressed herself against the stair wall.

The three men moved out into the hallway.

"Thanks for your time, Andy."

"Sorry we had to bother you at home, Sergeant Hagan."

The two men left.

Looking down, she could see the flash of anger in her father's face as he turned and walked into the kitchen.

* * *

Glancing into the rearview mirror, Carol saw flashing red and white lights on top of a Missouri Highway Patrol car. She looked at the speedometer. Eighty-five.

She slowed, turned on her blinker, pulled onto the shoulder, and reached for her wallet.

CHAPTER 21

Photos of a late model Buick, split in two by a tree, were on Carol's desk when she arrived in the newsroom Monday morning. A husband and wife from Burlington, Iowa, both fifty-five, were killed in the one-car crash on Riverview Boulevard at the north city limits early Sunday.

Charlie informed Carol that Chief Bryce had called him Sunday morning with an invitation to take pictures of the death car before it was towed. Not one to let his eggs Benedict be interrupted by a routine aim and shoot, Charlie had dispatched Kenny to the scene instead.

"The chief is really seeking you out these days, isn't he?" Carol said.

Charlie shot her a rare look of annoyance. "He called you first, but you weren't home."

She knew it bothered Charlie when she left town on the weekends, but she didn't know why he cared. On the slim chance that news did break out in Bethany on Saturday or Sunday, there was no newspaper to put it in until Monday, anyway.

Carol guessed it wounded Charlie's civic pride when she left town. But, so far, hurt feelings hadn't deterred her.

Neither did being pulled over by highway patrolmen.

Carol had learned early in her driving career that it didn't pay to play innocent. When the trooper informed her she'd been clocked doing eighty-five in a seventy mile-per-hour zone, she simply nodded her agreement. As usual, she got off with a warning. As usual, she kept her foot on the gas and kept a keener eye out for highway patrolmen.

"What's happening in St. Louis, Carol?" Tom asked, tossing a notebook onto his cluttered desk.

She looked up from the tickler file she had been looking through for feature story ideas. "It was great! Food. Drink. Friends. Movies. Tennis. More food!" she said, trying to mask a lousy mood.

She *did* have a problem with her trips to St. Louis, but not the same as Charlie's. In her brief time there this weekend, Carol had dined with friends at Favazza's on the Hill, gone to a late showing of *Paper Moon*, played two sets of tennis Sunday morning, had breakfast with her mother, and enjoyed a backyard barbecue with her brother Denny and his family before driving back up U.S. 61 late Sunday night. It wasn't a weekend in Paris, but it beat hell out of a weekend in Bethany.

Seeking to stave off the blues, she called to see if another St. Louis émigré was interested in company that evening.

CHAPTER 22

Driving out to the Sizemore farm, Carol looked forward to talking with Joan about the latest news from Washington, DC.

She had spent part of the afternoon watching John Dean, President Nixon's former White House counsel, in his first day before Senator Sam Ervin's committee, read from a 245-page statement describing his recollection of the events now simply being referred to as "Watergate." Under oath, Dean testified that the President became involved in the cover-up of the hotel break-in soon after it happened.

Some people doubted Dean's honesty since his version of events cast President Nixon as a criminal. But political biases notwithstanding, most Americans realized something historic was happening. ABC, CBS, and NBC were taking turns broadcasting the Senate hearings every day, and PBS aired taped replays every evening.

The revelations tumbling out of the capital all had their origins in the dogged reporting of Woodward and Bernstein, who had followed the scent of five burglars all the way to the president's closest aides.

Early on the morning of June 17, 1972, the burglars had been caught breaking into the Democratic National Committee headquarters in the Watergate Hotel. Frank Wills, a security guard, had noticed a piece of tape placed over the lock of a stairwell door. The first time he saw the tape, he simply removed it. But when he returned ten minutes later and found another piece of tape on the lock, he called the police.

Now, a year later, hundreds of reporters, as well as senators and staff of the select committee, were asking variations of, "Who in the White House knew what, and when?"

"Hi, Carol! How do you like my latest improvements?" Joan called to the preoccupied reporter when she pulled up in front of the farmhouse in her blue Maverick.

Joan was sitting in one of two new cushioned rattan chairs that flanked a glass-topped rattan coffee table on the covered front porch. Alongside the steps leading up to the porch, where weeds had grown just a few days ago, was an explosion of red, pink, and white petunias, purple impatiens, and orange and yellow marigolds. Two baskets filled with white and red begonias hung from the porch ceiling in macramé swags. The grass in the yard had been respectably trimmed.

"It looks great," Carol said. "You obviously have decided to stay put, in spite of the recent unpleasantness."

"I did it all myself. Except for mowing the grass, which is, of course, what God made teenage boys for."

After fixing drinks in the kitchen, the women returned to the porch, talking like old friends even though they'd known each other for only a week.

Joan confided that she was still steering clear of the barn but making the house her own. Besides purchasing furniture and planting flowers, she also had set up an office in a second-floor bedroom and already was editing a manuscript from Crawford Publishing.

When the conversation turned to Carol's work, Joan was glad to learn the reporter had no immediate plans for further articles on the "Sizemore skeleton." At the same time, she was surprised to hear about Chief Bryce's phone call to Charlie.

"I've never worked for a newspaper, but isn't it a bit unusual for an editor to be taking orders from a police chief? At least in the USA?"

"Yeah. I've been mulling over what to say to Charlie about that," Carol said. "I can't believe he's gullible enough to believe the chief's call was just a friendly gesture.

"I don't get the timing, either," Carol continued. "We weren't planning to run anything else about the skeleton unless we got word from the Department of Criminal Investigation in Des Moines, or maybe the sheriff's office in Fort Madison. When Charlie told me about the chief's call, my first thought was the body had been ID'd. I can't figure out why Bryce told Charlie he would give him any new information and then not have any new information to give him."

Before Joan could respond, the stove timer buzzed and the women moved back into the kitchen.

Over lasagna and Caesar salad, the conversation turned to John Dean's testimony before Senator Sam Ervin's committee.

Like Carol, Joan was among the pathetic thirty-eight percent of voters who had supported Senator George McGovern's run to replace Richard Nixon in the White House.

"I bet McGovern could chew nails," Joan said. "He tried to focus attention on the Watergate break-in last summer and was ignored. Now, finally, everybody is paying attention, and it's too late to change the outcome of the election."

"A lot of people thought McGovern was lambasting the break-in at the DNC headquarters just to make the White House look bad. Now the White House is looking bad all on its own," Carol said. "The more they try to stop the investigation, the more it looks like a cover-up."

Joan took a sip of Burgundy and swirled the wine in her glass. "Do you think anyone in town is trying to stop *you* from investigating the skeleton?"

When Ron had teased her about a Bethany version of Watergate on Friday, Carol had let it pass as a joke without admitting to him that the thought had crossed her mind. But now, hearing someone else suggest it, she was intrigued.

"Are you serious?" she asked.

"Why not?" Joan said. "Do you think all small towns are run like Mayberry?"

"No. Somebody *could* be trying to hide the truth about what happened out here, but it surprises me you would suspect it."

"Journalism schools aren't the only places that teach people to think critically," Joan said.

"I didn't mean to imply they are. But, except for reporters, not many people bother to dig beneath all the official stories and theories that come from the government."

"Well, then, now that you've heard the 'official theory' about how a murder victim ended up in my barn," Joan said, "what would induce *you* to dig beneath it?"

Carol smiled at the turn the conversation was taking. This was the woman who had been concerned a week ago about how the paper would report on a skeleton in her barn. This was the woman who, just an hour ago, was glad to hear Carol had no plans to report any more about it until she learned something from the authorities.

"Are you suggesting there's a cover-up going on in Bethany?" Carol asked.

"No. I'm just asking a question. You're the only real reporter in this town. What would provoke you to look deeper into something that might be fishy?"

Carol paused and smiled. "Well, let me see. Maybe if the police chief were to try to steer me away from a story."

"Where will you start?" Joan said.

CHAPTER 23

For the next hour, with dinner plates on the sink behind them and wine glasses on the table in front of them, Carol and Joan speculated.

Could the victim's killer or killers still be in Bethany? If there were people in town involved with the man's death, who were they, and what were they thinking now that the skeleton had been discovered? Did they have a next move in mind? Did they need a next move?

All of the people Carol had questioned said they knew nothing about the skeleton. But what else would they say if they wanted to avoid being connected to the crime?

Carol's mind wandered to Woodward and Bernstein. How had they penetrated the wall of silence in Washington? They had started with the DC police report of a break-in. They moved on to what they could learn from investigators and other sources. They kept putting one foot in front of the other, following a trail of names, addresses, and phone numbers. But Carol didn't have any fresh names and numbers. Her leads seemed as dry as the victim's bones.

She had to find more people to talk to. Charlie hadn't told her to stop working on the story. He just said he would be the one to receive any new information from the chief. But what if the most useful information wasn't going to come from Chief Bryce, anyway?

"Hey, where'd you go? What are you thinking?" Joan said across the table, interrupting Carol's soliloquy.

"Sorry. I'm just thinking about the work I've got to do. I've been taking what people are willing to give me. I think I've got to start all over again."

"Who's on your list?"

"I haven't talked to anyone in Des Moines for a while. I'll call the DCI tomorrow. I'll also go back to Sergeant Padgett and ask if any light bulbs have gone on lately. And what about your cousin Michael? Have you talked to him since last week?"

"No, but I can give him another call. Maybe he's remembered something about the handyman or the couple who leased this house after my aunt and uncle died. In fact, I think I'll go back to the real estate office and ask for the name of the couple and where they moved. If I can get a phone number, I'll give them a call. I'll also take another look around here to see if I missed anything."

Carol smiled, appreciating how quickly Joan ticked off the actions she could take.

She, on the other hand, had been inching around the edges of this cold homicide for four days. Her hesitancy wasn't because she had never investigated a murder before. She had always been able to solve the problem of not knowing how by learning how. No, Carol now realized, her hesitancy was because she had let the actions of Charlie Vogler and Larry Bryce lead her to doubt herself.

Shake it off, she said to herself, repeating what her brother Denny always told her when she used an ache or a pain as an excuse to stop playing.

Excuses wouldn't cut it here.

CHAPTER 24

Tuesday morning, the DCI investigator who answered the phone in Des Moines told Carol his office had nothing new on the skeleton and scant hope of ever putting a name to the victim. The case was cold, the killers were long gone, and the investigators had more current crimes to solve. Of course, he assured her, his office would continue to keep an eye on missing persons reports. She should feel free to call back now and then to learn if anything had turned up.

Carol decided that, for the time being, she wouldn't openly challenge Charlie's sheepish response to Chief Bryce's phone call. She was more than willing to stand up to her boss, but she wanted to pick the right moment. If she argued with Charlie now, just to make a point, she risked alienating him and accomplishing nothing.

Dr. Mallory had, by word and example, instructed her in the value of tamping down her tendency to favor confrontation over diplomacy. Still, he had respected her tough-mindedness. Once, she had turned in a profile on a university administrator for the campus magazine. The profile offered candid perspectives from both admirers and detractors, and Mallory had asked her to soften it. Carol refused her advisor's request, saying any changes would distort the honest portrait that had emerged as a result of thorough reporting. When she stood her ground, Mallory had apologized to his student.

Although Carol wasn't yet ready to go toe to toe with Charlie about the police chief's phone call, she also wasn't planning to ask his permission to investigate how the skeleton landed in Joan Sizemore's barn.

The managing editor rarely left the office before the day's edition was printed, but this morning he had a dental appointment. He asked Carol to postpone her lunch and take his place scanning one of the first papers off the press to make sure there were no mistakes so major that the run had to be stopped.

While she waited in the newsroom for a call from the pressman downstairs, Carol decided to have a private chat with Bob Hartman.

"Did Charlie say anything to you about the phone call he got from Larry Bryce?"

"What call?" Bob asked, lowering the briar pipe from his mouth and raising his dark, bushy eyebrows, eager to hear a fresh bit of gossip. The tall, sixty-something state editor combined urbanity with a small-town affinity for the grapevine.

Carol recounted Larry Bryce's Friday morning call to Charlie. "Doesn't that seem odd to you?" she asked.

"Never heard of the chief doing anything like that. He's cordial enough to Marg and me when we see him out socially, but he doesn't give two hoots about this newspaper. His calling Charlie to say he wants to give him information about a police matter is flabbergasting," he said, taking a squinty-eyed puff on his pipe.

"What do you make of it?" Carol asked. "We've run two short articles and a couple of photos. We've got nothing new to go on, no ID, nobody reported missing, nobody who saw or heard anything suspicious at the farm. The chief knows that. He told Charlie he wants to directly pass all information on the case to him, but why did Bryce even bring it up when there's nothing to pass?"

Bob shook his head and intertwined his fingers across his broad chest. "What do you think? You're the only one who ever talks to the chief—or anybody else at the police station for that matter."

"Based on zero evidence I've collected so far, I think the skeleton is connected to someone in Bethany," Carol said. "I don't know if Chief Bryce knows what the connection is, but I think somebody who does know asked him to make the call to Charlie."

"*Lawdy*, Carol Hagan!" Hartman exclaimed, leaning back so far in his swivel chair she thought he would tip over. "How on God's green earth did you jump to that conclusion?"

"It's not a conclusion. Like I said, I have no evidence. Let's call it a hypothesis."

She explained how Joan Sizemore had given her the push she needed to look into the police chief's odd attempt to interfere in the paper's coverage of a crime. Carol felt a little exposed voicing her flimsy suspicion to such a solid citizen. Bob socialized with virtually all of the big shots in town. Yet she instinctively felt it was smart to confide in him. If anyone had the nose to smell a rat in Bethany, it would be Bob Hartman.

He listened, at least not overtly dismissing what she was saying; he shoved the pipe between his teeth and left it hanging out the right side of his mouth, assuming the guise of a man tough and detached.

"Okay, Carol," he said. "Let's see. A man gets himself killed by someone who has some kind of a connection to the police chief. When the guy's body is found in its hiding place two years later, the criminal gets worried and tries to stop the newspaper from looking into the crime by going to the chief and asking him to tell the newspaper to lay off. Do I have it right?"

"That's good, Bob. You've summarized it well," Carol said. She could take the sarcasm as long as he was willing to consider what she was proposing. "Now, I only have about a hundred loose ends left to tie up. Any advice on where to start?"

Bob began to rummage through a desk drawer. "Let me find my manual on investigative reporting. I know it's here some place. I just used it back in August of '64."

They both laughed. But then the state editor turned serious.

"There's always got to be a motive," he said, leaning back in his chair with his hands clasped behind his head. "That's where I'd start. One man kills another man over money, women, revenge, power . . . oh, and did I mention money?"

"But the police think there's more than one killer," Carol said. "It would have taken two men to get the body up the steps. That's partly why Jack Padgett thinks it was fugitives who were passing through. They get into a fight. Somebody gets killed. The killers find an abandoned place to conceal the body and go on their way.

"It's an easy explanation for the police," she continued. "But if that's not what happened, why else would two or more men murder another man?"

Hartman looked at his watch and tapped the tobacco from the bowl of the pipe into the ashtray on his desk.

"Maybe you're getting ahead of yourself. Most of the time murder is the end game. What happened before that? Maybe they started out with one crime and, before they knew it, were involved in something else altogether."

Carol's mind wandered to the Watergate hearings.

"Like the 'third-rate burglary' at the Democratic Headquarters," she said, signing the quotation marks. "The break-in became important when people in high places were caught trying to cover up their knowledge of it."

"Shall we demand that the city council hold hearings to investigate the police chief?" he asked.

"Be that way, then," she said. "I told you I was hypothesizing. If I look into it and find nothing, all I'll have wasted is my time. Don't you think it's worth checking?"

Hartman shook his head. The reporter was talking about his circle of friends. He played golf with most of the men in town who might have the police chief's ear—bankers, doctors, lawyers, a judge, city officials.

"I don't know, Carol," he said, shaking his head again. "I'll have to think about it."

CHAPTER 25

Uneasy but determined, Joan Sizemore walked into her barn and looked around, trying to see the emptiness with fresh eyes.

Having urged Carol to take action last night at dinner, she felt obliged to live up to her part of the deal.

"The skeleton's gone," she told herself as she climbed the steps to the hayloft. "What's left to worry about?"

The loft looked just as it had a week ago, except now there were smudged shoeprints on the dusty floor. She opened the large wooden window on the loft's front wall. Her property looked much as it had that day, too, except now there were colorful flowers in place of weeds, new porch furniture, and a neatly mown lawn.

With daylight flooding through the window, Joan walked back to the space below the shelf and knelt down, surprised at her willingness to get so close to the place on the floor where the wood was darkened by decomposition.

In this familiar but unaccustomed posture, an old habit from her Catholic school days resurfaced.

"Eternal rest grant unto him, O Lord, and let perpetual light shine upon him," she said aloud. "May his soul, and the souls of all the faithful departed, rest in peace."

She rose from her knees, closed the loft window, and went back to the house.

CHAPTER 26

Mayor Jason Eberle hung up the phone and cupped a cool hand over his right ear. It felt like it was on fire.

"What the hell's going on?" he said loudly to no one.

Now Eugene Montgomery was calling him at his office in the middle of the day, warning him he'd better "get control of the situation." *What situation, for chrissake? The story's dead. Nobody's talking about it anymore. The paper isn't publishing anything. Why in hell doesn't Montgomery let this go? Is he trying to drive me crazy?*

Eberle composed himself and pressed the intercom button on his desk.

"Marjorie, please find Jeff and ask him to come to my office right away."

Four minutes later, Jeff walked in and found the mayor seated on his leather sofa, eyes closed, shoes off, feet up on the bird's-eye maple table.

"What's going on, Jason?" Ryan asked, not bothering to hide his irritation. "I'm in the middle of a meeting with the wastewater engineers from Davenport. It takes forever to get all these guys together. What do you need?"

"How much longer will you be with them?" Eberle said, opening his eyes. "We've got trouble with Montgomery, and I need to talk to you."

"Give me thirty minutes," the city manager said and strode out of the office.

Eberle closed his eyes again and pretended that when Jeff returned, the two of them would coolly make a decision.

A half hour later, the city manager came in unannounced and immediately loosened his tie, something he never did in meetings with subordinates or outsiders, no matter how hot it got. He went to the mayor's desk and pulled open the top right drawer where Eberle kept his supply of Bayer aspirin and Tums. Popping two aspirin into his mouth, he turned to the mayor's credenza, poured ice water from a silver decanter into a glass, and washed down the tablets. Only then did he break the silence.

"Jason, I've had it. We're dealing with a lunatic. We'll never be able to satisfy his desire for revenge or destruction, or whatever it is that's driving him. I think he wants to kill us both, and he's just tormenting us first, for the hell of it."

"So we need a different battle plan," Eberle broke in. "We've got to get more aggressive."

"What do you mean, 'get more aggressive'?"

"I'm not sure, yet," Eberle said. "He called to say he wants us to do what we promised. Why does he think we're *not* doing what we promised?"

"Because he's a raving lunatic out to make us both as crazy as he is!"

CHAPTER 27

Margaret Hartman observed her husband from the back porch.

Usually he was a fountain of conversation at home, sharing political tidbits he picked off the news wires or morsels of gossip from lunch with fellow Rotarians.

The last two evenings, Bob had been quiet. When she asked him about it, he said he was fine. But through forty-one years of marriage, "fine" had always looked a particular way. This didn't look fine.

Hartman was thinking. He had been thinking since yesterday afternoon's talk with Carol Hagan. In the short time she had worked at the *Bugle*, she had shown intelligence and good judgment. Still, what she was suggesting seemed far-fetched, to say the least.

If people in town had been involved in a murder here two years ago and he'd smelled nothing fishy the whole time, well, that was almost impossible for him to swallow.

He wasn't a native, but he'd lived in Bethany for more

than thirty years, and it was home. Although entrenched in the town's social life, he had inoculated himself against much of its parochialism with a good education and lots of reading. He often made fun of the town's foibles and the sometimes narrow minds of its citizens, but he believed they were good people who meant well and worked hard. That anyone he knew could have killed a man, abandoned the body, and gone on living in Bethany as though nothing had happened seemed way beyond belief. Provocative though it was, he knew in his heart nothing would come of Carol's suspicion that somebody in Bethany was connected to the skeleton.

His friends weren't saints. Some fudged on their taxes. One was hiding gambling debts from his wife. Another drove up to AA meetings in Burlington for fear of being labeled a drunk in his hometown. But Hartman knew of no secret so grave that the threat of exposure would drive any of his cohorts to kill.

As he mused on his patio, Hartman recalled a game he and his college friends used to play. The game began with someone describing a far-fetched occurrence. Often it involved a romantic fantasy, such as a lucky classmate seducing a famous and beautiful woman. Sometimes the unlikely event was an extraordinary physical feat, like surviving a fall out of a twenty-story building, or something ridiculous, like being discovered stark naked in the dean's office.

In the game, every player had three minutes to invent a logical explanation for how the improbable event could have happened; then, one by one, the friends would spin their scenarios. Whoever concocted the most believable story won a quarter from every other player.

By what scenario, Hartman asked himself, could any of the men he knew literally have gotten away with murder two years ago? Whom did they murder? Why did they do it? He mentally re-ran the litany he had recited to Carol yesterday. Sexual jealousy? Money? Revenge? Power?

Sex. Every one of his male acquaintances, except for Jeff Ryan, was at least moderately happy in his marriage. Almost every time he and a group of his friends were together *sans* wives, the talk eventually turned to sex. Having it, not having it, wanting it, wanting more of it, or thinking of having it with someone else. Hartman knew all the male talk was just a show for their best audience—themselves. None of his married friends pursued other women.

Jeff Ryan, on the other hand, had plenty of opportunities to enjoy the company of women when traveling, and Hartman had heard through the grapevine that the city manager wasn't averse to having overnight guests in his home. But there was no whiff of any passionate rivalry.

Besides, Hartman reflected, two men wouldn't be involved in murdering a third out of sexual jealousy.

Money. That could be a likely motive. Put enough money in the pot, and probably any man could become a murderer. Hartman again surveyed his circle of friends and acquaintances, trying to recall conversations about money problems or unusual windfalls. Just like sex, most of the men didn't hesitate to brag about their success in the stock market or fail to lament when they didn't get in on a good deal—or out of a bad one—fast enough.

Pete Eckles had confided to him about gambling debts he'd run up when he was making business trips to Nevada. But he hadn't started making those trips until last year. Besides, Eckles didn't have the status to go to Chief Larry Bryce with a complaint about Bethany's crime news.

"Honey, you want some iced tea? Aren't you getting bit up out there?" his wife asked from the screened-in back porch.

"No, thanks, Marg. I'm fine," Hartman responded distantly. Daylight was dimming to twilight, but the mosquitoes apparently weren't ready for dinner.

Who has the nerve, or the clout, to ask Chief Larry Bryce to run interference with the *Bugle?* Judge Ferguson certainly has the *cojones* to talk to anybody about anything, but he would consider it demeaning to go to the police chief for help, no matter what kind of trouble he was trying to evade. A city councilman might approach the chief, or maybe Ron Dalton over at the chamber of commerce. The mayor, of course. Or Jeff Ryan. Heck! Carol was just guessing that someone else had urged Bryce to call Charlie. Maybe it was Bryce himself who wanted to put the lid on news about a dead body.

Back to motive. The men he knew lived comfortably but not lavishly. All of his friends belonged to the Bethany Country Club. First, and most importantly, so they could play golf. And, second, to have a convenient place to take their wives out to dinner on Saturday nights.

Most couples took one vacation a year, usually to California, Florida, or Texas. The fanciest trip Hartman could remember was the mayor's two-week Mediterranean cruise with his wife a couple of years ago. What had Eberle said? He thought it was time to give his bride a special trip for putting up with him so long.

Bob Hartman laughed. Accounting for inflation, if he were playing with his Bradley buddies now, he'd be forking over twenty bucks.

CHAPTER 28

"Good article, Carol!" Charlie called to her when she entered the newsroom after lunch. He continued tapping out Friday's editorial supporting President Nixon's request that Americans reduce their energy consumption.

Waving her thanks, she picked up today's *Bugle* from her desk. Her profile of itinerant landscape painter Vincent Millerbaugh was on page one, below the fold, illustrated with her photo of the artist at his easel, demonstrating his duck-painting technique. With practice, Carol had learned from Millerbaugh, one could create a sky full of birds using a rapid, repetitive motion.

Underneath the newspaper, she found a pink message slip with Joan's phone number scrawled on it.

"Have you solved it yet?" Joan asked when Carol returned the call.

"Oh, yeah, sorry I forgot to tell you," Carol said. "Colonel Mustard did it in the kitchen with a lead pipe."

On her side of the conversation, Joan gave a report of her investigative work, summing up with the admission that she had learned nothing useful. Because Charlie was in earshot, Carol said only that she would call Joan again soon.

"I'll be in the morgue if anybody needs me," she said as she walked out of the newsroom.

Her plan was to begin an A to Z search of the *Bugle* files, looking for anything in the local news *circa* 1971 that suggested a possible motive for murder at or around the Sizemore farm.

She wasn't in the windowless little library five minutes before Bob Hartman walked in and sat down across the table from her.

"Did the Sizemore woman have anything for you?" he asked, matter-of-factly.

Carol looked surprised.

"I took the message while you were at lunch," Bob explained. "I figured she was following up on your mutual suspicions."

"Joan told me that she had revisited the hayloft, but didn't see anything newsworthy. She also called her cousin again to see if possibly he'd remembered anything unusual regarding his parent's property since they died. No luck there, either."

Bob sat forward in his chair, pushing his shoulders halfway across the table. "How well does Joan Sizemore know her cousin?"

"I don't know. There's a pretty big age gap. Michael was grown and gone when Joan started spending summer vacations with her aunt and uncle."

Bob drummed his fingers on the table. "I've been wracking what's left of my brain, trying to think of a reason for someone in Bethany to commit murder. But what about Sizemore himself? Did the police ever talk to him?"

"Sergeant Padgett told me he called him a day or so after the skeleton turned up. He doesn't think Michael Sizemore has any connection to the crime."

"Well, that may be," Hartman said, "but the fact is, the bones were found on property that belonged to Sizemore when the body was put there. Maybe he got involved in something out in California or Des Moines and dragged it back here, like a cat drags home a dead rat."

Carol smiled at the simile and shook her head. "From the way Joan talks, he sounds like a good guy. It's hard to believe he has anything to do with this."

"Well, my dear, it's also hard to believe a former U.S. attorney general could have had anything to do with the 'third-rate burglary' that found its way to a Senate hearing room."

CHAPTER 29

"Game, set, and match!" her tennis partner crowed across the net after smashing a backhand just inside the right foul line. "Something tells me your head wasn't in the game this morning, Carol."

"My head, my backhand, my forehand, my serve . . . you name it. Sorry I didn't give you more competition, Barb. Thanks for the exercise, anyway."

Carol approached the net to shake hands with her opponent, hoping she wouldn't spread word of today's preoccupied play. If she did, it could jeopardize Carol's chances of lining up good competition for the weekends she stayed in Bethany.

A few blocks from the park, Carol made a stop at Nicholson's Drugstore to pick up the thick Sunday edition of the *Des Moines Register*. A morning spent enjoying a good newspaper, a tasty breakfast, and leisurely cups of coffee was her usual reward for spending a summer Sunday in this small town that still didn't feel like home.

Preoccupation stayed with her all the way back to her apartment. At some point, very soon, she would have to disclose to Joan Sizemore that a *Des Moines Register* reporter was looking into her cousin's business associates.

After Carol and Bob's conversation Thursday in the morgue, Bob had decided to phone an old friend at the *Register* and ask him to check the paper's file on Michael Sizemore.

On Friday afternoon, the reporter, Dick Talbot, called back and told Bob that the file was slim. The one article he had found, from March 15, 1969, wasn't about Sizemore, but about a new shopping center being built by Whitlock Construction Company. The article stated that Michael Sizemore, a Los Angeles businessman, was one of the key participants in the center's development.

Talbot had read part of the article to Bob, quoting Fred Whitlock, the company's owner, saying how gratified he was to be collaborating with the Californian, who had worked at the construction company part-time while he was in school at Drake University. Whitlock praised Sizemore as an "innovator in the financial management of development projects."

The name "Whitlock" was vaguely familiar to the *Bugle*'s state editor, and Talbot reminded him that Fred Whitlock had been an Iowa highway commissioner for a few years before his sudden death in 1971.

"My friend Dick Talbot said he'll check into Fred Whitlock's clippings on Monday to see if he can find any links to the Sizemore property," Bob had told Carol before she left the office Friday.

"Do you think there might be something worth investigating?" Carol had asked.

"Frankly, I don't think it'll amount to a maggot on a meadow muffin," Bob had said. "But, I don't see any harm in checking it out."

Sitting at the kitchen table in front of a plate of Canadian bacon, scrambled eggs, buttered toast, and grape jelly, Carol's appetite was dulled by her ambivalence. She was happy to have a possible new lead, but she wasn't looking forward to telling Joan Sizemore about it.

CHAPTER 30

"Whitlock Construction was purchased by some of its executives after Whitlock died. They still do a lot of development work in Des Moines and elsewhere around the state," Dick Talbot told Bob Hartman Monday afternoon over the phone.

"Whitlock got a highway commission appointment in '68 and had a lot of political connections. There were too many mentions of his name in business articles and highway commission proceedings to read all the clippings," Talbot said.

"What'd he die of?" Hartman asked.

"Heart attack. Sudden. He was fifty-eight. What are you looking for, Bob?"

"I have no idea. Really. Thanks for your trouble."

Hartman hung up and started filling his pipe with fresh tobacco. Half the pleasure of pipe smoking was the ritual. Once the pipe was glowing, he turned to the ancient Royal manual typewriter he kept on the left side of his L-shaped desk, put in two sheets of copy paper with a piece of carbon paper between them, and began typing:

FW, d.'71, sudden heart attack, 58.
Succ. Constr.Co. Politically connected, hiway com. '68.
FW and MS's relationship? Who know in common? Bs.
relat.? Love relat.?
Money?
MS???? What do in Cal.? What connec. to WCC? How
long?
Who at WCC knows MS?

Hartman pulled the papers out of the typewriter, threw the
carbon paper in the waste basket under his desk, folded the
carbon copy, and put it in his lower right-hand desk drawer.
Then, he walked to Carol's desk and set the original down in
her view.

"Can you decipher that?" he asked through teeth that were
holding his pipe, vise-like, on the right side of his mouth.

Carol looked at it a moment. "I can decipher it. Where do I
find the answers?"

He shrugged his sloping shoulders, shook his head, and
strolled out of the newsroom puffing.

She put away her future file and studied the questions on the
sheet. To find the answers, she would have to talk to people in Des
Moines and maybe California. She needed names she wouldn't
find in the *Bugle*'s files.

Newspaper clippings were like a path into the life of person,
or a city. A reporter could gain a basic knowledge of newsworthy
people and events just by reading all the pertinent files. Carol
usually went to the morgue to check the spelling of names
and confirm titles and dates. But she was developing a better
appreciation for all of those painstakingly clipped and folded
pieces of yellowing newsprint. They not only could tell her about

the past, but also maybe give clues to what was going on in the present.

"Can I take another look at those stories you saved from '71?" Carol asked, coming up behind the rangy wire editor as he sat in his favorite position, chair tilted back, feet up on his desk, reading the latest edition.

"Sure. What's up?" Ron Davidson asked.

"Besides your feet? Probably nothing," she said. "I read the articles quickly the last time. I want to recheck them."

She took the envelope back to her desk, took out the Iowa stories, and laid them in front of her. Mutilated horses in Storm Lake. World War II vet in Fort Madison. Suicide woman from Des Moines.

The short AP article dated June 20, 1971, said the Des Moines woman's name was Amanda Mitchell. Her body had been found by a maid in the bathtub of her room at La Fonda Hotel in Santa Fe on Friday, June 18. Her wrists were slit. No note was found. Her husband had reported her missing the previous evening, after he returned home to Des Moines from a business trip. The couple had no children.

Carol read the article twice and took it back to Ron.

"What made you save this?" she asked. "A woman leaves her home to kill herself. Maybe punishing her husband. Maybe depressed because she never had kids. It seems pretty conclusive."

He took the yellowed paper from her and reread it.

"I don't know. I guess I wondered why a woman from Des Moines would travel to some hotel a thousand miles away to do something she easily could have done anywhere in Iowa. It could have been to make a point, but if so, why didn't she leave a note? There were loose ends."

"You never saw a follow-up on the wires?"

Davidson shook his head. "No. It probably turned out to be cut and dried."

Carol groaned and turned away, taking the article back with her.

CHAPTER 31

A trip to the state capital wasn't anywhere on Carol's list of how she would like to celebrate the Fourth of July. Nevertheless, Monday evening she was packing her overnight bag for Des Moines.

The midweek holiday presented a good opportunity to look in the *Des Moines Register*'s morgue for some answers to the questions Bob had typed out. As soon as Tuesday's articles were down the chute, she would make a quick stop at home to change clothes, put out enough food to last Simba until her return Wednesday night, throw her bag in the car, and hit the road.

When Joan called later than night with an invitation to come over for barbecued ribs on the Fourth, Carol hesitated and then immediately repented. Her friend had encouraged her to pursue this story, and Carol felt compelled to confide a largely accurate version of her reason for driving to Des Moines. She told Joan that Bob Hartman had suggested she look into Michael's business associates to see if any of them had connections in Bethany. The *Register*'s files might point to a possible link to the Sizemore farm.

Joan asked if Bob suspected her cousin of knowing more about the skeleton than he was saying. Carol assured her that at this point no one knew enough to suspect anyone of anything.

As she went to bed Monday night, Carol felt confident that taking the trip was a good idea. If any Bethany residents were involved in the homicide, they had covered it up seamlessly. In Des Moines, she might find a loose thread.

* * *

Her mother was sitting at the Singer sewing machine in the sunlit doorway between the dining room and kitchen, preparing to put the zipper in a newly made uniform skirt.

"Carol, I need your eyes to thread this needle!" her mother called out.

Obediently, she went over to the machine and pulled a strand of navy blue thread from the full spool that sat on the spindle, licked the end of the thread into a point as she had watched her mother do a hundred times, and, on the first try, pierced the needle's narrow eye with the thread and pulled it through.

She didn't want to talk to her mother right now. She knew it would be all about school starting soon and how it was time to go downtown to shop for saddle shoes and uniform blouses.

She turned and walked back into the living room, idly searching for something to do until her Aunt Sharon came to take her and her sisters to the Forest Park Highlands swimming pool.

Sections of the Globe-Democrat were strewn on the couch where her father had left them. She plopped down and scanned the front page, looking for something of interest. In the bottom right-hand corner, she saw a two-column article bearing the headline, "Officer Arrested In Gambling Sting."

Inset into one of the columns was a photo that looked like a school picture, except the man wasn't smiling. He was wearing a uniform hat just like her father's. Beneath the photo was the name, J. L. McCarthy.

"Patrolman John (Jake) Laurence McCarthy, a six-year veteran of the St. Louis Metropolitan Police Department, was arrested yesterday and charged with one count of embezzlement in connection with the July 30th gambling raid at a warehouse on Hall Street," the first paragraph read.

The article reported that about $10,000 of the $150,000 in cash seized in the raid never arrived at police headquarters. Patrolman McCarthy was the officer responsible for transporting the money downtown.

Farther down, the article named three "kingpins" who had been arrested during the raid and charged with several felonies. In the last paragraph, the article named four officers from the Fifth District who were on the team that had planned and executed the gambling raid. Her father, Sergeant Andrew Hagan, was one of the officers named.

"Mom, Daddy's name's in the paper!" she said from the living room.

"Oh, yeah?"

"Yeah. It's on the front page. Is he gonna get in trouble?"

"Shush! Where'd you get that idea?"

"Those men from the police department came to talk to him, remember? I heard them asking Daddy about 'Jake,' and that's the name of the policeman they say has been arrested," she said, walking back into the dining room.

"That doesn't mean Daddy's going to get in trouble. He's an honest policeman, you know that."

"What's embezzlement mean?"

"Since you've got so much time on your hands, why don't you go look it up in the dictionary?"

* * *

Suddenly Carol was yanked back to consciousness by Simba kneading her pillow. Awake, she knew that the dreamlike incident she had just relived was real. It had happened the same day she learned the difference between stealing something and stealing something that others trusted you to keep safe.

CHAPTER 32

"I've got to be here or I'll get fired," the twenty-something general assignment reporter said to Carol after they introduced themselves in the *Des Moines Register*'s newsroom. "What's your excuse?"

"Sheer ambition," she said with a smile. "So, Mike Duncan, can you direct me to the morgue?"

At Hartman's request, Dick Talbot had cleared the way for Carol to use the *Register*'s clippings library on the holiday, when the newsroom crew was a fraction of its usual size.

An assistant city editor sat reading and editing articles destined for tomorrow's metro section. A news editor sat in the slot of a horseshoe-shaped desk, scribbling head specs on the tops of the wire stories piled in front of him. As he finished, he shoved the marked-up articles over to the rim of the desk, where two copy editors checked the articles for typos and errors of fact, grammar, and punctuation, then wrote headlines to fit the type-size and column-width specs.

The remainder of the slim crew consisted of one other general assignment reporter and a police reporter, whose ears were trained to decipher the static-laden messages called over the police radio. Just by listening, the police reporter could determine which crimes, fires, and auto accidents were worth a trip to the scene, and which could be reconstructed from written police reports or phone calls.

Barring a disaster, these three reporters provided enough manpower to cover anything that might happen on this Independence Day.

Carol walked into the empty morgue, happy not to have to answer questions about what she was looking for. She would take notes on anything that caught her attention, get contact information for people with whom she could follow up, and call them from the *Bugle*'s newsroom in the next couple of days.

After setting up a place to work at one of the long tables in the room hemmed with narrow oak filing cases, Carol went to the Ws to hunt for "Whitlock." His fat four-by-six manila envelope was stuffed with a couple of dozen clippings, including an article from 1968 that profiled the newly appointed highway commissioner and Des Moines native at length.

Whitlock's was a riches-to-rags-to-riches story. His father had been a wealthy financier who committed suicide after losing everything at the start of the Depression. At the age of sixteen, Fred resolved to rebuild the family fortune, doing whatever it took. He dropped out of school and worked as a laborer. He learned how to paint, lay bricks, make electrical repairs, and install plumbing. A year-long stint as a Seabee on Guadalcanal in the South Pacific trained him to build foundations, pave roads, and construct ironwork.

When the country emerged from World War II, there was plenty to build and Whitlock was ready. At age thirty-two, he founded Whitlock Construction. He was smart, ambitious, and socially adept. His company grew fast, and so did his reputation as a man of action and influence. No one was surprised when the governor asked him to fill an open spot on the state's highway commission in 1968.

It all sounds good, Carol thought. Hometown boy makes good by determination and the sweat of his brow.

Next, Carol read a 1969 clipping, a duplicate of the one Dick Talbot had found under Michael Sizemore's name in the *Register*'s files. The article described a shopping mall with 500,000 square feet of retail space, the largest project in the history of Whitlock Construction Company. There was a picture of Whitlock in a hardhat, talking with crew members at the mall site. About halfway through the article, Carol found the reference to Joan's cousin.

"I'm thrilled to have Michael Sizemore with me again," Whitlock was quoted. "He came to work for the company while he was still at Drake University. I was impressed with his business savvy. Michael is an innovator in the financial management of development projects."

The next paragraph reported that Michael Sizemore had moved to Los Angeles in 1952 to work in real estate.

Most of the other clippings in Whitlock's file were there because his construction company was the contractor for notable building projects. Other mentions of Whitlock showed up in articles about the highway commission.

Carol unfolded and read each of the articles, doubting any villainy would come to light, but determined to be thorough. Toward the end of the stack of clippings, Carol found the article about Whitlock's sudden death.

"Fred Whitlock, Road Commissioner, Dead at 58," the headline from the Saturday, May 15, 1971, edition read. Whitlock had died of a heart attack in his office on a Friday afternoon. The obituary repeated much of the background information that was in the 1968 article.

"Fred Whitlock was known and liked by every government official in the state. He will be remembered as a vigorous leader in his industry and as an influential force for good in Iowa," the chairman of the highway commission was quoted as saying. "His death is a tragic loss to his family, his friends, and the whole state. He will be deeply missed."

As she prepared to leave the morgue, Carol recalled the conversation she had had with Ron on Monday about the suicide in Santa Fe; she detoured to the "Mi-Mo" filing case, where she found an envelope labeled "Mitchell, Amanda." There was one news article in the envelope, plus her death notice.

The *Register* article contained the same information about the Santa Fe suicide as the AP wire story. This one, however, also quoted Amanda Mitchell's brother, James McFarland, who said she was a wonderful woman and that her family was stunned by her death. He said his sister's husband, Frank, was holding up as well as could be expected and was grateful for the support of neighbors and friends.

Back in the *Register*'s newsroom, Carol copied Whitlock Construction's number from the Des Moines phone book. She looked in the phone book for the name "Frank Mitchell" without success. She flipped back a few pages and found "James McFarland." She scribbled the telephone number on a fresh page in her notebook.

Before leaving the newsroom, Carol called Bob Hartman at his home and gave a synopsis of what she had found on Whitlock.

"Doesn't look too promising, Bob. I'll call Whitlock's company tomorrow, though, and see if there's anyone there who can tell me more about him," she said.

"Besides that, maybe you should talk to Michael Sizemore," he said. "And heck, if Whitlock was so popular in the state's political circles, why not ask our mayor and city manager if they knew him?"

On the drive out of town, Carol stopped at Ewing Park on Indianola Road and purchased the "All-American Fourth of July Special" at the Lions Club barbecue stand.

Sitting on a grassy slope surrounded by "All-American" families, Carol relished the barbecued pork ribs, corn on the cob, coleslaw—and her independence.

CHAPTER 33

"Good morning, Mayor," Carol said, knocking on his open office door in City Hall. "Did you have a good holiday?"

"I had a terrific Fourth, Carol. How about you?" Jason Eberle said with a grin, putting down his pen and motioning her into the room.

"I visited Des Moines for the first time. Seems like a nice town."

"One of my favorite places. What took you up there?"

Driving to City Hall that morning, Carol had wondered about the best way to ask the mayor about Fred Whitlock and Michael Sizemore. She didn't want to lie, but neither did she want to tell the whole truth.

"I'm thinking that sometime I might write a series of articles in the *Bugle* about how Iowa has been evolving from a rural state to a more urban one. I went up there to do some research at the *Register*," she said, assuring herself that nothing in those statements was untrue.

"Interesting idea," Eberle said, rocking back in his chair.

"I found some information on a fellow named Fred Whitlock, the late highway commissioner who owned a big construction business in Des Moines. Did you know him?"

Eberle seemed surprised to hear the name. He furrowed his brow. "Fred Whitlock. I didn't know him well," he said, shaking his head. "I did see him occasionally at meetings in Des Moines. He died a while back, didn't he?"

"He died a couple of years ago. In one of the articles about Whitlock, I found a reference to Michael Sizemore. Apparently, the two men were close business associates. It was strange to see a reference to the guy who owned the farm where the skeleton was just found."

"What a coincidence," Eberle said with another shake of his head.

"Do you know Michael Sizemore, Mayor?" Carol pressed on.

Eberle shook his head again. "Nah. I think he left Bethany right out of high school. Never knew him myself."

"Well, I don't want to keep you. See you at the city council meeting tonight."

On her City Hall rounds, Carol didn't usually stop at the mayor's office unless she wanted his perspective or a direct quote on some city business. She had stopped this morning at Bob Hartman's suggestion. Jeff Ryan, however, was someone she regularly sought out. Today, she needed to ask him about the wastewater treatment plant, a multimillion-dollar construction project whose progress she reported on in the *Bugle* every couple of weeks. She ran into Ryan outside the mayor's office.

"Hi, Jeff, I was just coming to see you. Do you have a few minutes to update me on the treatment plant?"

"Sure. Let's go back to my office," he said, turning on his heel and pointing his thumb like a hitchhiker.

"By the way, did you happen to know Fred Whitlock?" she asked him.

Ryan pulled up and laughed quizzically. "Man, that's a strange question. I knew Whitlock a little. Did *you* know him?"

She was stung by his sarcastic tone. Ryan was usually cordial to her, but her question obviously had jarred him.

"No, Jeff, I didn't. Does it bother you that I asked about him?"

"It doesn't bother me that you asked; I just don't see why," he said. "I would think you'd be more interested in Bethany's business instead of wasting your time with questions about a dead man from Des Moines, that's all."

"I sure didn't mean to offend you," Carol said. "Please do fill me in on the progress Bethany is making in handling its sewage."

CHAPTER 34

Jeff Ryan walked into his office bathroom, threw up his breakfast, and returned to his desk, still queasy.

"Hold my calls, please, Lisa. Tell anyone who needs to talk to me that I'll get back to them after lunch," he said into his intercom.

Ryan folded his arms on his desk and put his head down on top of them. How did Carol Hagan make the connection to Whitlock? Why did Whitlock have to screw everything up by letting Montgomery in? He recalled Montgomery's excruciating intrusion that evening at Foley's.

* * *

"Jason! Jeff! Good to see you both again!" Michael Sizemore said, rising from the table where he and Whitlock were seated and extending his hand, first to Jason, then to him.

Whitlock also stood to welcome them to their favorite table at Foley's. The two partners already had their usual drinks in front of them, Smirnoff on the rocks for Sizemore and Chivas neat for Whitlock.

He asked the waitress to bring Budweisers for Jason and himself.

Before the beers arrived, Sizemore reached into his briefcase and pulled out a manila folder.

"I'm glad you were able to meet on such short notice, guys," Sizemore said. "I've got a very nice parcel that a friend in Los Angeles says is destined for great things. Granted, it doesn't look like much now, but I'm assured it will turn into something big in the next few years."

As Sizemore cleared the space in front of him and flipped open the folder, a man in a light blue, long-sleeved shirt approached the table carrying a tray with two bottles of Budweiser and two frosted Pilsner glasses.

"Hello, Fred! Hello, gentlemen! I understand the two of you wanted these cold, frosty brews. Here you go. It is my pleasure to serve you," the man said with a smile as he set the tray down with an exaggerated flourish.

The four men seated at the table looked quizzically at the man and at each other.

Awkwardly, Fred Whitlock stood up with a forced smile.

"Well, hello, Eugene. I wasn't expecting you today."

"Not a problem, Fred. I told you I would come by when I could, and today was good."

Sizemore, Jason, and he remained sitting, wondering who the man was and what he was doing there. Sizemore closed the folder and casually placed it on the floor alongside his briefcase.

"Gentlemen, let me introduce you to Eugene Montgomery," Whitlock said.

As if on cue, the three stood for the introductions and sat down again, expecting the man to go away. To their surprise, Montgomery reached for a chair at a nearby table and pulled it up to theirs.

"Please, don't let me stop the conversation," Montgomery said, motioning to the closed folder on the floor. "I'm fast, and I'll catch up," he said pleasantly.

Whitlock seemed almost as surprised as the others, but he forged ahead.

"First, Eugene, let me explain about you being here. This is the first time these fellows and I have been together since you and I talked in my office, so I have to bring them up to speed."

Montgomery chuckled. "Of course. I guess it's you guys who have to catch up, right?"

Fred Whitlock told of meeting Montgomery and being immediately persuaded he would make a good addition to the investment group.

"I hope you don't mind I made a decision on my own, but Eugene has my full confidence."

Absent the usual flair, Whitlock raised his glass and said, "Let's welcome Eugene to our group."

The three surprised men did just what Whitlock asked.

* * *

The intercom on the city manager's desk buzzed, and Ryan raised his head from his desk with a start.

"Sorry, Jeff. It's Gary Pearce calling from Davenport about one of the change orders on the treatment plant. He says he's got to talk to you right now."

CHAPTER 35

When she got back to the newsroom later that morning, Carol quickly wrote a two-page update on the treatment plant, plus a police roundup for all the items that had accumulated over the holiday. Once everything was down the chute, she would go to lunch with Tom and Ron and then go home as she usually did when she had an evening meeting to cover.

From the top right-hand drawer of her desk, Carol took the notebook marked "City Council, May '73-" and flipped through until she came to the page dated June 21. The brief notes reminded her that Jeff Ryan had missed the last city council meeting because of a conference in Omaha. His absence, although explained by the mayor that night, still struck her as odd. One of Ryan's most important duties was to report to the city council on all city projects and proposals and make recommendations for action. Why would he have given a higher priority to an out-of-town presentation that had been erroneously scheduled? Was he shopping himself around?

The instant the question occurred to her, Carol called the long distance operator to get the phone number for Omaha's City Hall.

"Guess what?" she said quietly, standing at Bob Hartman's desk a few minutes later. "Jeff Ryan didn't miss that city council meeting two weeks ago because of a schedule mix-up. I just talked with the Omaha mayor's secretary. She said Ryan gave his presentation on Wednesday morning, June 20. The conference ended that afternoon. There wasn't any scheduling glitch."

"Well, that is interesting," Bob said, rolling away from the desk till his chair stopped against the wall in back of him.

That men lied was not news to Hartman. What made news was *what* they lied about—and why. *Was Jeff looking for a new job? Did an attractive woman lure him into staying in Omaha? Had he been on a drinking binge? Did Ryan lie to Eberle about where he was, or did Eberle lie to the council members about where Ryan was? Were they both lying?*

CHAPTER 36

Carol looked around at the scattering of Howard Johnson's customers seeking relief from the summer heat and quickly spotted Bob Hartman motioning to her from a booth in the back. He had asked her to meet him here at four o'clock so they could talk freely.

"Do you think Jeff Ryan's absence from the council meeting had anything to do with Joan Sizemore's finding the skeleton?" Hartman asked as she sat down across from him.

The waitress came with two glasses of iced tea and stood ready to take an order.

"Thanks. This is all we'll be needing," he said. The waitress left them alone in the nearly empty section of the restaurant.

"Ryan was out of town both the day the skeleton was found and the next day when the news came out in the paper," Carol said. "I don't know what the connection would be. If he was in Omaha on the twentieth and back here on the twenty-second, he probably wasn't that far away on the twenty-first."

"If he was away at all," Hartman said. "It's possible he was in town and just not in any shape to attend the city council meeting."

"What do you mean, 'not in any shape'?"

"Jeff over imbibes sometimes. Maybe he was at home with a hangover."

"But we know he was in Omaha till the afternoon of the twentieth. If he drove and got back to Bethany late that night is it likely he would have drunk so much through the night or the next day that he couldn't come to a city council meeting on the evening of the twenty-first?"

"Probably not," Hartman said, shaking his head.

"Tell me about Ryan's drinking," she said, curious about the scenario Bob had suggested and reluctant to discard it without consideration.

The veteran editor had started his pipe ritual, tapping the old tobacco into an ashtray and scraping the ashy residue from the bowl of the briar. He furrowed his brow and reviewed his mental footage on Ryan.

"When Jeff first came to town, he was a happy guy," Bob said, digging the pipe into a brown leather tobacco pouch. "He seemed to love his work. He and Jason really hit it off. People liked him. But he doesn't seem as content as he once was," Hartman said, touching the flame of his Old Boy lighter to the fresh supply of tobacco and puffing till it smoldered. "Somewhere along the line he started drinking more than socially. I mentioned it to him once. Asked him if everything was okay. He just shrugged it off. Sometimes I think he misses having a wife and kids."

Now the pipe was clenched between his teeth, and Bob happily filled the air with the aroma of sweet cherry almond tobacco.

Carol's thoughts turned to John Dean, the Senate's key witness in the ongoing Watergate hearings. Like Jeff Ryan, Dean impressed people as a straight-arrow kind of guy, a non-politician in a political world. Now, Dean's ascendant career as legal counsel to the president was finished, and his name would forever be linked to what presumably would be the nadir of Nixon's administration.

"When did Jeff change?" Carol asked.

"I don't know exactly. Let me think," he said, closing his eyes to better see the memory. "Marg and I first noticed his heavy drinking at a couple of parties within days of each other. One was at Lyle and Ruth Novak's home. Lyle's the president of Hawkeye Bank and Trust. I remember the occasion because the Novaks don't usually throw large parties. This one was for a millionaire entrepreneur here from Germany. It was a beautiful summer evening, and Marg and I stayed out on the terrace the whole time, as did Jeff. Some people were teasing him about being the 'young mayor' of Bethany."

Hartman puffed and continued. "Yeah. That's when Jason and his wife were on their Mediterranean cruise a couple of years ago, and Jeff was more or less filling in for him. I remember saying to Marg that he was drinking like it was the night before the Volstead Act took effect.

"A few nights later, there was a smaller party at Doug Hurley's. Doug used to be on the city council. Marg and I just dropped by, didn't stay long because it was a school night. Jeff was there and, once again, pretty well oiled."

"So you first noticed Jeff's heavier drinking in summer, two years ago, when the mayor was on vacation. Has he kept it up?"

"Jeff and I don't socialize all that often, but I hear talk. I think the drinking is just part of his not being as happy as he was. Like I said, he may miss family life in a town where most men his age have kids running around at home."

"What if it's not that?" Carol asked. "The medical examiner said the guy in the loft was killed two years ago. What if that was the start of Jeff's unhappiness?"

Bob Hartman looked at her quizzically. "You think Jeff's the killer?"

"I'm not saying that. But maybe he learned something about what went on at the farm during the time the mayor was on vacation."

"Do you have anything specific in mind?"

She shook her head.

"I almost forgot," she said. "I stopped by the mayor's office as you suggested and asked Eberle if he knew Whitlock or Sizemore. He said he had met Whitlock at a few meetings in Des Moines but didn't know him well and that he only knew Sizemore by name. Later, when I mentioned Whitlock's name to Jeff Ryan, it seemed to disturb him. He asked why I would be concerned about a dead man from Des Moines."

Hartman puffed thoughtfully on his pipe and looked out the large window beside their booth, saying nothing.

"Do you think I should call Whitlock's widow and ask if Fred had any friends in Bethany?" Carol asked.

"You mean as a prelude to asking if her late, respected, and dearly beloved husband was a criminal?" he said with a wicked chuckle.

CHAPTER 37

Carol awoke to the buzz of her alarm clock on Friday morning, knowing it was time to give Michael Sizemore a call.

Before parting company at Howard Johnson's, she and Bob Hartman had reviewed the short list of facts she had gathered in her skeleton investigation.

An unidentified man had been killed by blunt force trauma to the head approximately two years earlier.

The skeletal remains were found on what, until recently, had been the property of Bethany native and current California resident, Michael Sizemore.

Sizemore had ties to Des Moines businessman and state highway commissioner Fred Whitlock, who died suddenly in May 1971.

Police Chief Larry Bryce had announced, without explanation, that he was going to give any new information he received about the unidentified victim to the *Bugle*'s managing editor rather than to Carol, but no new information was forthcoming.

Jeff Ryan or Jason Eberle, or both, had lied about why the city manager missed a city council meeting two days after the body was discovered.

So far, Carol hadn't found a thread that wove all these facts together. If there was one, Michael Sizemore probably knew what it was. He had told his cousin Joan he had no idea how a murder victim wound up on his vacated property. But maybe he just didn't *know* what he knew. Carol hoped she might be able to jog his memory.

She didn't want to have to ask Joan for Michael's number and then have to explain why. Instead, just before leaving the office on Friday, Carol called Whitlock Construction and asked the receptionist for the Los Angeles phone number of Mr. Michael Sizemore, a close associate of the late Mr. Whitlock.

That was the number Carol dialed from her kitchen wall phone Friday evening.

"Sizemore," a voice answered after three rings.

Carol introduced herself as the reporter who was with his cousin Joan when she called to tell him about the skeleton in the loft. She apologized for interrupting his evening and asked if he would take the time to answer a couple of questions. When Sizemore agreed, she posed the questions she thought might jog his awareness.

"I'm wondering, is there anyone in Bethany who, knowing you were so far away, might have used your property without your permission? Or," she continued, "do you have any acquaintances someplace else in Iowa who might have found themselves in a desperate situation and taken advantage of the fact that your property was vacant?"

She heard a soft chuckle on the other end of the line.

"I'm happy to report that I don't have any desperate friends, much less any friends who would be so rude as to criminalize my property behind my back.

"I really don't want to seem unsympathetic, Carol, but since my handyman was going out there on a regular basis, I'm sure he would have been aware if anyone was using the property without my knowing it. I think the barn had to have been a random pick, just like the police said."

"What about the handyman?" Carol pressed on. "I understand from Joan that you never met him in person. Is there any chance he might have been up to something?"

"The employment agency gave him a solid referral. I didn't have any reason to think he wasn't who he seemed to be," he said. "By the way, are you with Joan now?"

When Carol answered no, he asked her to be sure to say hello to his cousin the next time she saw her.

Sensing this was his signal to end the call, Carol thanked him and hung up. Her list of facts just as disconnected as before.

CHAPTER 38

Carol was jotting down names, dates, and offenses from the police log when she saw Chief Bryce enter the station through a side door. She interpreted this rare Saturday morning sighting as a sign it was time to ask him about his recent conversation with her boss.

"Did I do something to step on your toes, Chief?" she asked at the threshold of his office.

"Not at all, Carol. Why do you ask?" he said with a placid expression, waving her in.

"Well, the last time you and I talked, you said you'd keep me informed about any new developments with the skeleton. But since then, you've told my boss you wanted to talk directly to him about the case. I don't understand."

"It's not that I don't want to talk to you. There's just nothing new to say. If we keep rehashing this in the paper, all it does is reflect poorly on Bethany. We just thought it would be best if we waited till we have some real facts to give you."

"Who's 'we'?"

"Mayor Eberle and me, of course. Nobody wants this type of thing in their town's newspaper. It can negatively affect people's feeling of security and safety."

Carol swallowed a sarcastic response, suspecting it would be lost on Bryce anyway. The fact that he could sit there and tell her with a straight face that he and the mayor didn't like the inconvenience of bad news was absurd. But the bigger issue was that Charlie had been drawn into their absurdity.

"I understand that you and the mayor care about Bethany's image," she said, so tactfully it surprised her. "But people need to know what's going on. The *Bugle*'s not going to cover up bad news for you."

Larry Bryce stood up and awkwardly offered his hand for her to shake. "I would never ask you to stop doing your job, Carol. At some point, the DCI may figure out what happened and let us know. As soon as they do, I'll let the paper know. I promise."

Dismissed from his office, Carol knew the matter still was unresolved, but at least she had spoken up for herself and the paper. She was disheartened that Charlie had not.

CHAPTER 39

Except for Charlie, everyone cleared out of the newsroom by eleven thirty on Saturdays in order to squeeze every possible minute out of the weekend.

Carol had planned to go home, change clothes, put out Simba's extra food, grab her overnight bag, and be on the road to St. Louis by noon. But the conversation with Chief Bryce had left her uneasy. She knew she couldn't put off talking to Charlie any longer. She lingered, jotting next week's meetings and interviews on her desk calendar.

Bob, Ron, and Tom filed out together, wishing everyone a good weekend. Bob put a pink message slip on her desk as he walked by. "Call me if you want," he had scribbled above his home phone number.

Charlie was tapping out Monday's editorial, yet another on wage and price controls. He sensed Carol was waiting to talk to him; he thought he knew the topic, one he himself had been stewing over.

Mayor Eberle's assessment of the managing editor had been partially accurate. His phone conversation had left Charlie feeling more respected by a big wheel in town. He had justified accepting Bryce's request that he be the *Bugle*'s contact person on the skeleton case by telling himself there was no story, nothing to cover, nothing to follow up. If by seeming to comply with the chief's request he could improve their relationship, it could turn out to be a good trade.

Lately, he'd been having second thoughts.

At her desk, Carol knew it was time to start the conversation. She didn't want to be antagonistic, but she couldn't keep quiet about what had happened any longer. No matter what Charlie thought about the "arrangement" with the police chief, she knew it was way off the mark.

Before Carol could make her move, Charlie ambled over and sat down by her desk.

"What's cookin', ol' girl?" he said with a comradely wink.

"I need to talk with you, Charlie," she said, taking a deep breath. "First, I have to apologize to you. I've been working behind your back, trying to find out what happened at the Sizemore farm. I didn't know if anything would come of my research, and I didn't want to take the chance you'd tell me to stop. It was a sneaky thing to do, and I'm sorry."

Charlie nodded and started to speak, but she continued, unwilling to be sidetracked.

"I stopped and talked to Chief Bryce today and asked him why he wanted to give you information on the skeleton instead of me. He didn't answer my question. He said he didn't have a problem talking with me but that both he and the mayor were concerned the image of Bethany could be hurt if we kept the story in the paper.

"Charlie, I can't work for a newspaper that takes orders from the police chief or anyone else. No matter how much or how little information we have, or how much or how little we plan to cover a story, those decisions have to be ours. The minute we start letting anyone else tell us how to do our job, or even let them *think* they can tell us how to do our job, we're finished. We're not here to make life easier for them.

"I don't know if any city official is involved with what happened at that farm or not, but no matter what, they can't tell us how to report this story."

Again, Charlie nodded. He seemed embarrassed to be called out by his city editor for a journalistic sin, but also relieved.

"You're right, Carol. I really screwed up. I let it go because I didn't think anything would come of it. I know better. Whatever story there is to cover, it's yours. I'll tell Bryce you're the one to get any updates on this, as well as anything else that comes into his department."

"Thanks," she said, glad that her belief in Charlie's integrity was not unfounded. "If you have a few minutes, I'd like to tell you what I've been trying to track down."

"Sure. What have you got?"

She told the managing editor how the chief's call had triggered her suspicion that the skeleton might have a Bethany connection, that she had discussed it with Bob, and that together they had speculated about possible motives relating to business deals originating in Des Moines.

"Fred Whitlock and Michael Sizemore were good friends who did business together in Des Moines," she said. "When I looked through the clippings at the *Register*, I learned Whitlock apparently knew most of the politicians around the state. But when I asked Mayor Eberle the other day, he said he barely knew Whitlock and doesn't know Sizemore at all. I want to find out if, contrary to what Eberle said, he and Whitlock had more than a passing relationship. And if they did, why did Eberle lie about it?"

Charlie listened patiently. He didn't mind Carol's digging deeper into a story, but he couldn't believe this tangent would lead anywhere.

The conversation with her boss delayed her departure for St. Louis, but it was worth it. Despite his skepticism, Charlie promised he would support her investigation.

That evening, Carol and everyone else in the country learned that President Richard Nixon had refused to testify before the Senate Watergate Committee or permit access to presidential documents, citing "the constitutional obligation to preserve intact the powers and prerogatives of the presidency."

CHAPTER 40

As soon as Chief Larry Bryce got off the phone Monday morning, he dialed the mayor's direct line at City Hall.

"Jason, Charlie Vogler just called me. He said he's thought it over and decided Carol Hagan's the one I should contact with any information on the unidentified body. Said I shouldn't try to tell him how to run the paper. Can you beat that?"

Eberle had been clearing paperwork off his desk, looking forward to a round of golf at the country club.

"What the heck is Vogler doing?" he bellowed in the police chief's ear. "Is he out to ruin this town? Did he say they're running another article?"

"I have no idea," Bryce said, bewildered by the mayor's ferocity. "I can't imagine what they'd have to run. I checked with the DCI myself on Friday, and nothing's happening. Those fellas in Des Moines have too much other stuff going on to be dealing with this. Relax, Jason."

The mayor slammed the receiver down.

"Relax, sure, relax," he mumbled. "Two years later and I'm still screwing with this."

He picked up the receiver and dialed the city manager's office.

"Jeff, please come to my office. We've got a problem with the *Bugle*."

Jeff Ryan had tried all weekend to put last Friday's troubling conversation with the *Bugle* reporter out of his mind. He'd thought about calling to apologize to Carol for his rude reaction to her question, but he didn't want to resurrect the specter of Fred Whitlock.

"Why don't you invite Carol Hagan over here and talk with her directly?" Ryan said when the mayor told him about the chief's call. "Give her a pitch about Bethany's proud reputation as a safe, crime-free town. Tell her the only reason you're concerned about the paper's coverage is because you don't want citizens to be worried unnecessarily."

The mayor quickly agreed. He was a persuasive man who had not yet used his talents on the reporter. What was he waiting for?

CHAPTER 41

"Hey, where have you been?" Joan asked when Carol called her Monday afternoon. "I thought maybe the *Des Moines Register* had hired you away."

"Not yet. But I'm thinking maybe, if I go back for Labor Day . . ."

"Did you find anything in their morgue that helped?"

"I've got a couple of new leads. If you're not busy, why don't you come for supper tonight? We can catch up."

After giving Joan directions to her apartment, Carol decided it was time to call the widow Whitlock in Des Moines. When a woman on the other end of the line identified herself as Shirley Whitlock, Carol delivered her rehearsed lines about researching urban growth in Iowa.

"I know your late husband had quite an impact on Iowa's development because of his construction company, Mrs. Whitlock. Did any of his projects involve work in Bethany?"

"Well, I don't think Whitlock Construction ever did much work in those towns down there," Shirley Whitlock said. "There might have been a few things, but the company always kept pretty busy working in Des Moines and across central Iowa."

"I see. I guess, though, as a highway commissioner, Mr. Whitlock probably was familiar with development in Bethany and other towns around here. Do you know if he was acquainted with our mayor, Jason Eberle? Or maybe Jeff Ryan, the city manager?"

"Those names are familiar. I think they're fellows my husband had dinner with downtown occasionally. Fred had a good friend, Michael Sizemore, who was originally from Bethany. Fred would sometimes meet them at Foley's, his favorite dinner place."

"I've heard that Mr. Sizemore lives out in California," Carol said, wondering how far she could go. "Do you know if he worked on any projects with Mayor Eberle and City Manager Ryan, or did they just get together socially?"

There was a pause. "I really have no idea. Fred didn't talk shop much when he came home. He would tell me about meeting various people for drinks or dinner, you know, the after-hours side of it. I think he talked enough about construction and highway matters during the day."

Carol, sensing she had to end the conversation, thanked the widow for her help.

There was a little laugh on the other end of the line. "I don't think I've said anything that could be of use to you, Miss Hagan."

CHAPTER 42

No, it wasn't my customary Fourth of July. Yet enjoying fireworks bursting over a half dozen towns while cruising solo down Highway 34, car windows open and radio blasting, was a satisfying celebration of independence for this Iowa newcomer.

Finishing the first-person feature article about her holiday trip to Des Moines, Carol punched "save" on her computer. All she had to do was write a headline, and the story would be ready to send down the chute for Tuesday's edition.

She answered her phone on the first ring and was surprised to hear the voice of Mayor Eberle's secretary.

"Yes," she said, looking at her calendar. "I could be there at two. Did he say what it's about? . . . I understand, Marjorie. Thanks; you, too."

It was four o'clock. Ron and Tom both had left for the day. Charlie and Bob were at their desks.

"Here's some news," she said to both men. "That was the mayor's secretary asking if I can meet with him in his office tomorrow at two."

Bob let out a little whistle through his teeth. "Did Marjorie say what for?"

"I asked. Said she didn't know."

Charlie was pleased. He believed it was his earlier phone call to Chief Bryce, reasserting the sovereignty of the fourth estate, that had provoked the invitation. He didn't need to know why Jason Eberle wanted to meet with Carol. He just needed Eberle to know that the newspaper wasn't his public relations tool.

CHAPTER 43

Simba introduced himself to Joan by jumping onto her lap the minute she sat down at the kitchen table.

While Carol sliced a loaf of French bread, slathered each piece with a mixture of butter and pureed garlic, and wrapped the loaf in aluminum foil, Joan gave a detailed account of her latest research.

After revisiting the hayloft, Joan had examined the rest of the barn as well as the farmhouse and garage. She found no indication of violence anywhere. The only items in the house that Joan hadn't brought with her from St. Louis were two one-gallon paint cans in a basement storage room. One was half full of ceiling white; the other contained about a quart of pale yellow paint, the same color as the kitchen walls.

She also had telephoned the real estate agent who represented her in the purchase of her cousin's property. The agent gave her the name of the couple who had rented the house after the elder Sizemores died and a phone number in Ames, Iowa.

The wife told Joan that she and her husband had lived in the farmhouse from April 1969 to March 1971, paying rent only for the house and garage, since they didn't need the farmland, barn, or other outbuildings. In April of '71, they moved to Ames to work on their degrees at Iowa State.

Hearing Joan's report, Carol was satisfied that the barn had not seen normal use since the deaths of Ed and Kate Sizemore. Their son Michael had cleaned it out before returning to California, and his renters had no animals or crops to store there.

The empty barn would have been a perfect hiding place for someone who knew that Sizemore had no plans to live on the farm, sell it, or rent it again in the near future.

"What are you thinking?" Joan asked.

"I'm thinking the killers didn't just stumble upon a deserted barn; I think maybe they chose the barn because they knew the property was in limbo."

"The handyman," Joan said. "He would have known Michael had no plans to sell or rent the place during all that time he took care of the house."

"I had the same thought," Carol said, shaking her head. "But, 'Dan the handyman' told me your cousin gave him notice as soon as you purchased the house. If Dan Taylor was involved in the killing, he would have moved the body from the loft while he had the chance. Just in case, though, I called the employment agency on Friday to find out more about him. He's sixty-two years old, has lived in Bethany all his life, has three grown children and some grandkids, and takes care of his wife, who has MS."

Joan took a sip of her Scotch and water. "I should call Michael and ask if he had ever told anyone he owned an unoccupied farm in Bethany."

Carol put a fistful of stiff spaghetti noodles in a pot of boiling water before she came clean.

"I asked Michael about that Friday night."

"Well why didn't you just tell me straight out, instead of pussyfooting around?" Joan said.

"I was afraid you might take it the wrong way. I apologize for not giving you more credit than that."

"I accept your apology, but mainly because I don't want to miss out on this dinner," she said with a smile. "What did Michael say when you talked to him?"

"Let me take it from the top."

Carol took her notebook from the kitchen counter and sat down beside Joan at the maple table. While tomato sauce simmered and spaghetti swirled, Carol paged through the notebook in which she had written the facts gathered so far, as well as her unanswered questions about the skeleton. She had drawn a horizontal diagram across two pages, using solid lines showing the known connection between Michael Sizemore and Fred Whitlock, and the known connections among Jason Eberle, Jeff Ryan, and Larry Bryce. Dotted lines drawn between the various names showed the suspected connections.

"Did you ask my cousin if he knows Mayor Eberle or Jeff Ryan?" Joan asked, looking at the dotted lines flowing from Eberle and Ryan to Michael Sizemore's name on the diagram.

"No, I didn't. To tell you the truth, Joan . . ."

"Which, of course, is *all* you're going to tell me, right?"

"Of course. So here's the truth. Michael isn't obligated to answer my questions. He's a private citizen who can just hang up on me. If I tell him I'm suspicious of people who are friends of his, without having real evidence, he might not be willing to talk to me again.

"So far, the only thing I have that links them is Mrs. Whitlock's none-too-certain recollection that her husband occasionally had dinner with Michael, Jason Eberle, and Jeff Ryan in Des Moines. I need more than that."

Over dinner, the two women continued their conversation. Carol told Joan about the mayor's invitation to meet with him the next afternoon, and she recapped some of her and Bob's conversations.

"Bob Hartman thinks Mayor Eberle and your cousin might be involved in some kind of business deal."

"What do you think?"

"I don't think they knew each other when Michael lived here as a teenager. There doesn't seem to have been any connection between the mayor and your aunt and uncle. Michael left in 1948 to go to Drake and was in Des Moines till 1952, when he left for Los Angeles. He only came back here occasionally to see his parents.

"So I'm guessing Michael and the mayor met as adults, probably in Des Moines," Carol continued. "It simply might have been a case of getting to know one another through Fred Whitlock and going to dinner a couple of times because they were both friends of his."

Joan shook her head. "If that were the case, why would the mayor have denied knowing Michael when you asked him at City Hall? There's got to be something the mayor doesn't want you to know. Can you ask him?"

"I'm not going to ask Eberle anything more about Whitlock or your cousin until I have something solid," Carol said. "I don't want to tip him off."

Joan felt a chill. Two weeks ago, sitting around this same kitchen table, it seemed like a good idea to encourage the reporter to track down a possible cover-up. But, if Bethany's mayor was involved in the cover-up, it might turn out to be a very risky idea.

"Carol, you already *have* tipped him off," she said.

CHAPTER 44

Jason Eberle was standing by the sofa in his shirt sleeves, a smile spread across his face, his right hand extended.

"Thanks for coming over, Carol. I really appreciate it."

Right behind Carol came the mayor's secretary carrying a plate of cookies, which she placed on the bird's-eye maple coffee table.

"What would you like to drink, Carol?" she asked. "Coffee, Coke, lemonade, water?"

"Nothing, thanks," the reporter said.

Carol reached into her purse for her notebook and waited for a signal to be seated. She had never been invited to this area of the mayoral domain.

"My wife's chocolate chip cookies," Eberle said, nodding at the plate on the table. "Best in the state! You should try one."

The mayor gestured for her to take one of the tan leather chairs as he seated himself on the sofa.

Marjorie walked back in, carrying a cup of coffee, and placed it on the table in front of the mayor.

"Sure I can't get you something?"

"I'm fine," Carol said with a smile.

"You won't be needing that," Eberle said, eyeing the notebook. "I just wanted to chat with you a little about the skeleton found out in that barn. You and I haven't talked about it for a couple of weeks. Do we know anything more?"

Carol was surprised. "I thought Chief Bryce was keeping you informed. He told me you had some concerns about our coverage."

"Well, yeah," Eberle said, chuckling. "If you were the mayor, I don't think you would want that kind of publicity, either. All I meant when I talked to the chief was that unless there was something new happening, an identification of the body or something of that sort, I hoped it wouldn't be in the paper every day.

"I know you haven't been here all that long, Carol," he continued. "We can't expect you to know how people around here think. It's just that sometimes Charlie gets a bee in his bonnet and it antagonizes people. Don't get me wrong; I think Charlie's a great guy. I really do. And his wife's a doll. But, you know, he still has a little bit of a big city attitude. He can go a little overboard, and that affects peoples' opinion of the paper."

"Mayor, what are you referring to? We've only run two articles and a couple of photos. That's hardly going overboard."

"That's exactly my point, and it's why I wanted to visit with you," he said with a wink. "I want your assurance you'll continue your even-handed coverage of this thing. Just look at it from my vantage point for a minute. In the summertime, we've got tourists coming through here all the time on their way north to Nauvoo, east to Quincy, south to Hannibal. They stop to have a picnic by the river or get a bite to eat at HoJo's. They pick up the afternoon paper. They don't expect to see stories about skeletons in barns. We want to show them Bethany at its best, don't we?"

"Jason," she began, dropping the honorific, "if I were your PR person that is what I'd want to do. But that's not my job. I'm a reporter, and my job is to find out what's happening and tell our readers about it. I'm not out to make Bethany look bad or good."

"Well, of course," Eberle said. "I know you aren't a PR person, although, pardon my French, you'd probably make a damn fine one. But my point is if you don't have anything new to say about something, there's really nothing more to say, is there?"

Carol flashed back to Dr. Mallory. He had come to Mizzou from a newspaper in Texas and had years of experience dealing with politicians who thought they could win over reporters with charm or BS, the way they tried to win over voters.

Mallory was adamant that the reporters he trained should stand their ground with sources, no matter how high or low those sources happened to be on the news chain. "Remain polite, detached, and tough-minded," Mallory had admonished.

The *Bugle* reporter now found herself in the kind of situation Dr. Mallory had warned of. All she had to do was be polite, detached, and tough-minded. She had no axe to grind with Eberle. Even so, the more he talked, the cooler she played it.

The mayor was getting fidgety. He looked for some assurance that Carol Hagan was on his side.

"Don't you agree, Carol? If there's no *new* news, there's no use in trying to dig something up just to keep the thing in the paper." He put his hand to his neck and ran his index finger under the back of his white collar.

"Mayor, we're not trying to 'just keep the thing in the paper.' An unidentified body was found on local property. We're not going to ignore it. It's strange if you see anything out of line about that. Don't you want to know the truth about this crime?"

Eberle flinched.

"I think we do know the truth about this," he said. "At least as much as we're gonna know. The police suspect, and I agree, that the victim was some fugitive who was done in by double-crossing accomplices. I don't think it has anything to do with anyone around Bethany, and I don't see any need for the paper to waste time on it."

Barely taking a breath, Eberle ran on. "The police and the DCI will tell us when they know something. You don't really think you're better at investigating this than the police department and criminal investigators do you, Carol?"

He was trying to keep irritation out of his tone, but the conversation wasn't going the way he had hoped. Tiny beads of sweat had formed on his forehead but, nevertheless, he leaned forward and brought the cup of hot coffee to his lips.

Carol watched the easygoing mayor become restive, and her confidence surged. She doubted if either Charlie or Bob had ever seen this side of the famously unflappable Jason Eberle. Part due to J-school training, part due to sheer stubbornness, Carol resolved that no matter what Eberle said, she was not going to back down. She found it hard to imagine that this genial, well-respected mayor had something to do with a violent death, but it definitely appeared he was trying to hide something.

"You know, Mayor Eberle, I'm wondering why you're concerned about how I spend my time. Is there something you know about the events at the Sizemore farm that you'd prefer not be known by the public?"

Eberle flinched again.

"Don't be ridiculous!" he said, covering his reaction with a laugh. "What I know is exactly what everyone else knows. The residents of Bethany are all accounted for. The reason it looks like a waste of time to me is that whoever that fellow was, he's someone who didn't live here. Whoever is responsible for taking his life didn't live here, either. We don't have any missing persons, and we don't have any murderers. I'm just trying to help you save some time and trouble and, at the same time, keep things like old skeletons out of the minds of residents and summer travelers. That's all."

"Well, if that's all, Mayor, then I think I'll be getting back to the paper. There are a few things I'm trying to track down elsewhere," Carol said, putting her notebook and pen in her purse.

The mayor looked surprised as she stood up, put her purse strap over her shoulder, and walked toward the office door.

"Oh, so you do have some leads?" he asked with a weak smile. "What are you finding?"

"It's too early at this point. There's nothing I can write about, but I do want to check out a few things the police and DCI might not have thought of," she said with a smile. "Have a good rest of the afternoon, Mayor Eberle."

He closed the door behind her and called the city manager's office.

"I'll be damned if she isn't trying to screw us!" Eberle said angrily. "She acts nice and polite, but, I swear, she is trouble. She's working on something, won't say what it is. We're going to have to take the gloves off or Montgomery will have our balls on a platter!"

"Listen, Jason," Jeff Ryan said in a soothing voice. "She doesn't know anything. How could she?"

"She's chasing something, Jeff. She said she had some things to look into back at the paper but wouldn't say what. She asked me if I was trying to hide something, for chrissake!"

"I think she's playing with you, Jason. She's trying to act like a hotshot reporter. It's what they teach them in journalism schools these days. 'Go after the politicians. Don't give them a break.' Look at what the *Washington Post* has done to the president."

"Montgomery's not going to give us a break, either," Eberle said. "If one more word comes out in that paper, it's over. We can't wait. We've got to find out what she's doing and put a stop to it."

Ryan was alarmed at the panic in his friend's voice. "Calm down, Jason. Let me try to find out who she's talking to and what she's up to."

CHAPTER 45

Charlie and Bob were intrigued by Carol's report on Jason Eberle's demeanor. They thought it unlikely he was covering up a crime, but it seemed strange that he was so distressed about two newspaper articles.

"We've never had a murder in town while Jason's been mayor," Bob said. "Maybe he really is just trying to squelch bad publicity."

"Let's play this close to the vest right now," Charlie said. "There's no need for anyone else to know that Carol's investigating this. Not even our wives," he added, looking pointedly at Bob.

"What's your next step, Carol?" the managing editor asked.

She didn't have a next step, so she improvised. "I think I need to go back to Des Moines and find out more about the business deals Whitlock and Sizemore did together."

"Leave tomorrow after the paper's out," Charlie said. "I'll handle Thursday."

CHAPTER 46

Carol hadn't imagined returning to Des Moines so soon. But here she was, a week after the Fourth of July, seated again at a table in the *Register*'s morgue.

The last time she was there, she had focused her research exclusively on Fred Whitlock and Michael Sizemore. This time she scanned the Whitlock clippings for references to anyone from California. Within a half hour, she had found the names of four men.

Instead of continuing her search in the morgue, she gathered her belongings and went in search of a phone.

The *Register*'s newsroom was filled with the sound of clicking typewriter keys. With their fingers flying across keyboards, the dozen or so reporters looked like members of a one-instrument orchestra. Some cocked their heads to one side, holding telephone receivers to their ears. Some kept their eyes riveted on the scribblings in their Reporter's Notebooks. All were performing the nightly ritual of racing the clock to meet the deadline for the morning's edition.

The city editor sat in his habitual position, head down, eyes poring over the copy in front of him, tracking each line with a sharp lead pencil, ready to correct errors, eliminate redundancies, and clarify ambiguities with expert strokes.

When he looked up to grab the next article from his inbox, Carol caught his eye and got a nod of approval to use the phone at an unoccupied desk.

Benefiting from the two-hour time difference and the long-distance operator's assistance, she was able to catch the first man on her list at home. Ned Cantor, of Los Angeles, had been named in a 1970 article as the owner of a parcel of land on which Whitlock Construction was building a shopping mall in Cedar Rapids, Iowa.

Carol identified herself as a newspaper reporter researching Iowa's development projects.

"I'm interested in learning about the people from out of state who invest in land here," she told Cantor. "I found an article in the *Des Moines Register*'s files that named you as the owner of land in Cedar Rapids where there's a shopping mall. Is that correct?"

"Me and some other people," Cantor said.

"You're not the sole owner?"

"No way. I'm a member of a real estate syndicate. We look for good opportunities, pool our money, and invest it."

"May I ask what made your group decide to invest in the middle of Iowa?"

"Same reason we'd decide to invest in the middle of Texas or Pennsylvania, I suppose. You do research, find out what's happening, find out where people are going."

He wasn't telling her anything. Was he being secretive, or was she asking the wrong questions?

"Mr. Cantor, I'm afraid I have to admit to my ignorance about real estate syndicates. My paper's in Iowa, my readers are in Iowa, and I'm trying to find out why out-of-towners choose to invest in Iowa. Was there anything about the state that you and your partners found especially appealing?"

She heard a laugh on the other end of the line. Was she being a complete dimwit?

"Listen, Carol. It's Carol, right?" Cantor said. "You know that old telephone game? The one where somebody whispers to somebody else and they whisper to somebody else and they whisper to somebody else?"

"Yes."

"Well, I'm afraid I'm a little too far down the telephone line to be able to help you with your question. I get my ideas of where to invest through a network of people. I've never seen my land in Iowa; I've never *been* to Iowa. All I know is that whoever did the research on that piece of property was mighty good at it."

"Your investment is giving a good return?"

"A very good return."

"Mr. Cantor, now that I understand a bit better, may I ask a couple more questions?"

"Sure."

"If I wanted to talk to people who are higher up on the telephone line, how would I find them?"

Cantor didn't answer right away. She couldn't tell whether the silence was because he was thinking or because he thought she was getting too nosy. She had learned that matching silence for silence was the best course of action. Either he would answer the question or he wouldn't.

"There's a fellow by the name of Michael Sizemore who has a real estate company out here in LA," Cantor finally said. "I don't know him personally, but I hear his name, and I know he's done some deals in Iowa. If you can track him down, he might be willing to talk to you."

"Thanks. I'll look him up," Carol said. "Oh, this is a long shot, but would you happen to know a man by the name of Jason Eberle? Or Jeff Ryan?"

Another pause, then, "Sorry. I can't say that I do."

Carol thanked him and said goodbye.

Hanging up the phone in the busy newsroom, where every other reporter looked so productive, Carol questioned whether she was doing anything at all productive.

She had learned that at least one group of California investors got advice from a remote source about purchasing land in Iowa for profitable development.

She also had learned the name "Michael Sizemore" was familiar to one of these investors.

She could only speculate that if Californians had access to information about Iowa land, the reverse might be true of Iowans.

CHAPTER 47

"Erica! I'm so glad I caught you at home!"

Carol was making her last call from the *Register*'s newsroom to Erica Landers, a fellow J-school graduate student who had been in several of her classes. A California native, Erica had accepted a job at the *Santa Monica Outlook.*

The two spent a few minutes catching up, and then Carol made her request.

"I can't give you any details of the story I'm working on, but there may be Los Angeles real estate deals involved. Could you do some checking for me at the LA County Recorder of Deed's office?"

"I can give it a try," Erica said. "They keep all those documents at the Hall of Records. They're alphabetized by year, so if you give me a name and a year, it should be pretty simple."

"I'll give you three years: '69, '70, and '71, and three names . . ."

"Hold on a minute, girl," Erica interrupted, "I've got to write this down. Start over."

Carol repeated the years and spelled out the names: Jason Eberle, Jeffrey Ryan, and Frederick Whitlock.

Erica said she would visit the Hall of Records the next day and call Carol at home Thursday night.

Hanging up the phone, Carol noticed the reporter who had greeted her in the *Register*'s newsroom a week earlier; he was waiting with arms folded, leaning against a pillar near the desk she had borrowed.

"I see you've returned," he said with a smile. "Now, I'm really getting curious."

Carol rose from her chair and flipped her notebook closed. "It's Mike, isn't it?"

"Good memory, Carol Hagan."

"Oh ho!" she said laughing. "Remembering my *last* name means you win the Schwinn."

He bowed his head modestly. "When we get finished here, some of us go for a beer at a place called Porky's, across the street. If you don't have to rush off to your next secret assignment, would you like to join us?"

"I'd love to, Mike. I'm ready whenever you are."

CHAPTER 48

On her way to work on Friday, Carol looked forward to
getting Bob's and Charlie's thoughts about a strand
of evidence that linked both Bethany's mayor and city
manager with Fred Whitlock.

Erica Landers had found the names of Jason Eberle, Jeff Ryan,
and Fred Whitlock on deeds to the same three pieces of property
in Los Angeles County, purchased between 1969 and 1971. She
found Whitlock's name on five other purchases made during that
same period. The California reporter, anticipating Carol's next
line of inquiry, had looked through the property records from
1972, as well as the records for the first six months of 1973. She
found no more transactions bearing those names.

Carol now had proof that Eberle, Ryan, and Whitlock invested
together in California land, to go along with Shirley Whitlock's
recollection that Eberle, Ryan, and Sizemore had socialized in Des
Moines with her husband. Yet, the mayor had acknowledged only
a vague acquaintance with Whitlock and none with Sizemore, and
Jeff Ryan had denied knowing Whitlock at all.

"Why do you think Eberle and Ryan are being so secretive about their Des Moines pals?" Carol asked the two men as they stood in the middle of the newsroom.

Bob raised his dark eyebrows and opened his mouth to speak just as Carol saw Ron Davidson approaching the newsroom door.

"You can fill me in later," Carol said, cutting him off. "Right now, I've got to go find out who got ticketed last night for interrupting their drinking with a little driving."

Ron looked quizzically at the three editors standing in the middle of the newsroom. "What's happening? Did someone call a meeting and forget to tell me?"

"Naw," Charlie said with a grin. "We're just planning your surprise birthday party. When is your birthday, by the way?"

The lanky wire editor shook his head in mock exasperation, walked into the tiny, glass-enclosed closet with its clattering teletype machines, and collected the news of the world.

CHAPTER 49

Sergeant Jack Padgett's cruiser was idling at the curb on Fourth and Main when Jeff Ryan slid his red Buick Regal neatly into the space in front of it and walked back to the driver's side of the patrol car.

"How's it going, Jack?" he said, pushing his sunglasses back on his salt and pepper flattop and leaning down to address the officer through the open window.

"If I were having any more fun, I'd have to arrest myself. Everything okay with you?"

"Yeah. I'm just heading out to the treatment plant site. Thought I'd stop and make sure all is well."

"No complaints. Ask me next Friday, and it might be a different story."

Ryan hesitated. Then he remembered that the next Friday was the start of Bethany's annual street festival.

"Don't worry. We'll get through Bonanza Days okay."

"Yeah. I'm just hoping the weather cooperates. Last year, we baked."

"I remember," Ryan said absently. "Well, I better get moving. Take care of yourself."

He straightened up, and then leaned down again. "By the way, Jack, you worked the incident with the skeleton, didn't you? Anything happening with that?"

"No. From what I hear, I don't think DCI's doing much about it. Chief's called up there a couple of times, but he's not pressing it."

Ryan nodded. "Have you talked to the woman who owns the property since then?"

"I've said hello a couple of times when I've seen her in town, but we've never talked any more about the skeleton. She's stayed put, so I guess she's okay."

"Is she single?"

"Divorced."

"Good-looking?"

"I'd say so. Sandy blond hair, nice figure. What? You aren't getting any ideas are you, Jeff?"

"I'm always getting ideas about attractive divorcées. Is it possible I might accidently bump into her someplace?"

"I've seen her in town on Saturday mornings, shopping at the A&P and the bakery," Padgett said.

"You been tailing her? Tsk. Tsk. Jack, you're a married man."

"When you drive around in a patrol car all day, you notice a lot of people's routines."

"Well, good work, Sergeant Padgett. Thanks for the recon!"

Jeff snapped a salute, walked back to his car, and drove off.

CHAPTER 50

"I'll take one strawberry-cheese," Joan Sizemore said, pointing at the Danish pastries behind the glass counter. "And two apple turnovers, please."

At the sound of a bell, Joan looked over her shoulder and saw a tall, attractive man dressed in jeans, a navy polo shirt, and loafers. When their eyes met, they smiled and nodded. Joan turned back to watch the salesgirl ring up her purchase.

"Are you new in town?" he asked, standing alongside her at the counter.

"I've been here a few weeks."

"Welcome to Bethany. I hope we're living up to your expectations."

"Thanks for the welcome." She took a five-dollar bill from her wallet and handed it to the girl.

"I'm Jeff Ryan, the city manager. I guess you could say I've got a professional interest in newcomers' liking the town."

"I'm Joan Sizemore," she said, surprised that Carol had failed to mention how handsome he was.

"Oh . . . you moved into the old farmhouse on Route 2, right?"

"My late aunt and uncle's home, yes," Joan said, hating to think of the beloved home as just an "old farmhouse."

He nodded. "I'm sorry you were greeted with such a gruesome discovery. Must have been frightening for you."

"It was. Luckily, my pleasant memories of the farm far outweigh that bad one," she said with a smile. She accepted the white bag and her change from the salesgirl and moved toward the door. "It was nice meeting you, Mr. Ryan."

"Jeff. Everyone calls me Jeff," he said, following her out to the sidewalk. "I know we've just met, but I was going to head down to Howard Johnson's for a cup of coffee. Would you care to join me?"

Joan looked at her watch. She hadn't been to the A&P yet, so there was nothing in the car that would spoil. Her only other plans for the day had been to do a little housecleaning and a little gardening. She saw no harm in spending a little more time in town.

CHAPTER 51

Over coffee at Howard Johnson's, Jeff Ryan shared some of his background and some of Bethany's lore with Joan. She told him about her editing work, her ambition to write novels, and her decision last January to purchase her uncle and aunt's farm.

Joan found him both physically appealing and engaging, so when he invited her to join him for dinner that same night, she had accepted without hesitation.

Sitting with Joan in a booth at Schroeder's, a steakhouse across the Mississippi River, in Quincy, Illinois, Jeff asked, "Have you ever been afraid, living out there on the farm by yourself?"

"Not at all. I think about that day in the hayloft once in a while. It was so awful. But actually, I feel quite safe."

The waitress brought their drinks on a tray, J&B and water on the rocks for her and a Budweiser for him.

"Are you ready to order?" the waitress asked, beaming a smile at Jeff.

"Yes. I've praised Schroeder's prime rib to the sky, so I think we're both going to go with that, medium rare, plus house salads and baked potatoes. And we'll have a carafe of Gallo's Hearty Burgundy with dinner, please."

"I'll put this order in and bring you some fresh-baked rolls," she said, again to Jeff.

Joan liked sitting across from this man with a symmetrically chiseled face and steel blue eyes. In the months after her divorce from Dave Burton, she had had occasional dinner dates, usually in the company of friends who understood she wasn't ready for another serious relationship. Her dates were usually visitors from out of town or newly divorced guys trying to get back into the swing of single life.

Since her move to Bethany, dating had slipped way down Joan's list of priorities. Tonight she remembered how enjoyable it was to be part of a couple.

"It is a mystery, isn't it?" Jeff said, resuming the conversation as the waitress walked away. "The police didn't find any leads. The newspaper's had a couple of stories on it, but it's just kind of disappeared from view."

"Yes, I guess it has."

What Carol had told her about the investigation was confidential, and Joan intended to keep it that way. Even though she couldn't believe this man had anything to do with the crime, she wouldn't break her promise to Carol.

"Do you ever talk to the *Bugle* reporter who wrote about the skeleton?" Jeff asked, expertly pouring his Budweiser down the side of a frosted Pilsner glass.

"As a matter of fact, she and I have become friends over the past few weeks. Both of us are from St. Louis. It's great to have met someone from home."

"I'm glad," he said with a smile. "Carol and I have only talked about city business, but from the conversations I've had with her, she seems really nice. Has she been able to learn anything more about where the body might have come from?"

"Not that I could say," Joan said, casually shaking her head and hoping her indifference would prompt him to put the topic to rest. "Lately I've been pretty immersed in the manuscript I was telling you about."

"Well, I guess if the police don't know anything, she wouldn't either," he said, taking a swallow of beer.

Over dinner and a few glasses of Burgundy, the couple relaxed and conversed easily about movies, books, and travel. Afterward, they moved to the restaurant's lounge to sip Grand Marnier and listen to a jazz combo play bossa nova tunes.

About eleven thirty, they arrived back on the Iowa side of the river. Jeff parked on the levee's cobblestone parking lot where they had met a few hours earlier.

"Thanks, Jeff. I enjoyed the evening."

"Me, too. May I call you for another date sometime?"

"Sure, that might be fun," she said, exiting his car with a wave and sliding behind the wheel of her Malibu.

CHAPTER 52

Bob Hartman, a stack of newspapers by his side, was reading the *Des Moines Register*'s editorial page on his patio when Carol arrived at eleven thirty Sunday morning. She had stayed in town for the weekend and had accepted Bob's invitation to lunch.

"Good morning!" he said cheerfully, tossing the paper onto the stack. "Marg has fixed us some iced tea. If we're good, I bet she'll serve us a little food, too."

"That'll be terrific," Carol said with a wave, and seated herself in a lawn chair beside the state editor's.

"Sugar and lemon's already in the tea, is that okay?" Margaret Hartman asked as she filled a large tumbler for the reporter.

"Thanks. That's just the way I like it."

"If you need anything, you know where I am," Mrs. Hartman said to her husband, turning back toward the house. She had accepted his request for privacy, sure that eventually he would tell her everything.

"Discover anything new overnight?"

Carol shook her head and flipped to her latest entries in what she now called the "skeleton notebook."

"We know the critical year was 1971. The LA real estate deals for Eberle and Ryan apparently stopped in 1971, the year Whitlock died. The killing apparently took place sometime in late spring or early summer of '71. The mayor went on his trip in summer of '71. And, according to your recollection, Ryan started drinking heavily . . ."

". . . in 1971," they said in unison.

Carol stirred her tea deliberately, feeling as though no matter how many questions she asked, she kept going in circles just like the melting cubes in the glass.

"Sizemore might have been doing his California dealin' with more than just Whitlock, Eberle, and Ryan," she said. "Any of his business pals could have made use of the vacant farmhouse, with or without him."

"That puts you back where you were at the beginning, doesn't it?" Bob said.

"Not quite. At the beginning, I didn't know Eberle and Ryan had dealings with Sizemore. I'm convinced they know something they aren't saying."

"Tell me again what makes you so sure of that."

"Just look at what's been happening lately," Carol said. "Eberle and Ryan are very public people. Even people who don't really know them *think* they know them. They see them at meetings, on the golf course, at civic events. Everything they do seems to be completely out in the open. Right?"

"Right," Bob responded. "Except . . ."

"Yeah. Except for their lying to me about not knowing Whitlock and Sizemore, and the mayor's lying about Jeff's being at the Omaha conference, and the mayor's wanting the police chief to influence our coverage of the skeleton story, and then the mayor himself pressing me not to pursue the story.

"People have to have a reason for suddenly changing their behavior," she said.

"So, if the two of them acted suspiciously more often, you wouldn't suspect them now."

"Exactly. If the mayor was always telling us what he thought should or shouldn't be in the paper, we'd say, 'Oh, there he goes, trying to control things again.' Or if Ryan occasionally missed city council meetings, we'd say, 'What's he up to now?'"

"I think you've got a valid point," Hartman said. "But we sure as heck better have all our ducks in a row before anyone hears we suspect a connection between the unidentified body and our two highest officials. If the people of Bethany found out the *Bugle* was trying to pin a crime on their beloved mayor, Charlie would probably be ridden out of town on a rail. Can you prove what you suspect?" he asked.

"I don't know. And I'm not sure I want to," Carol said. "I believe Eberle and Ryan know something about what happened at that farm. That's scary. What's even scarier is they know where I live," she said, only half joking.

Bob was perplexed. Never in his years as a reporter or editor had he felt endangered by the events or the individuals he covered. Yet here he was encouraging a reporter who could be putting herself in jeopardy by following a hunch. Should he urge her to walk away from it?

"I hate to interrupt the two of you," Mrs. Hartman said from the back porch, "but the ham and cheese sandwiches are getting warm. Come and get 'em!"

CHAPTER 53

Monday afternoon's edition of the *Bugle* was going to contain an unusually high number of traffic citations and automobile mishaps. Carol guessed that a lot of the weekend's disorderly conduct had resulted from Bethany's residents trying to find relief from the summer heat with large quantities of beer.

When the lengthy police roundup was done, Charlie reminded his city editor there was still a large hole on page one waiting to be filled with a feature article on Bethany's upcoming Bonanza Days, held every year on the third weekend in July.

All week long, businesses would be running Bonanza Days tie-in ads in the *Bugle*, and the advertising department counted on Charlie to give generous coverage to the old-fashioned street festival in the news columns.

Carol's in basket held a stack of press releases from clubs and civic groups promoting their roles in the celebration. Each release touted items such as scrumptious shish kebobs, mouth-watering barbecue, heavenly homemade pies and cakes, beautiful arts and ingenious crafts, all available at the gaily decorated booths that would line Main Street on July 20, 21, and 22. Money raised at these booths would help fund everything from Bethany High's senior trip to Washington, DC, to baseball equipment, to songbooks, to new supplies of yarn for the brightly colored Afghans that eventually would adorn sofas, easy chairs, and beds in Bethany homes.

Hoping to find a fresh slant on a too-familiar story, Carol went to her Rolodex and made some calls to the heads of the chamber of commerce, Lions, Rotary, and Kiwanis.

The process reminded her of news-ed lab classes in J-school, where an occasional challenge was to pull together a lot of information in not a lot of time and shape it into an interesting story. Professor Mallory would start the lab by announcing the subject of the feature article and then provide, rapid-fire, an assortment of relevant and irrelevant facts, quotations, numbers, names, and titles. Everyone would scribble notes as Mallory talked, decide what was and wasn't important, check the accuracy of names, titles, and other factual information, insert quotations with the correct attributions, come up with an attention-getting lead, and hand in a typed, copy-edited article in about forty minutes.

"Thank God for news-ed labs!" Carol said, as she rolled up the punch-coded tape that clicked out of her word processor and sent it down the chute at eleven fifteen.

Heading out of the newsroom with Tom and Ron, she was glad when the sports editor asked if she'd heard about Nolan Ryan's second no-hitter of the season, pitched yesterday afternoon.

Her preoccupation with the skeleton investigation had made Carol feel awkward during their lunches recently. She would have loved to ask for her friends' opinions, but the topic was off limits.

Although she trusted Ron and Tom, she understood Charlie's position. If it ever got out that the *Bugle*'s editors suspected the town's leaders of involvement in a serious crime, and then the newspaper couldn't validate the suspicion, Charlie and she would have no credibility whatsoever.

Walking with her two companions onto a steamy, sun-filled Main Street, Carol was happy to have a no-hitter to lead off their lunchtime conversation.

CHAPTER 54

"Drawn like a moth to flame," Bob Hartman muttered to himself as he dialed Dick Talbot's number at the *Des Moines Register*.

At some point during his lunch with Carol yesterday, he had realized professionalism trumped paternalism. The reporter had to decide for herself how far to go in covering this story; he had no business interfering.

"Was there anything at all unusual about Fred Whitlock's death?" Bob asked when he heard Talbot's weary voice on the other end of the line.

"I've already talked with the Polk County ME," the veteran reporter answered. "Whitlock died of a myocardial infarction, a heart attack to you and me. He wasn't fat, but he was a big guy, fifty-eight, and sedentary. He wasn't doing anything physically exerting at the time of his death, which led the ME to suspect the heart attack was brought on by stress."

Carol had returned to the newsroom and was skimming through a stack of press releases in search of an angle for tomorrow's

Bonanza Days feature when Bob Hartman approached her desk and offered Talbot's terse recap of Whitlock's death.

"Brought on by stress?" she asked. "He's just sitting at his desk one afternoon and all of a sudden he experiences a burst of stress? Something had to provoke it, don't you think?"

Without waiting for Bob to weigh in, she spun her Rolodex to the *Des Moines Register*, dialed the number, and asked for the business editor. On the second ring, a voice answered, "Williams," and Carol identified herself.

"I'm following up on a local story from a couple of years ago, and I'm wondering if you can help me."

"Try me."

"Was there anything unusual happening in the construction business in Des Moines in the spring of 1971? Labor problems or maybe a downturn in development?"

There was silence on the line. Carol imagined Williams paging back in his file of memories the way Bob Hartman did, trying to recall something.

"I don't remember anything out of the ordinary."

Carol had to trust the business editor's discretion.

"I'm working on something that, for right now, requires confidentiality. May I ask you a question without giving you the background?"

"Shoot."

"I'm looking into something that may have involved Whitlock Construction. I was up in Des Moines earlier this month and I checked the *Register*'s files, but I didn't find any mention of what I'm looking for. Aside from Mr. Whitlock's death, was there anything unusual going on in his company at that time?"

Another pause. "Fred Whitlock suddenly dropped dead. *That* was a major unusual circumstance for his company."

"Yes, I know. But what I'm looking for is something that occurred while he was still alive."

"You sure you can't tell me why you're asking about this?"

"Not right now, I can't. But I promise to let you know if I find anything that would be of interest to the *Register*."

"It's funny," the business editor said after a long pause. "I'd forgotten about it till now, but a couple of years ago, I got a call from a guy who said he was a private investigator. He told me that in the course of another investigation he had learned something about Fred Whitlock that the paper might be interested in. I was in the middle of a big insurance fraud story and didn't have time to talk to him. I asked him to call me back in a couple of days."

"Did he?"

"No. Whitlock died a couple days later. The guy never called again."

"Did you get the investigator's name?"

"I probably made a note of it. Let me check my notebooks from back then. Call me tomorrow."

Carol hung up the phone, wondering if she might be on the verge of learning what "stress" had caused Fred Whitlock's sudden death.

CHAPTER 55

"Mitchell. The guy's name was Frank Mitchell," Ben Williams, the *Des Moines Register*'s business editor, told Carol the next afternoon. "I don't have a number for him, but I think he's a local."

She thanked Williams, and again promised to let him know if her research turned up anything the *Register* could use.

The name Frank Mitchell rang a bell. Flipping through her skeleton notebook, she found a page on which she had written, "Ron's '71 wire story." On the page were the notes, "Amanda Mitchell, 35, Santa Fe suicide, from Des Moines; Frank Mitchell—husband; James McFarland—brother; no kids." On the next page were the initials "JMc" and a phone number.

Carol had found the article on Amanda Mitchell's suicide in the *Register*'s morgue the last time she was there. The husband's name was Frank Mitchell, and James McFarland was the brother quoted in the *Register*. There had been no listing for Mitchell in the Des Moines directory, but there was one for James McFarland. Carol had jotted it down alongside the initials "JMc."

Was Amanda Mitchell's husband the same Frank Mitchell who told the *Register*'s business editor he had information about Fred Whitlock's company? Carol knew better than to assume it.

CHAPTER 56

"May I speak to James McFarland?"

"This is McFarland," the voice answered. "Who's this?"

Carol identified herself. "I'm trying to locate an investigator named Frank Mitchell who, I believe, used to live in Des Moines. Do you know him?"

"He's my brother-in-law."

"Do you know how I could reach him?"

"No, I don't. What do you want him for?"

She heard the familiar tone that almost always crept into people's voices when questioned by a reporter. For most people, even those with absolutely nothing to hide, the idea of giving information to a professional questioner was unsettling.

Carol adopted a casual tone. "Actually, I'm just trying to gather some background on a Des Moines resident for a possible story, and I think Mr. Mitchell had some contact with the person a few years ago. He may not even remember him, but I thought it might be worth a try."

"When Frank wants to be in touch with us, he sends us a card," McFarland said. "I haven't seen him since my sister's funeral two years ago. He sold their house and moved to California. I have no idea where."

"Does his PI firm still exist?"

"He worked for a law firm."

"Oh, I didn't realize that," Carol said, hoping to fish a little longer. "Somewhere I got the idea he was with a private investigation firm."

"No. Frank liked to hang around lawyers and policemen. He wanted to be a cop; when he couldn't do that, he settled for something close to it."

"Would you happen to remember the name of the law firm he worked for? I could give them a call."

"It was one of those long names," he said. "Began with an S. Stevens, something, and something. No, Sterling. That was it. Sterling, something, and something. I can't remember the other names."

"Thanks very much. I appreciate your help."

Carol could hear hesitation. She held on to the receiver a moment longer, thinking he might offer some bit of information.

"How about if I ask a favor of you?"

"What's that?" she said before she could stop herself.

"Who did you want to ask Frank about?"

Carol was caught off guard. She hated to give information to people she wanted to get information from, but this guy was minding his own business when she called him out of the blue. What harm could there be in telling him a name?

"Well, he's actually deceased. His name is Fred Whitlock, founder of the construction company. I've been researching some of the urban development around the state and his name has come up a few times, that's all. Do you know the name?"

"Sure, I've seen the name on construction sites around town; who hasn't?"

"Yes, of course. Thanks again for your help."

CHAPTER 57

Sterling, O'Connor & Foyle was a large and expensive law firm in Des Moines, handling both civil and criminal cases. The office assistant Carol spoke with on the phone was crisp, polite, and negative in every way.

"No, Mr. Mitchell no longer has any connection with the firm. . .No, I couldn't say what he might have been working on when he resigned. . .No, he certainly wouldn't have been investigating Whitlock Construction, one of Sterling, O'Connor & Foyle's own clients. . .No, I have no idea how to get in touch with him."

Carol put the skeleton notebook back in her desk drawer and began to work on a feature article describing the huge amounts of food to be prepared, purchased, and packed away by visitors to Bethany's three-day festival. The image of hot dogs, corndogs, bratwursts, barbecued ribs, funnel cakes, and snow cones being hawked on the streets of Bethany made her decide to fast for the next day and a half in preparation.

With her third feature of the week complete and no court session on her schedule, she told Charlie she was heading home.

"That's fine, Carol, ol' girl," he said, looking up from his keyboard. "Rest up for the weekend. I'll want you and Kenny out on Main Street taking lots of photos. I'm planning a two-page spread of candid shots for Monday: kids with cotton candy, kids with animals, kids with parents, kids on rides, etc., etc. We'll have a round up on attendance, contest winners, money raised, police issues, the clean up, and whatever else you've got. We'll wanna wrap the whole shebang up with a bow on Monday."

CHAPTER 58

Following the managing editor's advice, Carol reclined on her living room sofa that afternoon, watching the Watergate hearings on the little portable she'd brought with her from St. Louis.

She envied the DC reporters. Woodward and Bernstein had turned up enough evidence to engage the entire country in their investigation. Sam Ervin's committee was pushing the Nixon administration hard. Since learning two days earlier that Oval Office meetings were routinely taped, the committee had asked the White House to turn the relevant tapes over. Nixon had refused, but public sentiment was running against him.

Carol, so far, had received no such validation for her investigative efforts. Charlie had given her leeway to follow up on her suspicions, but he was getting edgy. He had never been faced with the prospect of accusing a local official of crime or corruption.

If it weren't for her, the case of the long-decomposed body would probably have been permanently relegated to four thin manila folders in four steel filing cabinets at the Bethany PD, the Lee County sheriff's office, the ME's office in Fort Madison, and the DCI in Des Moines.

By five o'clock, the Senate hearing had ended for the day, and Carol found herself thinking about Frank Mitchell; no relation, as far as she knew, to the recently indicted John Mitchell, former U.S. attorney general and director of Nixon's reelection campaign.

How was she going to find this Mitchell in California?

As much as she didn't want to call Joan's cousin with more questions, she realized he might be the shortest route to Frank Mitchell. If Michael Sizemore was on the road, he probably wouldn't be home yet, but she dialed his number anyway.

"Sizemore," he answered.

Carol reintroduced herself and apologized for interrupting his work day.

"I've come across the name Frank Mitchell while trying to track down a lead on the skeleton your cousin found in the barn. I know it's a long shot, but by any chance do you know him?"

"Frank Mitchell? Sorry, but I don't know anyone by that name. How do you think he might be connected?"

"I was doing some research and his name came up. I learned from his brother-in-law in Des Moines that Mitchell lives in California. I'm trying to locate someone out there who might know him."

"What makes you think I would know him?"

"Well, I'm told he worked for the law firm used by Whitlock Construction, and I know you've worked with Mr. Whitlock," she said.

"Fred Whitlock? He died two years ago. How could he have anything to do with this?"

Carol knew she had to back off. Sizemore was starting to sound annoyed, and she couldn't blame him. She was calling him for the second time in less than a week, asking vague questions about a case the Bethany police were ignoring.

"I'm really sorry to have bothered you. I knew it was a stretch. I'll let you go. Thanks for your time."

She hung up before he could say anything else.

"You are an idiot!" she said, slamming her notebook on the kitchen table.

She wouldn't be surprised if Michael was calling his cousin right now to tell her that her reporter friend was nuts. She decided to try and beat him to the punch.

When Joan heard Carol's voice, she suggested that instead of catching up on the phone, Carol come out to the farm where they could visit over dinner.

No sooner had Carol said yes than she regretted having accepted the invitation. She seriously doubted she'd be able to hold up her end of a cheerful evening.

As she washed her face and applied a little makeup in an effort to brighten her mood, Carol felt foolish and alone.

* * *

She stood in the doorway of the upstairs bathroom watching her father brush the thick white lather over his dark whiskers. She let out a giggle. It seemed like fun to cover your face with soapy bubbles and then erase them with dramatic strokes, gliding the straight-edge razor down each cheek, then drawing it upward from neck to chin, finishing with quick, deft touches to the upper lip.

He bent over the sink and rinsed the remaining thin, white lines of lather from his face.

"What's so funny?" he asked, drying his face with a towel.

She was startled by his rough tone.

"Not so funny," she said sassily, trying to hide her hurt feelings. "Just laughing at how you look when you're shaving."

"Go on, get out of here, now. I don't have time for any nonsense this morning."

She left him without a word and went downstairs.

Several minutes later, her father came down, his face a solemn mask. Even though it was his day off, he was in uniform: sharply creased navy blue trousers, starched light blue shirt, black tie, navy blue coat with shiny brass buttons down the front, and a sergeant's badge on the left breast pocket. His black leather Sam Browne belt, holster, and handcuff case were all polished to a luster, thanks to an electric buffer, her father's all-time favorite Christmas gift. He wedged his uniform hat under his left arm as he went into the kitchen to say goodbye to her mother.

From her spot in the living room, she saw her mother walk him to the front door.

"It'll be okay, Andrew. They know you didn't do anything wrong. Just tell them what they need to know."

Her mother raised her right hand in a halfhearted wave as her father left the house.

"Where's Daddy going? Isn't he off today?"

"He's got some police business to take care of at the courthouse. He won't be long."

"Why is he mad? Is there something wrong at work?"

"Oh, musha! Why do you always have to ask so many questions?

* * *

Carol knocked her makeup case off the edge of the bathroom sink, spilling most of the contents on the floor. After collecting the tubes and plastic cases, she hit the back of her head on the edge of the sink as she rose from her knees.

"Damn!"

CHAPTER 59

Joan Sizemore had spent the day in her upstairs office editing a dry manuscript and resisting the temptation of the pond's cool water below.

Now, she was glad for an excuse to punch out and put together an easy supper. Scanning the pantry and refrigerator, she found red beans, rice, sausage, green pepper, and onion, everything she would need for a spicy jambalaya. A tossed salad and some Jiffy cornbread would complete a tasty meal.

Except for their brief exchange a half hour earlier, the two women hadn't talked since her date with Jeff Ryan on Saturday. She was eager to tell Carol about the chance meeting in the bakery that had led to coffee, then dinner.

Joan noticed the reporter's glum mood as soon as she opened the door.

"Are you okay?"

"You can tell I'm not?"

"What happened?"

"I got into a fight with myself over what I'm doing and why

I'm doing it. That's all."

"What *are* you doing?" Joan asked.

"Trying to find out what happened two years ago, a hundred yards from this house. People think I'm crazy."

"Who thinks you're crazy?"

"Your cousin is at the head of the line."

"What makes you think so?" Joan asked, returning to the stove to sample the simmering jambalaya and sprinkle more creole seasoning into the pot.

Carol told Joan about her call to Michael and the impatience in his voice when she inquired about Frank Mitchell and mentioned Fred Whitlock.

"I'm to the point where I have to go one way or another with this," Carol said. "Either I give up and say, 'Everyone's telling the truth. Nobody knows anything. The fugitives who put that body up in the loft are long gone. The victim's long dead. Nobody cares. Including me.' Or I continue asking questions, alienating the city fathers, and annoying the relatives of friends, hoping eventually someone will come forward and say what really happened. To me, neither is a good choice."

"Who else could help you find Frank Mitchell?" Joan asked, ignoring Carol's self-pity.

"What?"

"Who else could help you locate this guy in California? There's got to be somebody out there. What about your friend who went to the Hall of Records for you?"

"Of course. Why didn't I think of that? I can ask Erica to go through the phone books of California cities, looking for the names, Frank Mitchell, Francis Mitchell, and F. Something Mitchell, and calling each of them to ask if he happens to be the private eye from Des Moines who two years ago had a suicidal wife and a hot news tip about Fred Whitlock's business operations."

Joan laughed. "Erica wouldn't have to call all of them. She could stop as soon as she found the one who answered 'yes' to all of the above," Joan said, taking two hand-painted bowls from the table to the stove. "C'mon, Carol, let's eat. I've got some news to tell you about last weekend."

Joan dished up the steaming, savory stew while Carol poured glasses of the Burgundy she had brought with her. Then, without preamble, Joan described how she had met Jeff Ryan at the bakery, joined him for coffee, and accepted his invitation to dinner in Quincy. She recapped their evening at the restaurant, including Jeff's concern for whether she felt safe living on the farm alone and his curiosity about Carol's reporting on the skeleton.

The news of her friend's date with Ryan caught Carol off guard, but she didn't want to be a wet blanket. Joan obviously had enjoyed the date, and Carol couldn't fault her for it. She figured Ryan's reputation as a charming bachelor was deserved.

"He was smart, but really sweet and easygoing," Joan said. "I never would have guessed he was such a nice guy."

"I haven't been slandering him, have I?"

"Not a bit. It's just that you haven't said much at all about him, except that he hasn't been very open about his business dealings with my cousin."

"Dr. Mallory made his mark," Carol said. "He always urged us to keep our distance from news sources. I guess I look at Jeff Ryan differently than most people do. Besides, talking about a waste water treatment plant doesn't exactly bring out the 'sweet and easygoing,' side of a person."

"He said he wanted to ask me out again," Joan said as she buttered a piece of cornbread. "What would you think if I started to date him?"

"I think you should do whatever you want to do."

"What would you *think about it*, though?" Joan repeated.

"Does that make any difference?"

"It could. It depends on what you think—and why."

Once again, the reporter found herself wondering whether to withhold her concerns from Joan. Michael Sizemore and Jeff Ryan could have been entangled in a serious crime. Joan was related by blood to Sizemore, and now she was getting friendly with Ryan. Was it Carol's business to say anything that would cast more suspicion on them?

"Well, are you going to share your opinion with me or not?"

Carol was grateful to have a friend who talked straight and wasn't afraid to hear the truth.

"You're always candid with me, and I appreciate that. Part of me feels I should be just as straightforward with you."

Joan smiled, and tapped her head with an index finger. "That's the part of you that is highly intelligent."

"Okay," Carol said, plunging in. "If I were you, I wouldn't get involved with Ryan."

"Why not?"

"Because, right now, you're just somewhat interested in him. If you don't get further involved, you'll simply miss out on the chance to date a 'smart, sweet, easygoing' man. If you do get involved, you could get hurt. That's why not."

"You think Jeff's a bad guy?"

"I think there's something bad going on that he knows something about. Whether or not he's 'bad,' I'm not sure. I believe that, somehow, he's been entangled. I could be wrong, but you asked my opinion, and that's it."

"Thanks for being honest with me," Joan said, refilling their wine glasses. "Let me ask you, is there anything I could tell you that would alleviate your suspicions?"

Carol thought for a moment as she gathered another spoonful of stew. "What did he buy?"

"What do you mean, 'What did he buy?'"

"What did he buy at the bakery?"

Joan was surprised by the question and flashed back to when she first saw Jeff in the bakery. She had just ordered her Danish pastry and apple turnovers when he walked in. They smiled, and he started talking. She paid the clerk, put the change in her purse, took the package, and walked to the door. He followed her out.

"He didn't buy anything, now that I think of it," Joan said, puzzled.

"Maybe he abandoned his plan to buy bakery goods because he was afraid he would miss the chance to ask you out. But maybe he only came into the bakery to find you."

"Why would he have done that? He doesn't know me. It doesn't make any sense that he would come in there looking for me."

For the first time since she had known Joan, Carol heard a tad of impatience in her voice. This is what she had wanted to avoid, annoying her friend with suspicions she couldn't validate.

"You're right, Joan. It doesn't make any sense. Unless he just wanted to meet the woman who had found the body of a man he knew so he could learn if she knew anything that could cause trouble for him."

"My God, Carol, are you serious?" Joan said.

"Or just crazy?"

"Fair enough," Joan said, nodding her head. "I asked you what you thought, and you told me. Now, can you tell me what you think you should do about this?"

"That's where I came in, isn't it?" Carol said. "Wondering what the heck I'm doing and why. Frank Mitchell may be the source I'm looking for, or maybe looking for him is a total waste of time. Your cousin may not know him, like he said. Or, then again, Michael may know him and not want me to know he does."

Joan took a sip of wine, set the glass on the table, and exhaled. Since she and Carol had first talked about the reporter's suspicions, Joan occasionally had wondered what her cousin Michael was really like. As she listened to Carol, who was within a hair's breadth of suggesting Michael was lying, Joan's questions were there again.

Who was Michael? Sure, he was her father's brother's son. Blood in common, name in common, and a natural family loyalty. But she didn't know him. When she was little, she thought his name was "Poor Michael." That's how her relatives often referred to him because he was an only child and all of his cousins lived in St. Louis. He still sent occasional cards or gifts to his aunts and uncles but never visited. He'd lived away for so long nobody expected anything of him. He had become the "distant" cousin, too busy with his West Coast life to deal with the only family he had left.

Michael had quickly disposed of his deceased parents' belongings, briefly leased the house, and inexplicably let fertile land sit unfarmed. He was amiable enough when she called him about buying his property. But he didn't come into town to complete the deal.

It was Carol's turn to break into Joan's soliloquy.

"Did what I said about Michael upset you?"

"No. What you said just reminded me of all the questions I've been accumulating. I don't know him any better than you do. Maybe he is involved somehow in whatever crime took place here. I hope not, but my hoping won't change the truth, and I know you only want to discover the truth."

"Thanks. I hope he's not involved, either."

CHAPTER 60

Standing in line at a Des Moines Airport ticket counter was the last thing James McFarland had expected to be doing on Wednesday evening. He had left his wife, Claire, in a sullen state because of it. She objected to his spending money they didn't have on a wild goose chase.

McFarland fully agreed with her characterization. But here he was, shoving his suitcase ahead of him with his foot as he advanced in line. He would try to make it up to her when he got back. First, though, he had to try to make up for two years of sitting around on his duff, hoping someday he would understand his sister's death.

The call the day before from Carol Hagan had jarred him from inertia. McFarland knew the reporter's attempt to contact his brother-in-law had nothing to do with his sister. But he didn't believe in coincidence. The phone call was a sign from a higher power.

Ever since Amanda's suicide in the summer of 1971, he had prayed for the strength to accept her death. He had gone over and over in his mind their visits and phone calls in the months beforehand. His sister hadn't given him the slightest hint she was desperate or depressed. Although the medical examiner in Santa Fe was unambiguous in his finding that Amanda had bled to death from self-inflicted wounds to the arteries in her wrists, McFarland never got an answer to the most important question: Why did she do it?

She had left no note. Her husband had had no warning. Frank Mitchell had acted strong at first. He flew to Santa Fe to accompany Amanda's body back to Des Moines. He made the funeral arrangements and endured the ceremonial grieving process with family and friends, holding himself together. Then he seemed to fall apart. Within three days of the burial, Frank Mitchell went off to mourn alone. He had called James and Claire from Pueblo, Colorado, saying he would be gone for a while. He promised to stay in touch.

Staying in touch consisted of Christmas cards and birthday cards for their son, Jamie. Mitchell always wrote that he was okay and that he hoped James, Claire, and Jamie were well. There was never a return address on the envelopes, only postmarks with names like Palmdale, Hidden Hills, Cerritos, and Artesia.

McFarland hadn't been close to his brother-in-law, but he could see that Mitchell had a certain charm, mixed with intelligence, and a persistence that equipped him well for his job as a private investigator.

They would never be buddies, but that was okay as long as Amanda was happy.

On the day his sister was buried, McFarland had a flicker of hope that together he and Frank might be able to answer the question they couldn't answer alone. When his brother-in-law went away, so had McFarland's hope.

"How can I help you?" the woman behind the counter asked.

"A ticket to LA, please."

CHAPTER 61

J eff Ryan walked down the corridor to Mayor Jason Eberle's office, remembering the times when these Thursday afternoon meetings had been enjoyable.

Sitting in the leather chairs with their feet up on the coffee table, eating the homemade cookies supplied by the mayor's wife, they were like big boys playing office. Tidbits of local gossip and laughter at the foibles of their fellow citizens were spread like mortar between the bricks of city business.

This particular meeting wasn't going to go that way.

After his dinner with Joan Sizemore Saturday night, Ryan had felt a measure of relief. He had conveyed his good feeling to the mayor in a phone conversation late that same night. Joan had as much as told him that Carol Hagan knew nothing about the origin of the skeleton. He had brought up the topic several times to see if she would engage, but Joan clearly had no insights into the case—nor any interest in speculating about the remains in her barn. She seemed satisfied with the theory of random violence by fugitives.

If the reporter had learned anything in her snooping around, Ryan told the mayor, she surely would have shared that information with her friend who had found the body, wouldn't she? Jason's worry was pure paranoia.

Eberle had remained skeptical and unsoothed on the other end of the line.

"What if the Sizemore woman just didn't want to tell you what she knows?"

"But if the reporter had told her anything that implicated us, do you really think Joan Sizemore would have agreed to go on a date with me?"

"If you ask me, your date resolved nothing," Eberle had said. "We can't keep standing around with our thumbs up our asses waiting for the newspaper to make a move. We've got to find out what in hell Carol Hagan's doing. Who is she talking to? I'll be damned if I'm going to let the house burn down around me!"

Feeling like a scolded child, Ryan's resentment had resurfaced.

"Wait just a damn minute, Jason!" he said at a volume neither of them was used to hearing. "You're the one who has refused to deal with this. We knew the body would be found sooner or later. At least I've done something to try to find out what's going on, and I'm telling you I don't think the reporter has anything that can hurt us. If she knew something, we'd know it by now."

"Jeff, listen to me. I've talked with this gal. She's got something by the tail. The way I see it, we've got one more chance to head this off before it blows up. We've got to find a way to shake it out of Charlie Vogler, or maybe Bob Hartman."

That was the way their phone conversation had ended Saturday night.

Eberle was still seated at his desk when Ryan walked into his office. The city manager positioned the straight-back visitor's chair directly across the desk from the mayor. Eberle took off his reading glasses, closed his eyes, and pressed his right thumb and forefinger to the bridge of his nose.

"Here's what we're going to do," he said, opening his eyes. "We've got Bonanza Days all weekend. On Monday night, we're going to throw a little soiree at your place in celebration of a successful festival. We invite Vogler and Hartman from the *Bugle*, with their wives, Ron Dalton from the chamber, and Larry Bryce, with their wives.

"I'll have Anne call everyone at home this evening and invite them. We'll make it an informal buffet on your terrace, around seven. Anne and Marjorie can put the food together and get over to your house Monday afternoon to set everything up."

For as many years as Jeff Ryan had known the mayor, he was still amazed at the man's confidence. Just days earlier, Jason was frantic with the thought of being exposed, or worse. Now he talked as though all he had on his mind was a cozy get-together.

"What do you hope to accomplish with this?" Ryan asked.

"The mood will be easy and relaxed. We'll have cocktails and a little supper. In the course of conversation, we'll ask Charlie and Bob some questions and see what we can learn. Why don't you invite the Sizemore woman as your date?"

Ryan realized it was no accident the mayor was still at his desk. This was not meant to be a give-and-take session. It was the mayor's unilateral ruling on their next step. Ryan nodded agreement.

"Great!" Eberle said, standing up as he pressed the intercom button on his desk. "Hey, Marj, can we get some cookies and cold Cokes in here for Jeff and me, please? We've got a council meeting to prepare for."

CHAPTER 62

McFarland opened the suitcase that lay on the bed in his motel room. On top of two folded sports shirts was a five-by-seven cardboard-framed photograph of his sister and brother-in-law. The couple was seated at an outdoor table with a view of blue ocean and palm trees in the background. Beautiful Amanda, her raven hair pulled back, wore a red and white sundress in a floral pattern; a white orchid covered her left ear. Frank wore a yellow and white Hawaiian-print shirt. His right arm was casually draped over Amanda's shoulders. Each was saluting the photographer with a raised cocktail and a smile.

McFarland felt queasy looking into the eyes of the unsuspecting couple.

No matter how little he and Frank Mitchell had in common, no matter how remote their relationship had been, McFarland felt sorry for him.

Eighteen hundred miles from home, he realized he might never learn why Amanda had committed suicide. Maybe the reporter's phone call hadn't been God's cue to look for the source of his dead sister's despair, but simply his own excuse to look for his living, breathing brother-in-law.

Frank Mitchell didn't make it easy, though. The postmarks on the occasional cards suggested that Mitchell lived in the Los Angeles area, but they didn't say where. McFarland's inquiry at the law office of Sterling, O'Connor & Foyle had almost led to a dead end. But McFarland held a trump card. He had told the law firm's office manager there was an urgent family matter that needed Frank Mitchell's attention.

"I know my brother-in-law did investigative work for a number of your clients," he said to the cool woman on the other end of the line. "Doesn't your firm have a California connection that might help me locate him?" he had asked.

Faced with the familial appeal, the office manager warmed up a degree. She informed McFarland that one of their clients, Whitlock Construction Company, had a previous association with a developer in Los Angeles by the name of Michael Sizemore.

"It's possible Mr. Sizemore might know of Mr. Mitchell," she said. "I can give you Mr. Sizemore's phone number in Los Angeles."

McFarland had scribbled down the Los Angeles number with a new burst of hope.

Dialing that number from his motel room and hearing the phone ring without interruption, James McFarland wasn't so hopeful. If he couldn't connect by phone, he'd need a street address.

The desk clerk at the motel pulled the massive LA phonebook from beneath the counter and shoved it toward McFarland. In the voluminous list of Angelenos with the surname Sizemore, he looked first for "Michael." When he didn't find a match for the phone number he'd been given by the women at the law firm, he paged back to the "Sizemores" whose first names started with M. There, alongside the listing "M. E. Sizemore," McFarland found a phone number that matched the one he had in his possession. Beside the phone number was the address: 403 San Gabriel Drive.

McFarland headed northwest toward Los Angeles in his rented Chevy Nova.

CHAPTER 63

Main Street was blocked off at six thirty Friday morning, so Carol approached the parking lot of the *Bugle* by way of Jefferson Street, one block south.

In the relative cool of night, workers had constructed game booths and food and beverage stands. Now, with the temperature already at eighty degrees, volunteers were decorating the booths with multicolored crepe paper and plastic sheeting.

Carol felt more than the usual deadline pressure as she prepared for her day. She had to get last night's city council article written and her local news roundups down the chute by nine thirty. Then she would take a walk along Main Street to survey the last of the setup crews and the first of the fair-goers. She would jot down what she hoped would be colorful, non-clichéd observations of this heartland ritual. If she was as good as she thought she was, she'd have a feature article worthy of page one down to the composing room by eleven fifteen.

Kenny had already been out taking pictures of carnival crews assembling rides on the Mississippi levee and Lions Club men fueling fires in the half-barrel pits where slabs of pork ribs slathered in barbecue sauce would slow cook all weekend long. He already had developed three rolls of film and placed the contact sheets on Carol's desk by the time she got into the office.

"Thank you, Kenny!" she exclaimed when she saw his work. If her Bonanza Days feature ran short, she and Charlie could select more photos and write some clever cutlines.

"Ready for a wild weekend, Carol?" Charlie said cheerfully when he entered the newsroom at seven and saw her typing from her notes.

"I'm taking it one step at a time," she said, not looking up for fear of losing her train of thought on the city council story. "Kenny's in the photo lab ready to take your order for hot Bonanza pics. The contacts are over here. They look pretty good."

Charlie examined the contact sheets with a magnifying glass, used a grease pencil to mark a red X through the shots he wanted enlarged, and took the sheets to Kenny in the photo lab.

"Oh, by the way," he said on his return. "Got a call from hizzoner's wife last night. Seems they're throwing a little party Monday night at Jeff Ryan's house and want me and my wife to attend. What do you think of that?"

"Interesting," Carol said, unwilling to become too interested.

"What's interesting?" Bob Hartman asked, walking through the newsroom doorway.

"The invite from Anne Eberle," Charlie said. "You get one?"

Carol was relieved to have Bob there to maintain the conversation with Charlie so she could keep writing. Her curiosity would be satisfied later.

"Oh, yeah," Bob said. "A Monday night dinner party. Kind of unusual, don't you think?"

"Anne said it's to celebrate the success of Bonanza Days. Let's hope the Days are successful, or Jason may close the bar early."

"Not when the party's at Jeff Ryan's house," Bob returned.

Both men laughed.

CHAPTER 64

"First, I wanted to tell you again that I enjoyed our dinner last Saturday very much," Jeff Ryan said over the phone. "Thanks for accepting the last-minute invitation."

"You're welcome," Joan replied. "I had a nice time, too."

"Second, you said you would consider another date, so here I am. I thought this time you might enjoy meeting some of Bethany's leading citizens."

"Oh?"

"The mayor and I are hosting a casual dinner at my house on Monday evening. It will be Mayor Eberle, Chief Bryce, Ron Dalton, head of the chamber of commerce, and two longtime editors from the *Bugle*, plus all their wives, of course. I'm hoping you can join us."

"That's quite a lineup. What's the occasion?"

"This is the weekend for Bethany's annual street festival, and we wanted to cap it off with a little gathering. They're all good folks, and I know they'd be happy to meet one of our newest and prettiest residents. Can you make it?"

Since Thursday night, Joan had been weighing Carol's caution against dating the city manager. She hadn't made up her mind what to do, but now she had to make a decision on the spot. She was curious about the people Jeff had just mentioned. Besides, a dinner party with the town's leading citizens seemed a respectable enough occasion.

"Yes. I'd like that."

CHAPTER 65

Carol spent parts of Friday afternoon and Saturday strolling along a muggy Main Street, sampling a good amount of fair fare—pork ribs coated in sweet barbecue sauce, teriyaki chicken on a skewer, roasted corn on the cob, a powdery funnel cake washed down with a cherry snow cone, and just *one* of the Presbyterian Women's Club's decadent brownies, embedded with gooey caramel, pecans, chocolate chips, and coconut.

Mostly, she observed and interviewed festival-goers and took notes that would help her recall sights, tastes, sounds, and smells on Monday morning when she wrote the final chapter of the Bonanza Days saga. She took candid shots of the round, sun-reddened faces of toddlers and the tanned, leathery faces of nomadic carnival workers.

On Sunday, she steered clear of the food concessions altogether and busied herself gathering quotes and fundraising estimates from the volunteers.

By two o'clock, she decided she had enough notes scribbled in her "Bonanza Days '73" notebook to fill Monday's entire edition. She was ready to quit work and spend the last slice of a hot weekend in Joan's backyard pond.

When she arrived around three, Joan was sitting on the porch, already in her swimming suit and a pale blue terrycloth cover-up. Carol changed while Joan gathered plastic cups, a jug of iced lemonade, towels, and other beach necessities. Then the women headed for the lawn chairs stationed on the pond's grassy bank.

"Just so you're not surprised when you hear this from Bob or Charlie, I'm having dinner with them tomorrow night at Jeff's house," Joan said, as she applied Coppertone to her tanned face and arms.

Carol simply nodded at Joan's disclosure. She wasn't surprised and wouldn't pretend she was. Bob had told her all the men who were on the guest list, and they all were coupled by marriage except Ryan. Carol had figured Joan would be his likely date. Not bothering with lotion, Carol waded into the cool, refreshing water. Swimming a few laps would give her time to let go of her reaction to the news about Joan's second date with the city manager.

If he was the amicable bachelor everyone seemed to think he was, there was nothing to worry about. Carol was determined to keep whatever paranoia she felt about the possible opposite of amicability under wraps today. Unless Joan brought it up, she would say nothing about Ryan, the dinner party, or the skeleton. The afternoon would be simply a refreshing break from heat and work.

After swimming vigorously for several minutes, Carol turned on her back and floated in the middle of the pond, tiny waves lapping against her skin as the sun bore down. She felt she could almost fall sleep right there, floating on the water.

Joan was engrossed in *The Odessa File*, but when Carol returned from the pond and settled into the lawn chair beside her, Joan put the novel aside.

"Tell me something about the people I'm going to meet tomorrow night."

"You'll like Bob Hartman. He acts like he's just a small-town guy, but he's got a worldly side, and he's pretty funny. Charlie wants people to think he's sophisticated because he's from Chicago. His male chauvinism is a bit much, but he has a good heart, so I just let it roll off."

"What about their wives?"

"Bob's wife, Margaret, is pleasant and motherly. Haven't talked to her much. I've only met Charlie's wife once, so I don't really know her."

"Not to change the subject," Carol said, changing the subject, "but that was a pretty big bombshell Alex Butterfield dropped about Nixon's tapes, wasn't it? I wonder if the Senate committee will get access to them."

"That would be the last straw," Joan said. "How ironic it will be if, after his landslide victory, Nixon goes down because of a stupid burglary."

"It won't be the burglary that takes him down. It'll be all the lies that were told to cover it up," Carol said.

After a pause, Joan took her turn at changing the subject. "Are you going to keep the skeleton investigation to yourself now because I've decided to see Jeff again?"

Carol hesitated. "It *is* a bit awkward. You're becoming friends with a man who's hiding something, and I need more time to learn if what he's hiding is connected to the skeleton."

"Don't you think you can trust me not to say anything to Jeff?" Joan said. "When he asked me the other night at dinner if you had any leads on the skeleton, I didn't bite."

"Joan, I know you won't talk to anyone about it. But you've decided to date Jeff, and that means you've got a good opinion of him. I don't want to tell you you're wrong, but I can't pretend I don't have serious misgivings about both him and the mayor. I don't think they're as reputable as they'd like people to believe."

After a few minutes of silence, Joan got up and took her turn in the pond, treading water in the deep center. Carol sat with her eyes closed, absorbing the late afternoon sun, mindful that even good people don't always tell the whole truth.

* * *

She was finished washing the dinner dishes but pretended there was still work to do at the sink. She rinsed out the dishcloth several times, wiped and re-wiped the counter tops, and then industriously cleaned the salt and pepper shakers.

Her father and brother, Denny, sat at the cleared table on the other side of the kitchen, talking in low voices.

Supper had been over for about twenty minutes. Her mother had gone next door to talk with Mrs. Bayer on her front porch swing. Her sisters Peggy and Maureen were playing in the front yard with the kids from across the street.

In a few minutes, she would go outside too. It was getting dark a little earlier now that it was late August, but all the kids from both the Catholic schools and public schools were still on vacation. Their only job was to play as long after supper as their parents would let them.

Tonight, though, she wanted to hear what her father and Denny were talking about. She strained her ears, trying to learn what had been making her father so grumpy lately.

"Was there anything you could have done?" Denny asked.

Her dad ran his hands through his short-cropped dark blond hair. "If only I'd taken it myself. I don't know. I didn't think there'd be a problem."

He picked up his cigarette from where it rested in the ashtray, inhaled deeply, and scratched his head again as he blew a long plume of smoke toward the kitchen ceiling.

"Jake told me they were having trouble," her father said. "But, heck, I never put it together. You never think that somebody you know . . ."

"What did the other guys say?" her brother asked.

"Heck, I don't know for sure, Denny. None of us could be in there when we weren't on the stand. All we could do was sit and wait. Nobody was talking."

"Do you think anybody else is gonna get in trouble, Dad?"

Her father crushed his cigarette out in the ashtray, shook his head, pushed his chair away from the table and stood up. "Let's hope it's done."

* * *

"I don't know about you, girl, but I'm ready for something stronger than lemonade. Why don't you tend bar, and I'll get a couple of steaks ready for the grill?"

Carol's wistful memory dissolved in the sound of her friend's lighthearted invitation.

She was grateful for Joan's easygoing temperament. She didn't want to mess up their friendship. They simply would have to accommodate each other's views of Jeff Ryan.

Until something happened to prove one of them was wrong.

CHAPTER 66

Carol had just returned from a "Bonanza Days are Done!" celebratory lunch with Tom and Ron when her phone rang. From the other end of the line came a familiar voice.

"Hello, Carol. Do you know who this is?"

"Michael Sizemore."

"Hey, you got it right! Listen, I'm in Bethany, but Joan doesn't know I'm here yet. I want to surprise her, so don't say anything."

Carol was taken by his friendly tone. Her only previous phone conversations with him had been official in nature, and the last one had ended awkwardly.

"I'm sure she'll be surprised and happy to see you," Carol said. "What can I do for you?"

"First, I want to apologize for how rude I was the other day when you called. I was having a bad day, and I'm afraid I took my impatience with clients out on you. Will you accept my apology?"

"Don't worry about it. I called you with a pretty far-fetched question."

As she cradled the phone to her ear, Carol wrote in large letters on a notepad, "M. Sizemore is in town!" and held it up in Bob Hartman's direction so he could see it from his desk. When he saw the note, Carol pointed to the receiver, signaling it was Sizemore on the phone.

"You were just trying to do your job," he said. "Anyway, I've got some business in Des Moines and I just decided at the last minute to make a quick stop to see Joan. I've been feeling bad I didn't turn the family homestead over to her in person. Is there any chance you and I could meet this afternoon?"

Surprised, she hesitated a second. "That would probably be okay. Hang on, let me check my calendar."

She put him on hold and walked over to Bob's desk.

"Michael Sizemore wants to meet me this afternoon," she said quietly. "I told him I have to check my calendar. What does my 'calendar' say?"

"Go to a public place—and take a notebook," the state editor said.

"Yes, Michael," she said into the receiver when she got back to her desk. "I can meet you. What time is good, and where?"

"I just had a sandwich in the little park by the bridge. It's nice down here. Could you come down about two fifteen? I'll be waiting on one of the benches. I'm wearing a dark blue, short-sleeved sport shirt and gray slacks."

Carol agreed to the meeting place and hung up the phone. It was ten to two. She had a few minutes to think of what she would ask him. Fred Whitlock's widow had told her she believed Bethany's mayor and city manager had socialized with her husband and Michael Sizemore. Carol knew Eberle and Ryan had purchased land in Los Angeles, but she was not yet positive that Sizemore was their agent. The two Bethany men claimed they didn't know Sizemore. Could Shirley Whitlock possibly have been mistaken about who had dined with her husband in Des Moines? Was it too big of a leap to suspect that if Michael Sizemore brokered land deals in Iowa for Los Angeles investors he was doing the same for Iowans in California?

She took a new notebook from the metal supply cupboard and walked back to Bob's desk.

"Here's the situation. The man who used to own the property where the skeleton was found wants to meet me at the river. Should I beat around the bush, or should I just come right out and ask him, 'Michael, about this homicide, what do you know and when did you know it?'"

"He asked to meet with *you*. Just go see what he's got. Maybe he's thought of a likely suspect. Or, on second thought," Bob said with a grin, "maybe his cousin told him you were an attractive girl, and he's just looking for an excuse to meet you."

"Well, now that you mention it, that might be true," she said. "But if I don't show up for work tomorrow morning, tell the police to scour the park on the levee."

Carol headed for the door. "Have a good time at the city manager's party. I'll expect details."

CHAPTER 67

Carol spotted the Californian as soon as she pulled into the cobblestone parking lot along the murky Mississippi. He was in his early forties, medium build, lean but muscular, with an even tan. Carol placed him in the "ruggedly handsome" category.

"Hello, Carol. Good to meet you."

"Same here, Michael," she said, shaking his extended hand. "When are you planning to see Joan?"

"I'm driving out there a little later this afternoon. I thought for fun I'd just knock on the front door and see if she recognizes me. She probably won't. She was just a little girl when I moved away."

"Better not make it too late today. I know she has dinner plans this evening."

"Is that right? I'm glad she's getting into Bethany's social life."

The two sat down on the open bench, and Carol opted to skip the small talk.

"So what's on your mind, Michael?"

"I know you've been looking for information about the body Joan found in the hayloft. I wish I could tell you I have an idea about what happened. The last time I was at the farm was when I cleaned out my mom and dad's things after they died. I leased the house for a while and hired a handyman to keep the house and yard in shape till I figured out what to do with it. Then, last January, Joan called and said she wanted to buy it."

"That's what I've heard," she said, pretending patience.

"Joan told me the police are pretty sure the victim was a fugitive," he said, "maybe someone double-crossed by his partners in crime or something like that."

"Yeah, I think that is what the police believe."

"What do *you* believe, Carol?"

"I don't believe anything," she said, shrugging noncommittally.

"Well, you did call me trying to track down some guy. And Joan told me you've had questions. You must not agree with the police's view."

"There's really nothing I can tell you. I came to meet you because I thought you might have some information for me. Do you?"

"Why don't you ask me something, and we can both see if I have any information?" he said with a smile.

"Okay. This is none of my business, but I've wondered why you kept your parents' farm so long after they died. If you weren't going to live there, why not sell it?"

His face became somber and he looked away from her, toward the river.

"I always felt I was a disappointment to my parents. They loved farming. They loved that piece of land. It would have made them so happy if one day I'd have come back from California and told them I wanted to be a farmer. But that was never going to happen. I think not selling the property after they died was my way of trying to keep them alive. If someone from my father's side of the family hadn't asked to buy it, I probably would still be hanging on to it."

"I see. Thanks for telling me."

"No problem. Got another question?" he said, his face brightening.

"Do you have any idea why a private investigator would have called the *Des Moines Register* offering to give a reporter some information about Fred Whitlock just a couple days before Whitlock died?"

"I have no idea," he said, shaking his head. "The last time I talked to Fred he mentioned that he hadn't been feeling like himself. Next thing, I get word he'd had a massive heart attack. What possible connection could there be between Fred and the body found down here anyway?"

Carol wasn't biting. "It's just a question I want to find an answer to."

"Sorry I can't be of help with that one. Got another?"

"I know you haven't lived here as an adult, but have you ever done business with anyone here in town?"

He again looked toward the river for a moment and then turned back to her and shook his head. "No, I haven't."

"Is there anyone here you've stayed in touch with?"

"Only the handyman and, more recently, Joan, but that's all."

She felt torn as the two of them sat on the park bench on this sunny, summer afternoon. She wanted to confide in the cousin of her friend. She wanted to tell him she suspected the mayor and city manager knew something about the body on his property. But Dr. Mallory's counsel was etched in her brain. Sizemore wasn't her friend; he was a potential source. A source's job was to give information, not collect it. If he had nothing for her, there was no point in continuing the conversation.

"I should be getting back to my office. Are you going to see Joan, now?"

"First I want to stop at the cemetery. I've never seen the headstone I ordered for my parents' grave. The least I can do is make sure they spelled Edward's and Katherine's names right," he said with a melancholy smile.

Carol rose from the bench and shook his hand again. "It's been nice to meet you, Michael. I'm sure Joan will be happy to see you. Enjoy your visit."

CHAPTER 68

"He seems like a nice enough guy, but he didn't have any new information for me," Carol told Charlie and Bob when she got back to the newsroom sooner than she expected. "He asked what I think. I didn't tell him."

Carol's phone rang.

"Guess who just called me?" Joan Sizemore asked on the other end of the line. "My cousin Michael's in town."

"I know. I just met him down at the park on the levee. Didn't he mention that we talked?"

"He didn't say anything about that. What did he want to see you about?"

"I'm still not really sure. Said he wanted to surprise you later today. I told him you had plans this evening and suggested he not wait too long to get out there."

"It's odd he didn't mention talking to you," Joan said. "He asked if we could have dinner together here at the house this evening. When I said I had plans, he said he would catch up with an old friend over in Quincy tonight and see me tomorrow before he leaves for Des Moines."

CHAPTER 69

Something was gnawing at Carol as she arrived home from the *Bugle* that afternoon, but she couldn't put her finger on it.

Charlie had praised her writing and photos in today's Bonanza Days wrap-up. She was proud of herself for having gotten through the weekend without complaining. And now, thank God, the Days were done for another year. Her uneasiness wasn't about work.

Was she upset Joan was going to Jeff's dinner party tonight? She ruled that out as well. She would be interested to hear about the gathering tomorrow, but she wasn't going to lose any sleep over it tonight.

Carol changed from her work clothes into shorts, a T-shirt, and tennis shoes, looking forward to taking a long walk before making dinner. She decided to lie down just for a minute next to Simba, who was napping on her pillow, his furry chest rising and falling serenely.

Suddenly Carol felt the kitten's paws kneading her face. She awoke, startled and groggy. Was it morning? No. Thank God, she thought, as she sat straight up on the bed. The soft light coming in the bedroom window was the sun on the downside of a long summer day.

"Hey, goof boy, look what you made me do!" she said, pretending to scold him.

It was too late for a walk but too nice outside to end the evening indoors. Carol carried Simba out to the yard and placed him on the ground beside her, letting him indulge his instinct to terrify tiny prey in the grass.

The unscheduled nap hadn't erased her concern that something was off kilter. She had ruled out work, as well as Jeff's party. It was something about her earlier meeting with Michael Sizemore.

It seemed odd he had chosen to phone her first and see her first, instead of his cousin. It also was odd he hadn't told Joan about their meeting at the park. And, if he so regretted not having visited Joan before now, why was he satisfied to wait till tomorrow?

One thing in their conversation that had made sense to her was his obvious love for his parents and his plan to visit their gravesite that afternoon.

"That's it!" Carol said out loud, jumping up from her cross-legged position on the grass. Surprised by her sudden movement, Simba sprang straight up, all four paws leaving the ground at once. She gathered him in her arms and hurried back inside.

CHAPTER 70

After changing back into the navy skirt, yellow sleeveless top, and low-heeled pumps she had worn to work, Carol arrived at the *Bugle* eager to check out her suspicion about the afternoon's conversation.

The newspaper's front entrance was locked for the night, so she used her key to the side door off the parking lot. She went up the narrow steps that led to the second floor and headed straight for the morgue.

With a flick of the switch, she turned on the overhead fluorescent lights in the windowless room, went to the narrow, alphabetized file drawers, and found the one marked "SH–SM." The thin envelope she selected from the drawer was marked "Sizemore, E. L." Inside, she found the death notice for Michael Sizemore's father. The brief notice confirmed the recollection that had made her jump to her feet in the yard. Michael had said he wanted to make sure "Edward's and Katherine's" names were spelled correctly. But the elder Sizemore's given name wasn't Edward. It was Edgar.

A chill ran over Carol's bare arms. A son as devoted as Michael surely would know his father's given name. She looked quickly at the door of the morgue and listened for any noise in the building, admitting to herself that she was being paranoid.

The man who had phoned her at the newsroom was the same man whom she had called in Los Angeles twice before. Joan had expressed no doubt it was her cousin Michael who had called her today.

Carol felt she had to do something, but she wasn't sure what. She told herself to stay calm and think it through. She remembered Dr. Mallory exhorting her and her classmates to conduct themselves professionally on the job, no matter what circumstance they found themselves in and no matter what their personal opinion happened to be.

The best interpretation was that Michael Sizemore had misspoken his father's name. But that was so unlikely as to be absurd. She could think of no second-best interpretation.

Carol's watch showed 8:20 p.m. Jeff's party would be at full tilt. Should she call his house and ask to speak with Joan? Or should she wait till later tonight and call her at home?

Intuition told her to call now.

She found Jeff's home number on her Rolodex in the newsroom. He answered the phone on the fourth ring.

"Jeff, this is Carol Hagan. I'm sorry to interrupt your dinner. Joan told me she was going to be there this evening. Could I please speak to her for a moment?"

"I'm sorry, too," Jeff responded. "She called me around five thirty and said she wouldn't be able to make it. Said she wasn't feeling well."

"Wow, that must have come on really fast. I talked with her about three thirty."

"Yeah. She told me it struck without warning. Is everything okay?"

"Everything's fine. I just needed to check something with her," Carol said, realizing that calling a friend at a party just "to check something" was beyond peculiar.

"You should be able to reach her at home. It might be a good idea anyway to call and see how she's doing."

"Yes, I'll try her at home. Enjoy the rest of your evening."

Carol hung up, worried. Joan had been fine this afternoon and gave no indication she was thinking of skipping the party. What had happened? She dialed Joan's number and listened to the phone ring over and over again. She tried a second time, in case she had misdialed. Again, no answer. Could Joan be so deeply asleep the phone didn't awaken her?

CHAPTER 71

Joan could see her blurry, naked legs, arms, and torso lying in the reddish water, but she couldn't move them. It felt good, this lazy warmth climbing through her. The soft, dizzy feeling of slipping into sleep felt so good. She would just stay here . . . .

Craaaack! Thud!

Far away, wood was ripping in her ears.

"Joan! Joan, where are you?"

"Joan! Answer us!"

Muffled voices floated from space, intruding into the peaceful dream of a red, watery heaven.

"Wha . . .? Wha . . .?" Joan tried to answer with paralyzed lips. Her words came out in half bubbles. There was something she was supposed to do, but she didn't know what. Couldn't anyway. She needed to sleep.

Carol and Jack Padgett rushed up the stairs and into the bathroom. They found Joan almost fully submerged in the tub of water. Blood was leaking from both wrists, sliced vertically down the veins.

The cop and reporter reacted immediately, without words, reaching down into the tub of cool, magenta water and pulling Joan's body into a sitting position. Carol put both arms around Joan's chest, while Padgett grabbed two hand towels hanging from a rack on the wall and pressed them hard on Joan's wrists.

"Keep applying pressure like this with the towels. I'll lift her out of here and onto her bed," Padgett told her.

The two switched positions and Padgett reached his arms under Joan and pulled her up out of the tub.

In clumsy tandem, the soggy rescuers backed out of the bathroom and carried the unconscious woman a few feet down the hallway to her bedroom. Padgett gently placed her on the white chenille bedspread. Instinctively, he checked the back of the closet door, found her robe, and covered her with it.

Even though they had caught her friend at the edge of death, they still might not be able to stop her from slipping over. Feeling panic rising, Carol reined in her emotions and pressed hard on both wrists, trying to force life back through the ugly cuts on Joan's arms.

"You're gonna be okay, Joan, honey," she said in the most soothing voice she could muster. "You're gonna be okay."

Using the phone on Joan's nightstand, Padgett called for an ambulance.

"Stay calm," he said to the reporter. "They'll be here right away." Then he took Carol's place on the bed while she got another towel and gently began to dry Joan's hair.

When she heard the urgent wail of the ambulance as it flew over the now-dark Route 2, Carol's emotions broke through and she began to cry, relieved that help was close, terrified that death was closer still.

What force of evil had dared to harm this beautiful, good-hearted woman?

CHAPTER 72

By ten thirty, all the guests had said their thank-yous and good-byes, leaving Jeff Ryan to clean up the remnants of their dinner on the terrace. Collecting ashtrays and candles from the tables where he and the five couples had dined on shrimp cocktail and beef tenderloin, he felt self-righteously irritated about the waste of time the whole charade had been.

Neither he nor Jason Eberle had learned a single thing about the newspaper's plans for future coverage of the skeleton, even though both had had ample time to talk with the editors, Vogler and Hartman. At the end of the evening, the mayor had spoken briefly to Jeff, asking the city manager to meet him first thing in the morning and assess where things stood.

From Ryan's perspective, things stood in exactly the same place they had over a week ago when he took Joan Sizemore to dinner. He made a mental note to call her tomorrow to see how she was feeling.

"Hello, Jeff," said a smooth voice from the shadows of the terrace. "How was the party?"

The unexpected, unmistakable voice of Eugene Montgomery jolted Ryan from his reverie. He wheeled, squinting toward the unlit edge of the terrace near the wrought-iron fence. At first, all he could see was a red tip on the end of a cigarette. Then his eyes adjusted to the darkness, and he saw the man he hated and feared.

"You SOB! If you don't get the hell away from here, I'll make sure you rot in prison!" Ryan's voice shook. The hair on his arms and the back of his neck stood on end.

"My friend," Montgomery said, "you seem to be forgetting that if I go down, you go down with me."

"None of us has to go down, you bastard! All you have to do is leave this alone."

"I'm going to leave it alone, all right. But before I do, I've got to be sure you and Jason don't mess up my reentry."

"For God's sake, what more do you want us to do?

"First, I want you to call the mayor and tell him to get himself over here right now. The three of us need to have a little talk."

CHAPTER 73

Sergeant Jack Padgett called his wife on a pay phone in the corridor outside the ER to tell her he was helping a friend and would be home soon. Then he bought two cups of coffee from a nearby vending machine.

Sipping coffee and flipping distractedly through outdated magazines, Carol and Jack sat waiting for someone to tell them how Joan was. The last time they had seen her, she had tourniquets below both elbows and an oxygen mask over her mouth. One of the ambulance crew had nimbly carried her down the stairs, lain her on a gurney, and rolled her to the ambulance that then sped, siren screaming, toward Bethany Memorial Hospital.

After hastily repositioning Joan's front door, Jack and Carol headed in the same direction, arriving at Memorial several minutes after Joan had been wheeled behind closed doors.

Now it was ten thirty. A white-jacketed physician walked into the almost-empty waiting area looking for relatives of his suicidal patient.

"I'm Dr. Neely. Are you Miss Sizemore's family?" he asked, approaching the two of them when they stood up expectantly.

"She doesn't have any family in town. I'm her friend, Carol Hagan, and this is Sergeant Jack Padgett, with the Bethany police. We're the ones who found her. How is she?"

"She'll pull through. We've given her several units of O-negative blood and admitted her to a nursing floor. I've left orders for a nurse to stay close by her through the night to monitor her vital signs."

"Can we see her?" Carol asked.

"Not tonight. She ingested a stiff dose of phenobarbital. The good thing is the drug will help ease her agitation as she comes around. She needs to rest and stay calm. There's nothing you can do for her right now. Leave your phone number at the desk in case we need to reach you, and come back in the morning."

Carol shook his hand, squeezing it hard.

"Thank you so much, Dr. Neely," she said, for the first time in her life able to understand why ordinary mortals sometimes regard doctors as gods.

CHAPTER 74

Neither of them spoke on the drive back to Osco's. Reassured by the ER doctor's confident manner, each ruminated on what had happened.

Carol had called Sergeant Padgett at his home right after talking to Jeff Ryan. She rarely made feminine appeals to masculine strength, but this was a time she felt one was warranted. Of the men she knew in Bethany, Jack Padgett was the man whose strength she felt she could count on.

Fortunately, the police sergeant was home, enjoying a day off before switching over to the three-to-eleven shift. His wife had taken their two kids to see *Charlotte's Web* for the second time.

Trying to seem only mildly concerned, Carol had asked him if he would drive out with her to check on Joan, who had taken ill suddenly and was not answering her phone.

"Sure, I'll go out with you," he had responded. "Where should we meet up?"

Osco Drug's parking lot had been their choice, and it was where they now sat in Padgett's Ford Falcon.

"Did you know Joan was so depressed?" he asked.

"She isn't depressed," Carol said, matter-of-factly.

He tilted his head. "She tried to take her own life. People don't do that unless they are *very* depressed."

Carol turned in the passenger seat so she could look directly at this man whom she didn't know well but now needed to trust.

"Listen. I know what it looks like. But I don't buy it, Jack." She hesitated. "There's a story I've been working on that I've had to keep confidential. The only people who know anything about it are Charlie Vogler, Bob Hartman, and Joan. I'm not sure, but I think what happened tonight is somehow connected to what I've been investigating."

Padgett ran his right hand through his curly black hair and tapped the fingers of his left hand on the steering wheel, making a soft clicking sound with his wedding band. He took in a long breath and exhaled. So far, all of his official dealings with death had involved natural or accidental occurrences, except for the recent case of the unidentified skeleton. When he saw Joan Sizemore in the tub, he was determined suicide would not be added to his list of fatality reports.

"Are you telling me you think we walked into a crime scene, not a suicide attempt?"

"I know it sounds crazy," Carol said. "I'm really sorry, but I didn't feel I could tell you more on the way out there. When Jeff Ryan told me Joan had suddenly become ill only two hours after I had talked with her, I was afraid she might be in trouble, and I didn't want to go out there alone. But if I had told you my reasons for being suspicious and then it turned out Joan just wasn't feeling well, I would have broken my word to my boss for nothing."

"Well, she sure 'just wasn't feeling well,'" he said, failing to keep irritation from his voice. "How can you be so sure she hasn't been hiding her depression from you? People do that, you know. There was no sign of forced entry, no sign of violence in the house. What if the illness that suddenly overcame her this afternoon was a bout of depression she couldn't handle this time?"

Carol shifted back in the passenger seat and turned her eyes from the police officer to the parking lot, empty except for her Maverick. She had no answer.

"Okay. Maybe you're right," she said, looking back at him. "Tomorrow morning, I'll talk to Joan and find out what happened. Can I ask just one more favor of you, though?"

"Sure, why not?" he said, with a tired smile.

"When you're cruising around tomorrow, would you mind driving out to Joan's house to see if anyone's around?"

"Are you expecting someone to be there?"

"Well, let's say that's another thing I'm not sure of," she said, getting out of the car. "Thanks a lot for coming with me tonight, Jack. Thank your wife, too. I'll talk to you tomorrow."

CHAPTER 75

"What's going on that couldn't wait till daylight, Jeff?" Jason Eberle said, following the city manager into his living room barely ten minutes after Ryan had called and asked the mayor to return to the house on Riverview Drive.

"*This* couldn't wait till daylight, Mr. Mayor," Eugene Montgomery said, walking in from the hallway, holding a .38-caliber Charter Arms in his right hand.

Seeing the gun, Jason's body tensed. He flashed back to the battle of Argentan-Falaise, where German land mines or sniper fire had felled every infantryman who took a wrong step.

"Don't do this, Montgomery. Let's talk," Eberle said.

"Shut up. We've had enough talk already," Montgomery said, his gun hand motioning Eberle closer to where Ryan stood by one of the blue velvet easy chairs.

"Let's see . . . we've got two guys who got too greedy and had to kill their golden goose. Hey, that's kind of poetic, isn't it?" Montgomery said with a humorless chuckle. "When the dead goose's bones turned up, the boys figured their goose was cooked, and they decided to go meet their maker together.

"Who shall go first in this 'murder-suicide pact'? Jason, how about I shoot Jeff for you?"

At a distance of about five feet, Montgomery raised the revolver, cocked it, and pointed it at Ryan's chest.

Time froze for Jason Eberle. He looked at his best friend, standing there impassively, apparently not grasping that he was in the last moment of his life. A bullet was going to explode in the center of Jeff's heart, and that would be his end. All because of the wrong steps the two of them had taken.

"No!" Eberle shouted as he threw himself in front of Ryan, intercepting with his head the bullet that spiraled toward the upper left side of the city manager's torso.

The crack of the revolver exploded in Ryan's ears and he felt blood, bone and brain spray across his face and chest. Eberle's body sagged to the floor,

"You idiot!" Montgomery barked at the crumpled heap and moved nearer to the still-standing Ryan.

Crack! Crack! Two more gun blasts sounded in the living room.

Montgomery yelped as a bullet struck him in the left arm; Jeff Ryan dropped to the floor. Montgomery swiveled his head toward the front door, turned back to see the bloodied city manager lying with eyes closed, then bolted through the dining room.

Police Chief Larry Bryce fired one more shot at the retreating gunman as he fled through the French doors to the terrace. Then Bryce strode from the foyer into the living room, his face flushed and perspiring.

Ryan, splattered with the warm remains of Jason Eberle, rose from his prone position and grabbed the dead man's left wrist, trying to find a pulse. Blood from the head wound was leaching into the plush white carpet.

"Are you okay, Jeff?" the police chief asked.

The city manager nodded.

Bryce shoved the Smith & Wesson .38 into its holster and sank to his knees beside Eberle's body. The bullet from Montgomery's gun had pierced the mayor's right temple, cracking his skull and pushing brains and blood through a gaping hole on the left side of his head. The chief put his hand on his friend's heart, already knowing there was no life to save. He shook his head in grief and disbelief. Then he rose from the floor, went to the phone, and called for an ambulance and all of his on-duty officers.

CHAPTER 76

Carol watched Padgett drive away from Osco's parking lot as she sat in her car with the engine idling.

The thought that Joan might have tried to kill herself was now swirling among all the other uncertainties in Carol's mind.

Maybe it was the *Bugle* that had gotten the elder Sizemore's name wrong, not the man who claimed to be Michael Sizemore. And maybe the mayor and city manager were just trying to hide harmless white lies from the public they served. And maybe the people who really knew what happened at the Sizemore barn were long gone or long dead. And maybe the police chief was just too comfortable to be bothered with the grimy details of a homicide investigation.

Maybe Joan *was* depressed and hiding it. They had known each other only a month. If the situation were reversed, would she confide that to a new friend?

Joan was divorced, living alone in a new town, and working without the usual companionship of office colleagues. Who knew how a change in circumstances, either subtle or momentous, could impact a person's state of mind?

* * *

Her mother, her brother, Denny, and her sisters, Peggy and Maureen, sang "Happy Birthday" to her around the supper table. It was April 5, 1959–her twelfth birthday.

"It would have been Daddy's birthday today, too," she said matter-of-factly, trying not to act too proud that she and her father had shared a birthday.

"That's right, Carol. He'd be forty-eight," her mother said.

"He'd probably be a captain by now, don't you think, Mom?" she said.

"Captain, hell!" Denny said. "He'd be running the whole damn police department by now!"

They all laughed, but her mother said, "Watch your language, Buster! Daddy wouldn't want you talking like that around here."

"Denny, do you think Daddy could have been chief of police if he was alive?" she asked.

Denny gave his mother a look of frustration across the table before answering and, almost imperceptibly, shook his head. "Sure he could have been! He was one of the best cops in St. Louis."

"Do you think he liked being a policeman?" She directed the question toward both her brother and mother, but all of a sudden, her mother got very busy stacking the dinner plates and clearing the table, a task she normally left for her daughters.

"Are you kidding? You know he loved his job," Denny said. "Don't you remember how he used to polish his Sam Browne belt and his holster till they could just about blind somebody?"

All five laughed again.

"Yeah. The thing I remember most," she said, "is how he would wave the pressing cloth around like he was a magician when he ironed the creases in his uniform pants."

"Daddy was so proud of his uniform," her mother said from over at the sink.

"What happened that he changed?" she asked her brother. "He seemed sad . . ."

Their mother had returned to the table, and Denny seemed to be looking to her for a signal.

"Hey now," her mother said, cutting Denny off before he could speak. "I was planning to serve up this devil's food cake before it gets stale. Peggy, get the ice cream from the freezer. Maureen, get the cake plates and forks from the counter. Carol, you get the first piece."

* * *

Carol heard her stomach growling.

Driving east on Main, she made a quick detour into HoJo's for a carryout hamburger and fries. The fact that she cared about eating while her friend was lying in a hospital bed gave her a pang of guilt. But hunger pangs prevailed.

The pleasant evening she'd envisioned—a long walk, a good dinner, and a couple of hours reading Tom Wolfe's new book before bed—had devolved into disaster.

"Woman plans, God laughs," she said to herself as she turned the key in the lock. From the entrance of the small apartment, Carol could see into her bedroom. She was surprised Simba was neither at the door to greet her nor sleeping on her pillow, his favorite retreat when he got tired of waiting.

"Simba!" she called out, setting her purse on the oak-veneer coffee table. "Where are you, my little fur ball? I've got a hamburger to share with you!"

The floor lamp she had turned on before going back to the *Bugle* earlier in the evening now illuminated the way past the brown and yellow plaid sofa and matching easy chair, through the bedroom and toward the kitchen. She expected Simba to come sauntering out, tail straight up, now that he had heard her voice. But no Simba appeared.

"Simba?" She walked into the dark kitchen and flicked on the wall switch to her right. "Jesus Christ!" she shouted, jumping backward and dropping the HoJo sack on the floor.

Sitting at the far end of the kitchen table was the man who had introduced himself to her as Michael Sizemore. His right hand was in his lap; his left arm was resting on the table, swathed in one of Carol's bath towels, whose original pale green was darkening to fuchsia.

"What are you doing here? How did you get in here?" she demanded, in a voice she didn't recognize.

The smile was the same one she had seen several hours earlier at the park on the levee. But it was eerily different. *He* was different.

"More questions for me, eh, Carol? Always questions," he said, shifting his smile into a sneer. "It's very easy to get into your apartment, in case you didn't know. When you don't lock your windows, anybody can get in. Even a one-armed man."

"What do you want? Please tell me what's going on," she said, as she assessed her chances of running out the way she had just come in.

As though reading her mind, the intruder raised his right hand from his lap so she could see a short-barreled revolver pointed at her.

"What I want is just a couple of things from you. What's going on, you may never know. First, I want you to bandage me up. You can do that, can't you, my dear? Then I want you to drive me to Des Moines. We'll take my car. It's all gassed up and ready to go."

Carol's knees trembled with dread. This man was maniacal. The last thing she should do was get in a car with him.

"Tonight? You want me to drive you to Des Moines tonight?" she said, realizing too late that her question absurdly presumed a rational person on the receiving end.

"Ah, Carol. It has to be tonight. We don't know if we'll even be around tomorrow, do we?"

The phone rang, and she reflexively started to move toward where it hung on the wall in back of him.

"Stay right there!" he said, lifting the gun higher. "Let it ring."

They both waited in silence until the caller gave up after seven rings. Carol wondered who would be calling her this late. The hospital? Jack?

"Let's get moving," he said, rising to his feet and removing the towel from the wound on his arm to show it to her, like a trophy. The bullet from Larry Bryce's Smith & Wesson had torn through the flesh on Montgomery's left triceps, creating a mess of skin and muscle.

"My God, you'll need stitches for that," Carol said. "You've got to get to an emergency room."

He laughed. "*This* is my emergency room. And *you* are my ER nurse, Miss Hagan," he said, hissing the double s. "I assume you've got gauze and tape in your bathroom closet. Get it fast. Move!" he ordered, waving the gun toward the door off the hallway between the bedroom and kitchen. He followed close behind, kicking the sack of food out of the way as he went.

Carol shuddered. The man who had been so cordial to her this afternoon had tonight climbed into her home through an unlocked window, waited for her in the dark to scare her witless, and now he was threatening her with a pistol.

She was on the verge of becoming one of those women about whom she had read so many times in the newspaper. Victims of lunatic gunmen, serial killers, enraged ex-husbands or ex-boyfriends.

As she opened the bathroom closet door, a strange, inexplicable calm came over her. Some impersonal force was infusing her with defiance.

"*Polite, detached, tough-minded. Polite, detached, tough-minded. Polite, detached, tough-minded,*" she silently repeated Dr. Mallory's lesson like a mantra.

"I said move!" he yelled at the back of her head. "How goddamn long does it take to find the goddamn gauze and tape?"

"I'm looking for the merthiolate. It will help sterilize the wound," she said, stalling.

"Forget that! Just bandage this! We've got to get on the road!"

CHAPTER 77

"What should I call you?" Carol asked as she situated herself in the high-back bucket seat of the '73 Oldsmobile Cutlass S, an Avis rental.

The man was crouched low in the backseat of the sedan, out of view of anyone who might be on the street at this hour. His upper left arm was thickly wrapped with several layers of gauze, tightly secured with adhesive tape. He wore a makeshift sling, fashioned out of a square Carol had cut from a cotton bed sheet and folded into a triangle. In his right hand, he held the Charter Arms revolver.

"I've got many names," he answered. "If you don't like Michael, how about Eugene? Or Martin? Or Frank?"

The names Eugene and Martin meant nothing to her, but Frank was familiar. "Would that be Frank Mitchell?" she asked matter-of-factly, as though seeking accuracy for some future newspaper article.

"Yes, Miss Reporter, it would be Frank Mitchell. You are very clever to have figured that out."

The man's behavior in their short time together had careened between sardonically polite, impatient, and angry. She needed to avoid provoking him and his trigger finger.

"May I call you Frank?"

"You don't need to call me anything. All you need to do is drive me to Des Moines."

After two trips to the capital this month, Carol was familiar with the route. North on U.S. 218 to 34 west, to 63 north, which became State 163 at Oskaloosa and stayed that way into Des Moines.

"I've been known to have a lead foot," she said, as she headed toward the highway. "Do you want me to step on it or keep to the limit?"

"Just drive the damn car! I'll tell you what I want, when I want."

Her smartest course of action, at least for the time being, was to obey orders. For the next four hours, he needed a driver. That meant he probably wouldn't be shooting her. The route would be almost deserted. Perhaps silence and the monotony of the road would tranquilize him. He might let down his guard and give her an opening for escape. She had to stay alert and do nothing to cause a violent reaction.

CHAPTER 78

Charlie Vogler drove down Harrison Street on his way to Jeff Ryan's. When he saw Carol's car in front of her apartment, he thought about stopping but decided to let her keep sleeping. Whatever had happened at Ryan's, it would only take one of them to report on it, and he was already up and out.

The chief's phone call had come shortly after Charlie had dropped off to sleep. Bryce's voice was serious, and the message was brusque.

"Charlie, you need to come back on over to Jeff Ryan's place," he had said. "Something's happened." Click.

The chief had given him no chance to ask questions, a fact Charlie didn't appreciate. It had only been two weeks since he had set Bryce straight about who was running the show at the *Bugle*.

Hanging up from the police chief, Charlie followed his first impulse, which was to call his city editor and ask her to get out of bed, go over to Ryan's, and find out what was going on. He was surprised Carol didn't answer her phone.

"I sure wish I could sleep as soundly as she does!" he had groused to his wife as he got dressed.

Turning onto Riverview Boulevard, Charlie let out an involuntary whistle. Two police cars were double-parked in front of Jeff Ryan's house with their red and white lights flashing. A few of the neighbors were standing on their front lawns, some in robes and some in T-shirts and trousers. Yellow tape was draped across the front yard.

"What the devil's going on?" he muttered.

Charlie parked two doors down from Ryan's residence, picked up his notebook from the seat beside him, got his camera out of the trunk, and headed toward the house that had become a crime scene.

A young patrolman nodded soberly and let him pass into the brightly lit foyer. Charlie's eyes immediately were drawn to the bloodstains on the white living room carpet and then to Jeff Ryan. He had removed his bloody sport shirt and was sitting slumped on the couch in a formerly white, now garishly pink, T-shirt.

Sitting across from Ryan in matching blue arm chairs were Chief Bryce and a Bethany police sergeant holding a pen in one hand and a notebook in the other.

"My God, what happened?" Charlie said to the three men.

The chief rose from his chair. The city manager remained seated, his eyes puffy and red. The crisp confidence was gone; in its place were shock and grief.

"It's bad, Charlie," Bryce said. "The mayor's been murdered. Shot to death. The perpetrator was wounded but managed to escape. I've got two-thirds of the force looking for him right now. He's armed and dangerous. I've given shoot-to-kill orders."

The managing editor took a deep breath and briefly closed his eyes. Then he placed his camera on a side table, pulled out his notebook and pen, and jotted down the chief's telegraphic statement.

"Who was the guy?" Charlie asked, looking at Jeff.

"Jeff doesn't know who he was," Bryce intervened. "He thinks he's deranged. The guy barged in here and said he had to talk with Jeff and the mayor. He said he'd been defrauded by Michael Sizemore in a business deal. He wanted his money back, and he thought since Sizemore had lived in Bethany, the city should give him some money. He forced Jeff at gunpoint to call Jason. Once Jason got here, the guy said he was going to kill them both. If I hadn't come when I did, he would have. I got three shots off but only wounded him with one before he escaped," the chief said, pointing to drops of blood that formed a trail through the dining room.

"You got here while the killer was still here?" Charlie asked. "How'd you do that?"

"Jason called me right after he got the call from Jeff asking him to come over. He told me he didn't like the way Jeff had sounded on the phone. He thought Jeff might be in trouble and asked me to meet him over here, just in case. I thought Jason was going to wait for me outside, but he didn't. I was at the front walk when I heard a shot. I pulled my weapon, ran up, and pushed the door open just in time to fire at the intruder. If I hadn't, Jeff would have been killed, too."

Charlie looked to the city manager for verification. Jeff nodded and looked down, cradling his head in both hands.

The editor felt sorry for Jeff and what he had been through, but he wanted to hear something directly from the survivor.

"Jeff, did this guy just force his way in here?"

Again, the police chief ran interference.

"The guy showed up on the terrace while Jeff was cleaning up out there from the dinner. He pulled his gun and demanded that Jeff call Jason."

"Do you know what kind of gun it was?"

"Not sure. Maybe a Colt or a Charter, short muzzle," the police chief said. Charlie hesitated, realizing that pressing Ryan in his dazed condition would be futile.

"Chief, Jeff," he said, looking first at Bryce, then Ryan. "I know this is very difficult, especially because of your close relationship to the mayor. But I'll need to get as much information as possible in tomorrow's edition. Can you both be available to talk to either Carol Hagan or Bob Hartman early in the morning?"

The men nodded.

Charlie picked up his camera and headed for the front door. Then he turned.

"I appreciate your calling me, Chief."

Outside Ryan's house, Charlie took several photos from different angles to include the front of the house, the crime scene tape, and the two police cars.

Back in his car, the managing editor turned the key in the ignition but didn't move.

What he had just heard and seen seemed unthinkable for this small, peaceful town. A nut case, looking to revenge a bad business deal with a former resident, murders a total stranger just because he's the mayor? Charlie shook his head.

Tomorrow's edition of the *Bugle* would not only have to eulogize the life and accomplishments of Mayor Jason Eberle, but also try to explain the circumstances of his tragic death, report on the search for the killer, and provide reactions from city leaders and citizens.

"I might as well not even go to bed," he said to no one but himself.

He considered ringing Carol's doorbell and asking her to join him in the newsroom. But he thought better of it. It was almost one o'clock. He would head to the paper, call his wife, and then get to work. He'd pull the clippings file on Jason Eberle and write a basic obituary that Bob could embellish in the morning. At five, he would make wake-up calls to Carol, Bob, Ron, and Tom and tell them to get to the newsroom ASAP to start assembling a special edition of the *Bugle*.

CHAPTER 79

A short distance from Ottumwa, about two hours beyond Bethany, Carol decided to ask her captor if she could take a bathroom break. There would be a twenty-four-hour truck stop coming up as they approached 63 north. She might be able to signal a trucker that she needed help.

"Any chance we could make a stop when we get to Ottumwa?" she said, looking into the rearview mirror.

They had been riding in silence since leaving Bethany. Carol wondered a few times if her captor was unconscious, but every time she glanced into the mirror, his eyes were staring back at hers. His right hand, holding the revolver, rested lightly on the back of the driver's headrest. His body was perched on the edge of the rear passenger seat, with knees jutting forward and the weight of his legs braced on the balls of his feet: a position devised for alertness, not comfort.

"Why do you need to stop?"

"A bathroom break and a cup of coffee would help me keep my mind on the road for the next couple of hours."

"Nix on the coffee. You can pee on the side of the road if you need to go that bad."

"I can wait."

"God, I hate this town," Mitchell said minutes later when they passed the sign that said, "Welcome to Ottumwa."

This was the first utterance he had volunteered since the trip began. Until her request a moment ago, Carol had obeyed his demand for silence, but his spontaneous disgust might be a chance for conversation. Maybe she could learn who he was and what he was up to.

"I've only driven through Ottumwa a couple of times, never stopped. What's so bad about it?" she said.

Silence.

Then, "This is where my life went to hell."

CHAPTER 80

Frank Mitchell's left shoulder throbbed with pain. He could feel the tepid sliminess of his blood as it oozed from the wound under the gauze. The blood vessels in his head felt like they would explode from pressure. And now he was reduced to squatting in the backseat while the bitch reporter whined about wanting to pee. He wanted to sleep but couldn't let himself.

* * *

Exhausted, he lay in the backseat of his car, parked on Lambert Field's short-term parking lot, and tried to appease a throbbing headache with an hour of sleep before boarding Ozark's morning flight from St. Louis to Quincy, Illinois.

Whose head wouldn't throb after spending thirty hours behind the wheel, driving twenty-one hundred miles from Des Moines to Santa Fe to St. Louis?

As hard as it had been, the trip to Santa Fe had been equally rewarding. The pleasure of seeing Amanda's shock when he appeared at the door of her fancy hotel room had made it all worthwhile.

He was her husband, but he wasn't the man she was expecting. What a stunning surprise for the whore! She thought he was fooled by her pretense of innocence, her apparent acquiescence to his wishes. She believed he was deceived by her clever cover-up of infidelity, the betrayal of their sacred wedding vows.

What a distressing turn of events for her, realizing a midweek tryst was turning into a midweek suicide. She had, indeed, brought her death upon herself. He assisted, of course, after she was sedated, in making sure her wrists were slit in just the proper way. Nevertheless, it was a suicide. The authorities had had no doubt.

Just like his mother had thought his father a fool, Amanda had thought the same of him. But unlike his father, he wasn't a fool. He hadn't spent all those years watching and learning from people who ran their cons on both sides of the jailhouse bars to emerge a fool. Maybe he appeared to be a teenage flunky, mopping floors and fetching coffee for the cops. Maybe to the patronizing lawyers at Sterling, O'Connor & Foyle, he was a nobody trying to be somebody. Maybe all those bimbo secretaries in short skirts and tight blouses thought he was panting after them just like the junior partners were.

They were all wrong. Just like his mother. Just like Amanda.

No punk, no flunky, no "nobody" could have planned revenge the way he had and taken action the way he had. In just an hour or so, he would be on his way to execute the next stage of his . . . executions. He smiled. The sweetness of revenge requited the pain.

* * *

"What happened? What happened to you in Ottumwa?"

He heard the bitch reporter's voice coming from the front seat and opened his eyes, meeting hers in the rearview mirror.

"What do you care?"

CHAPTER 81

She had to tread cautiously. Frank, Michael, Martin, Eugene. Whoever this guy was, he wasn't stupid. Desperate, wounded, full of rage, but not stupid. She could never convince him she cared about him.

"I'm a reporter," she said, deciding to give honesty a try. "For over a month, I've been trying to find out about the skeleton and getting nowhere. Everybody says they don't know anything about it. I have a feeling you know something. Does what happened to you in Ottumwa have anything to do with the remains found in Michael Sizemore's barn?"

She learned immediately that the "honesty is the best policy" adage wasn't true in this case. She felt the cool metal of the gun barrel shoved up hard against the right side of her neck, under her ear.

Shocked by the unexpectedness of his action, she momentarily jerked her head and the wheel of the car to the left side of the road. Luckily, there was no oncoming traffic.

"Listen, bitch," he hissed in her ear, "you want to know why

I'm going to answer your stupid questions? Because, just like your girlfriend, nobody's ever going to hear from you again."

He again pressed the revolver against her neck, as though placing an exclamation point, and then pulled it away, keeping his gun hand on the headrest.

"*Detached and tough-minded*," Carol said to herself, giving up on "polite." Without turning her head, she scanned the road from left to right. Except for a few fluorescent-lit signs marking the roadside businesses of west Ottumwa and an occasional car heading southeast on U.S. 63, the road was dark. She saw nothing that offered an escape. A better chance might show up closer to Des Moines. If she lived that long.

She drove on without a word. At least now she knew for sure that Joan hadn't tried to commit suicide. And even if Carol couldn't save herself, at least Joan would be alive to tell the police what she knew about this lunatic. Cold comfort, but better than nothing.

"Don't have so many questions now, do you, Carol? Nothing like the prospect of imminent death to squash curiosity is there?"

"You're right. If I have an option, I'd prefer you don't tell me anything and let me live."

Mitchell laughed at that, and then ran his tongue over his lips, licking away the remnants of amusement.

"Too bad, sister! You already know too much, anyway. We've got maybe a couple of hours to kill, so to speak. I might as well pass the time by telling you how I took Michael Sizemore's life."

"You killed Michael Sizemore?"

"Well, that too."

Carol knew the man meant to shoot her, but not until they arrived at some unnamed destination in Des Moines. All she could do was to keep driving, try to keep him calm, and find a way to escape somewhere between here and the capital. The man in the backseat had answers to the questions she had raised a month earlier when she sat at Joan's kitchen table. From where she sat now, it didn't seem like a news story she would live to write.

CHAPTER 82

"Honey, it's almost two-thirty; why don't you come to bed and at least try to get some rest?" Claire McFarland said softly to her husband who sat in semidarkness on the living room couch.

Since he'd returned from Los Angeles on Saturday, James McFarland had slept little. Doubt and anguish over what he had discovered while trying to learn his brother-in-law's whereabouts had left him immobilized. Unwilling to confide the details to his wife, he had simply told her he needed time to think things over and pray.

But thinking had brought no enlightenment. Prayer, no consolation. The last few days he had spent mostly on the couch, trying to accept as real something that did not happen in real life—at least in the lives of people *he* knew.

* * *

No one answered the doorbell at 403 San Gabriel Drive. He peered through the gauzy curtains and saw vague signs of life in the foyer and living room. Some mail lay on a console table, a newspaper lay on the coffee table.

He decided that since he had nowhere else to go he would just wait.

He was still waiting at five o'clock, seated on the low steps in front of the townhouse, when a middle-aged woman parked a silver '72 Pontiac Firebird in the driveway next door.

"Hello," she said as she got out of the car. "If you're looking for Martin Sizemore, he's out of town."

"No, ma'am. I've come here looking for Michael Sizemore. Isn't this his home?"

"Used to be," she said, walking across the narrow strip of fescue that separated the townhouses. "Now his cousin, Martin, lives here. He's been holding the fort while Michael's in Europe. I'm Nona Reynolds. May I ask who you are?" the woman said, holding her hand up to shield her eyes from the lowering sun in order to get a better look at the stranger in front of her.

"Excuse me," he said. "I'm James McFarland, from Des Moines, Iowa. I don't know Michael Sizemore personally. I was just hoping he might help me find someone."

"Martin probably could tell you how to get in touch with him. He handles Michael's affairs, keeps the real estate business going. But, like I said, Martin's not here. He left town yesterday evening. Sorry about that."

He had a thought.

"Perhaps you know the person I'm looking for. His name is Frank Mitchell. I think he was a business associate of Michael Sizemore's, and he might also know Martin Sizemore."

The woman pushed back a lock of silver-flecked brown hair and shook her head. "The name isn't familiar. Martin sometimes meets business associates here, but I don't know their names."

"No, I guess you wouldn't. Would you mind looking at a picture to see if you recognize Frank Mitchell?"

"Sure, if you've got one handy."

He went back to the Nova and retrieved the framed photo of his sister and brother-in-law.

"This is the man I'm looking for. Have you ever seen him?"

He wasn't prepared for the neighbor's shocked reaction when she looked at the photo of Frank and Amanda Mitchell smiling happily with cocktails in hand. She took the photo, turned her body slightly away from him to cut the sun's glare, and drew the photo closer to her face.

"Why, that's Martin and Amanda! This is Martin Sizemore, the man I've been talking about, Michael's cousin. The woman is Michael's girlfriend. I don't understand. Why are Martin and Amanda together like this? Why do you say his name is Frank Mitchell? That's Martin Sizemore," she said, emphatically tapping Frank Mitchell's image.

"And that's Amanda," she said, pointing at his sister. "Poor thing died a couple of years ago. Michael and she made a lovely couple."

He couldn't make sense of what she was telling him. He stood staring at her, dumbstruck. This woman recognized his deceased sister Amanda and his brother-in-law. But not as themselves. She was calling Frank Mitchell "Martin."

The neighbor seemed surprised, but not nearly as much as he was. She handed him back the photo and put a hand on his left forearm.

"This is none of my business. I'm sorry for whatever upset this has caused you, Mr. McFarland. I don't know what to say." She stood there sympathetically, seemingly unsure if she should wait or simply leave him standing frozen on the sidewalk.

After a moment, he pulled himself together enough to ask a question.

"How do you know she was Michael Sizemore's girlfriend?" he said, pointing to Amanda. "Have you seen other pictures of her?"

"Why, I've seen her! Here. Before she died. She didn't live here, but she would visit every once in a while. Michael told me they were planning to get married as soon as they could work things out.

"*Then, a couple years ago, she died very suddenly. It was meningitis— viral or bacterial—whichever one is the deadly one, I always forget. Michael was out of town at the time. We found all this out because Martin arrived one day and said his cousin had asked him to watch over things for a while. Michael was devastated by Amanda's death, Martin said. He was going to get away, travel to Europe and get a fresh start on life. Michael hasn't come back since.*"

He found it difficult to continue standing in the face of the reckless untruths that were pouring from this woman's mouth. He sat down on the low step, placing the photo down beside him. He put his head between his knees, trying not to vomit.

The neighbor waited briefly in silence, then offered her condolences for his unexplained sorrow, and retreated to her house.

After several minutes, he picked up the photograph, rose from the steps, walked to the rental car, and drove until he found an Albertsons Supermarket.

He returned to the San Gabriel Drive neighborhood forty minutes later with a new flashlight and batteries, and parked on an adjacent street, where several other cars were already stationed in front of their bungalows and townhouses for the evening.

Lying down in the backseat of the Nova, he tried to make some sense of the story he had just heard.

How could his sister have had an affair with Michael Sizemore? How had she met him? Why would she do it?

The only thing he had ever heard about Michael Sizemore was that he was a possible California link to his brother-in-law Frank. What had the law firm's receptionist said? Sizemore lived in California and had done some work with one of their clients, Whitlock Construction Company. And why had the reporter called him in the first place? She said she wanted to locate Frank Mitchell to ask him about Fred Whitlock.

He felt as though he had just been spun in circles.

Why was his brother-in-law Frank pretending to be Michael Sizemore's cousin? And why did he tell people that Amanda had died of an illness instead of telling them she had committed suicide?

Waves of apprehension floated over him as he lay there waiting for nightfall. He felt no certainty about anything. He didn't know how to act in this world where nothing was as he thought it was.

When darkness finally fell on the southern California street, he left his car and walked back to the townhouse on San Gabriel Drive, watching for activity in the home of the neighbor woman. Except for an upstairs light in the front of her house, he saw no signs of life.

He moved across the lawn and alongside the jacaranda trees planted between the townhouses, feeling drops of perspiration rolling down his neck and torso. He stayed close by the side wall until he came to the back of Sizemore's two-story townhouse. He entered the unlocked gate of an enclosed patio whose dawn-to-dusk light illuminated a dusty grill, a wrought-iron table, and two wrought-iron chairs.

He had no prior experience breaking into other people's homes, but he acted without hesitation. He first tried the backdoor on the chance it was unlocked. It was not. A window, to the right of the door, was at shoulder height. Raising his arms to the edge of the window screen, he could feel the clips that secured the screen. Even though the clips were on the inside, there was enough slack in the mesh for him to position his thumbs against the clips and release them. He then raised the screen to slide it out of its tracks and remove it. Just as he had hoped, the kitchen window, left unlocked, opened easily. He climbed up on one of the patio chairs and hoisted himself through.

Finding his way to a living room window, he once again surveyed the neighbor's house. Seeing no movement, he pulled the flashlight from the waistband of his trousers and turned it on, directing the beam around the room at a height below the windows to avoid drawing neighborly attention to the darkened house.

It was a white-walled townhouse; he guessed it was no more than seventeen hundred square feet in total. The adjoining living and dining room were furnished uniformly, with a Mission style sofa, coffee and end tables, and a dining room table and chairs. The space was decorated with a few colorful prints on the walls and some earth-toned ceramic bowls on the tables. There were no photographs or personal mementos.

The kitchen had the customary furnishings—counter, stools, refrigerator, stove, and cabinets. In the refrigerator, he found a partial carton of milk, a loaf of white bread, some eggs, butter, and ketchup. Nothing to reveal a man's tastes. He found his way up carpeted stairs to a small hallway that gave onto a bedroom, office, and bath. The bedroom, painted in pastel green, was neat and uncluttered, with nothing hidden and nothing exposed. There was a double bed, two nightstands with table lamps, a telephone, and a chest of drawers with a jewelry tray on top containing loose change.

A walk-in closet was arranged with trousers and sports jackets on one side and shirts on the other. The trousers were doubled over their hangers. The jackets hung together. Starched blue and white dress shirts hung with their long sleeves overlapping each other. Short-sleeved sports shirts hung in the back. Pairs of black and brown lace-ups sat on the closet floor.

He walked into the second room, white-walled. A cherry wood desk and a black leather swivel chair dominated the space. In front of the desk was a brown side chair with a padded leather seat. A cherry wood credenza was against the wall behind the desk. Judging from the anonymity of the rest of the house, he doubted the office would tell him anything important about the person who lived here. Still, he was hungry to find even a hint of what Sizemore—or Mitchell—was up to.

On the top of the desk were two small gold-plated trays and a banker's lamp. Both of the trays contained stacks of business cards that bore an embossed imprint, "Sizemore Real Estate & Development Strategies." In smaller type, below the company name, one stack of the cards bore the name "Michael E. Sizemore," with the San Gabriel Drive address and a phone number. The other stack of cards was imprinted with the name "Martin E. Sizemore" and the same address and phone number.

Growing bolder, he turned on the desk lamp and pulled out all of the drawers in the desk and credenza. In a bottom drawer, he found a small stack of Christmas cards in envelopes postmarked St. Louis, Missouri, addressed to Michael Sizemore. They had all been mailed the previous December. He opened the first card. It had a Christmas wreath on the outside and the message: "Wishing you the best the season has to offer." A handwritten note inside said, "Michael, thanks so much for the box of California oranges! They won't last till New Year's! We hope you're doing well. If you come through St. Louis, give us a call. It would be great to see you again! Love, Aunt Margaret and Uncle Joe." Another card showed a Nativity scene with the words, "Peace on Earth." Printed inside were the words, "May the peace and joy of Christmas fill your heart." Enclosed was a photo of a man and woman and two teenagers sitting by a fireplace. It was signed, "Love from Beth and Tom, Laurie (13!) and Matt (15, driving by next Christmas!)"

"Who is this man?" he said out loud as he quickly examined three more greeting cards that had been sent last Christmas. "He's been in Europe for two years, yet relatives still send cards to this address, and he sent them oranges from California?"

Continuing his search, he found an assortment of blank documents used in real estate transactions and boxes of checks from Golden State Bank & Trust some printed with the name "Michael E. Sizemore" and some with "Martin E. Sizemore."

On the credenza sat a telephone and a Rolodex. He spun through the alphabetized entries filled with a variety of contact names, some printed business cards and others handwritten. He turned to the tab labeled "Mc" and went through each card. He found a handwritten card that read "McFarland, James and Claire," with his address and phone number.

He looked at it for a long moment. Among the couple hundred other contacts for businesses, professional firms, and acquaintances, this card would mean nothing to anybody except him, the one person who was never supposed to see it in a million years.

This was neither Michael Sizemore's office nor Martin Sizemore's office. It was the office of Frank Mitchell, doing business as one or the other—or both—of these men.

He leaned back in the leather office chair and took deep breaths.

He had come here to find his brother-in-law. Instead, he had discovered his brother-in-law's cruel deception.

There was no way in hell Frank Mitchell would have let Michael Sizemore live once he knew Sizemore had stolen his wife.

There was no way in hell Frank Mitchell would have let Amanda live after learning she had been unfaithful to him.

Michael Sizemore was not living in Europe. Amanda didn't die by her own her hand.

* * *

James McFarland sat up straight on his living room couch. The nausea of last Thursday had long since passed, but his outrage over what he had heard and seen in Los Angeles remained.

CHAPTER 83

The wipers were moving at full speed, pushing raindrops and smatterings of refracted light back and forth across the windshield. Carol was relieved to have to concentrate on driving in the downpour. It helped take her mind off the killer in the backseat who had a revolver aimed at the right side of her head.

Over the past several minutes, Frank Mitchell had served up a story in which he starred as both innocent victim and brilliant protagonist. It began in Ottumwa, where he had gone to collect evidence of marital infidelity for a client and wound up discovering his own wife's infidelity.

A less gifted man, finding his faithless spouse and her arrogant lover together, would have gone into a murderous frenzy right then and there. And he would have paid for it for the rest of his life in the state penitentiary. Mitchell, according to himself, had stayed calm and meticulously sought proof that he'd been wronged.

When satisfied his suspicion was accurate, he devised a malicious plan by which his wife and her lover would be murdered more than one thousand miles apart, both having plenty of time beforehand to learn why they were going to die and who was going to kill them.

Frank Mitchell had spent the past two and a half years focused on achieving revenge and escaping detection. He was not driven by sex, money, power, status, or reputation. Once his imagination became absorbed in the task of retribution, his actions were single-minded. Nothing and no one could stop him. Everything he did was in the service of the self-righteous course he had chosen.

It hadn't been difficult for him, a seasoned investigator, to learn that the adulterer was Michael Sizemore, who had acquaintances in Des Moines. How convenient that one of Sizemore's business partners was construction magnate Fred Whitlock, the same Fred Whitlock whose company was represented by Mitchell's firm, Sterling, O'Connor & Foyle. When Mitchell sneaked a peek into Whitlock's business operations, he found a route into Michael Sizemore's life.

Bethany's mayor and city manager, Mitchell told Carol, were just two saps who got caught in the wrong place at the wrong time.

"It's too bad you had to come along and interfere the way you did," he said to Carol. "Because of you, three more people had to die. And you'll have to die, as well."

Those words rattled in Carol's ears as she gripped the wheel and studied the dark, watery road.

She had no way to separate fact from fiction in the tale he had spun, but right now, that didn't matter. Escaping was all that mattered.

Without some dramatic change of course, Mitchell would shoot a bullet into her head or heart without remorse. Any action, no matter how risky, would give her a better chance of surviving than if she continued to follow his orders.

The oncoming traffic was gradually increasing as they drew closer to Des Moines. Drivers passing the Cutlass sedan saw just another motorist heading toward the state capital. Carol saw no way to signal her peril without alerting Mitchell at the same time.

She imagined herself jerking the wheel hard to the left, deliberately steering into the path of an eastbound car and letting the passenger side take the brunt of impact. But unless the other driver was in a heavy truck, he or she would certainly be killed or maimed. An unacceptable tactic.

Both behind and in front of them, the road was now clear of traffic except for one car, whose distant headlights she could see through the rain.

Carol was approaching an overpass on 163, and she knew the time had come.

Just as the Cutlass went under the overpass, she gripped the wheel as tightly as she could, slammed her foot on the brake pedal, and threw the gearshift into park.

The car shuddered to a stop on the dry pavement.

Mitchell had been leaning forward, balancing most of his weight on the balls of his feet. At the moment Carol slammed on the brakes, he screamed in pain. The force of inertia pushed his body through the space between the bucket seats, squashing his wounded left arm against the driver's seat. Staring at Carol in dumb rage, he started to raise the revolver. Reflexively, as though backhanding a drop shot, she reached out and swatted the gun from his hand onto the car's dark floor. As he reached down to try to find the weapon, Carol unbuckled her seat belt and swung the driver's side door open. Mitchell turned back toward her and grabbed her right arm, but she was able to tear away and spring from the car, running for her life across the lane where the other motorist was approaching from the west.

She had only an instant to decide. She could head for open land and hope to outrun a bullet or run westward on the eastbound shoulder and hope the oncoming car would stop to give her refuge. If she ran away from the road, she had a chance of distancing herself from the madman. If she put her trust in the driver of the other car and he didn't stop, she would again be facing Mitchell's gun and at his mercy.

Without hesitating, she kicked off her pumps and sprinted in the early morning darkness through a rain-soaked field of soybeans.

A moment later, stopping to catch her breath, she turned and looked back toward the highway. Both Mitchell's rented Cutlass and the car that had been approaching from the west were out of sight, shielded by the overpass.

Carol turned and continued running, low to the ground, as far into the field as she could go, looking for a farmhouse door to knock on or an outbuilding in which she could hide.

Seconds later, she heard a gunshot.

CHAPTER 84

"Charlie? It's me, Carol."

The managing editor looked at his watch as he cradled the phone's receiver on his right shoulder. It was 4:40 a.m., still twenty minutes before his planned wake-up calls to his city editor and the rest of the newsroom staff.

"Carol, have you heard about the mayor?"

"Your wife just told me. I called your house to let you know I won't be able to get back this morning. I'm really sorry. I know you need me there."

"Where are you? What happened?" he asked, hearing the weary tension in her voice.

"I'm at a farmhouse in Prairie City, just outside Des Moines. I'll tell you everything, but first I want you to know I'm okay. You've got too much to handle this morning; don't spend any time worrying about me."

With that intro, she recapped the events of her night and morning. As his city editor talked, Charlie took notes, quickly connecting Jeff Ryan's story about the mayor's killer with Carol's report of being abducted by a wounded gunman named Frank Mitchell.

"Troopers from the state patrol want to talk to me," Carol said, ending her narration. "I'll get back to Bethany as soon as I can."

"Thank God you're safe, Carol," Charlie said. "I want you to sit tight until they make sure this guy is running away from them and not after you."

"Don't worry about that," she said.

CHAPTER 85

Chief Larry Bryce was standing somberly by the police cruiser on Main Street, his uniform cap under his left arm, when Charlie Vogler pulled up at 6:30 a.m. Bryce was wearing a starched, long-sleeved white shirt adorned with two gold stars on each epaulet and two gold stars on each tip of his collar, a navy blue tie, and sharply creased navy blue trousers.

Charlie and Bryce had agreed to meet outside the Hawkeye Hotel, where Jeff Ryan had spent the night. Never friends in the thirteen years they had known each other, now the managing editor and police chief were allies in the effort to elicit the truth from the city manager.

After learning details of Carol's abduction in an early morning call from Charlie, the chief no longer believed Jeff Ryan was an innocent bystander in the shooting of Jason Eberle. He knew Ryan was genuinely grieving the death of his close friend, but he also knew Ryan had lied about the circumstances of that death. Until he could learn the true story, the chief wanted to go slowly. Rather than put Ryan on the defensive by interrogating him, he had asked Charlie to proceed with the scheduled "interview." Charlie had consented to the pretense, but he felt uneasy. Working alone in the newsroom overnight, adrenalin surging, his focus had been razor-sharp. Besides drafting Jason Eberle's obituary, he had written a tight story of the mayor's murder, trusting that Carol would add fresh details after interviewing Ryan and Chief Bryce. He also had dummied up the front page; developed and printed the photos he had taken last night outside the city manager's home, and made out the reporting assignments.

Bob would burnish the mayor's page-one obit, drawing upon personal recollections and making calls to Eberle's closest friends to gather anecdotes and words of praise.

Ron would edit any must-run wire stories, select photos of the mayor for a montage on page two, and report on the overnight search for the shooter.

Tom would call members of Bethany's City Council and other prominent citizens and get their reactions to the tragedy.

Charlie would stay at the wheel and keep everything rolling until the special edition was ready for the press.

But everything had turned upside down with Carol's call from Prairie City. Charlie's plan for covering the mayor's murder with a neat package of articles was insufficient. The truth was still missing.

CHAPTER 86

The unlikely allies found Jeff Ryan tense and red-eyed when they entered his hotel room. He was dressed in a white T-shirt, khaki pants, and brown loafers.

"How are you feeling this morning, Jeff? We brought up some coffee," Bryce said, directing the patrolman who had accompanied him to wheel in a coffee service provided by the hotel.

Charlie grimly shook hands with the city manager as the police chief began pouring steaming coffee into white ceramic cups.

"To tell you the truth, not good," Ryan said. "I couldn't sleep. I kept replaying last night over in my mind. I still can't believe what happened. I can't believe Jason is dead. Have you found the guy or heard anything about him?"

"No, haven't found him yet," Bryce said. "Got a heck of a lot of people looking, though."

Charlie stirred cream and sugar into one of the cups and took a sip, thinking about how to begin a conversation he knew would not end well.

"I know you were really shook up last night, Jeff," he said. "Maybe it would be good if you started from the beginning. You were so out of it, I didn't get to hear what happened directly from you."

Charlie set his cup and saucer on the coffee table and took a notebook and pen from his back pocket.

"Mind going over it again? From the point where the guy confronted you. Was that on the terrace? Or did he come to the front door?"

Unlike last night's questioning, Chief Bryce made no attempt to intervene. He had placed his white cap with its gold stars and black patent leather visor on a side table and seated himself in an armchair by the window.

Ryan sat on the sofa, leaving Charlie to pull out a straight-back chair from behind the escritoire. He placed the chair to the side of the sofa so the chief could have a clear line of sight to Ryan.

The city manager began to recite the events of last evening exactly the way he had given them to the chief. He restated that he didn't know the gunman, had never seen him before, and believed the man had to be out of his mind, perhaps high on drugs.

Charlie took notes, wondering as he wrote when the chief would interrupt and challenge Ryan's account.

"Can you tell me about the conversation you had with the gunman?" Charlie asked. "Did you ask him anything about himself? Like where he was from?"

Ryan closed his eyes and rubbed the thumb and fingers of his right hand along the bridge of his nose. "It was so fast," he said looking down at his lap. "One minute I was on the terrace picking up ashtrays, and the next minute the guy was standing there with a gun on me, telling me to call the mayor and ask him to come over to my house immediately. He didn't give me time to ask questions. He pushed me inside with the revolver and forced me to the phone. I called Jason and just said, 'Get over here quick.'"

"What did the two of you talk about while you were waiting for the mayor?" Charlie asked.

"I asked what he wanted. He said he had come to collect what was owed him. He said Michael Sizemore had embezzled money from him and he wanted it back. He couldn't get it from Sizemore, so he planned to get it from the City of Bethany."

"Did you ask him why he couldn't collect from Sizemore himself?"

Ryan shook his head.

Rising from his chair, the chief broke in. "Isn't it true you didn't ask him that because you knew Michael Sizemore was long dead?"

The city manager looked up wide-eyed at the police chief.

"What? What are you talking about?"

The police chief walked over to the sofa, glaring at Ryan with contempt. He'd had enough of the bogus interview. His longtime friend had been murdered in cold blood. He himself might have been able to save Jason if he had acted more decisively when the mayor called for help. This man sitting here, a city official he had trusted and respected, was telling lies and wasting his time.

"Jeff, I'm going to give you a chance to tell the truth about what happened. From the beginning. If you talk straight, I'll make sure your cooperation is noted. If you don't, you and I might as well have never known each other, and I couldn't care less what happens to you. You got that?"

The chief opened the hotel room door and motioned for the patrolman to come in.

"What'll it be? You want to talk here? Or shall I arrest you on suspicion of aiding and abetting the murderer of Jason Eberle?"

CHAPTER 87

The usually self-assured city manager of Bethany, Iowa, put his head in his hands and wept. After a moment, the chief, unmoved, tapped Ryan on the shoulder with a box of tissues.

"I'll tell you what you want to know," Ryan said, pulling a couple of tissues from the box and wiping his eyes.

Bryce nodded and pulled the armchair from its place by the window to a spot across from Ryan.

Charlie checked his watch. He would have to trust Bob Hartman to keep today's edition on track.

"Who shot Jason, and how do you know him?" Bryce asked.

"His name's Eugene Montgomery."

The police chief and the managing editor exchanged skeptical glances but said nothing.

"Jason and I were introduced to him by Fred Whitlock, a fellow we met a few years ago in Des Moines," Ryan continued. "Fred had invited us to do some business with him and his partner, Michael Sizemore, who lived in California. We took him up on the offer."

"How did Montgomery enter the picture?" Bryce asked.

"He somehow had made a connection with Fred Whitlock. We never understood how or why. When Fred died in 1971, Michael Sizemore told us he was going to end all of his business dealings in Iowa; Montgomery didn't like that. He insisted on having a meeting with Michael, Jason, and me to talk things over.

"Michael was reluctant to meet, but I think he wanted to end the thing on agreeable terms. He said he'd fly to St. Louis from LA on June seventeenth, and then drive up here in a rental car in time for a three o'clock meeting.

"Jason and I got to the farm at three that afternoon." Ryan closed his eyes and sat silently for a moment.

"Go on," Bryce said. "What happened?"

"When Jason and I pulled up, there was only one car in the driveway. It was a rental. Montgomery was standing in a grassy area, toward the side of the house. I wondered what he was doing out in the yard and where Michael was. When we got out of Jason's car, Montgomery waved us over."

The city manager paused, his face losing color.

"As we got closer, we saw Michael . . . his body, lying face down in the grass. Montgomery had struck him at the base of his skull with a baseball bat. There wasn't much blood, but we could tell he was dead."

Larry Bryce stood up and walked to the hotel room window, trying to collect his thoughts. He had no stomach for what he had seen last night or what he was hearing this morning. Violent crime was not what he had signed on for. Yet he had to keep going.

"Did this 'Eugene Montgomery' tell you why he had killed Michael Sizemore?" Bryce asked, turning back to Ryan.

"No. He just sneered at us when we asked him. He said he

wasn't there to answer our asinine questions, that we were his now and that we would do what he told us."

"Did he threaten to kill you?" Charlie asked, looking up from his notebook.

"Not in so many words. He didn't have to. As soon as we got close enough to see Michael's body, Montgomery pulled a gun that he had hidden behind his back, in his belt. He had gone from being an annoyance to a ruthless killer, right in front of us. We were scared out of our minds."

"So what did he tell you to do?" Bryce asked.

"First, he made me turn the body over. He gave me the key to unlock a pair of handcuffs on Michael's wrists. Montgomery had a bag, like the ones they use for softball equipment. He put the cuffs, the key, and the bat into the bag. Then he made me go through Michael's pockets and take everything out. I removed his wallet, some keys, a handkerchief, and some change and dropped it all in the bag. Then he ordered me to remove Michael's watch, a ring off his right hand, and a medal from around his neck and put those in the bag, too.

"Montgomery said it was our job to hide the body where it wouldn't be found. If we did it right, he'd never come back. Then he walked to the car, carrying the bag, and yelled to us, 'Don't worry. I'll make sure Sizemore's rental car gets back where it belongs!' and drove off."

"What did you do after Montgomery left?" the chief asked.

"We panicked. We wanted to come and tell you, but we didn't believe Montgomery would leave the area till he was sure we'd gotten rid of the body. If we had reported the murder, it would have been in the newspaper. We were afraid Montgomery would read about it and find a way to kill us before anybody could stop him. The only thing we could do right then was hide the body as best we could. I found the paint tarp in the basement of the farmhouse. We put the body in it, rolled it over to the barn and hauled it up into the hayloft.

"We didn't mean to leave him there forever. We thought when there was no news of the killing in the paper, Montgomery would go away. And then, after a while, we could tell you what happened. But whenever I brought it up to Jason, he wasn't ready to deal with it."

The police chief stood up again and walked away. Then he turned and strode quickly back to the city manager.

"I can't believe you could have been such frigging idiots!" he exploded, spraying saliva in Ryan's face, his own face turning red. "The highest officials in our town and you help a killer cover up a murder and let him get away! How could you look at yourself in the mirror every day?"

Ryan said nothing. He lowered his head and slumped deeper into the sofa, motionless.

"Jeff Ryan, I'm placing you under arrest for aiding and abetting the murderer of Michael Sizemore and obstructing justice in a felony investigation."

CHAPTER 88

It was 4:30 p.m. when Carol arrived home in a black, unmarked Plymouth Fury, driven by an on-duty trooper from the Iowa State Patrol. She was surprised to see Jack Padgett sitting out front in his police car.

"It's real good to see you in one piece, Carol," he said, approaching the passenger side of the car.

"Thanks, Jack. Are you my welcoming committee?"

"Actually, I am. I got a key from your landlord a little while ago, and me and Wilson went through your apartment, dusted for prints, and took the towel that's got the guy's blood on it. We left everything else the way it was. I want you to take a look around while I'm here."

Carol turned to the trooper behind the wheel. "I guess this means you don't have to go inside with me. Thanks a million for driving me home."

She got out of the car dressed in a pair of borrowed jeans, a blue and white striped sleeveless blouse, and a pair of white Keds. She opened the car's rear door, retrieved a brown paper bag containing her clothes, and gave a wave to the trooper.

"Oh, just so you know, Carol," Padgett said as he pushed the key into the lock and opened the door of her apartment, "I made sure all of your windows are now *locked*."

Walking into the kitchen, Carol saw a mess scattered on the kitchen floor. An empty HoJo's bag, French fries, ketchup packets, pickles, and a lonely bun. "Simba, you little devil!" she said with relief as she picked up the kitten. "You ate the whole hamburger!"

CHAPTER 89

Padgett took notes as Carol walked through her apartment and described the sequence of events from the time she had arrived home the night before until she escaped the killer's car on the road to Des Moines.

Then she turned the conversation to her friend.

"Have you seen Joan today?"

"I saw her, but she didn't see me," Padgett said. "She was sleeping soundly when I went by around nine thirty this morning. The nurse said she'd had a pretty restful night, all things considered." He looked at his watch. "You going to make it over there today?"

"That's my plan. First, I've got to find my spare keys. Couldn't manage to get both myself *and* my purse out of the car."

"That reminds me," Padgett said. "You should get your door lock changed tomorrow."

Just as he spoke, the phone rang in the kitchen.

"Well, that's some good news, anyway," she said into the receiver after listening for a moment, giving a thumbs-up to

Padgett. "No sign of Mitchell though? Okay. I really appreciate that. Thanks a lot. I will."

"The state patrol found the Cutlass abandoned on a farm road near Colfax," Carol said as she hung up the phone. "The officer said they found my purse, with wallet and keys, still in the car. They're going to get it down to me via a relay of patrol cars. He said they should have it here by nine tonight."

"But no trace of the bad guy?" Padgett said.

"Not yet. He might be sneaking through farm fields on foot, or maybe he thumbed a ride with somebody who hasn't heard there's a bloody murderer on the loose. Who knows?" Carol said with a shudder.

CHAPTER 90

On the elevator ride up to the fourth floor of Bethany Memorial Hospital, Carol urged herself to remain cheerful and composed. But when she saw her friend lying in the hospital bed, both wrists covered with white gauze bandages, emotion overtook resolution. Tears welled up as she gently hugged the friend she had come so close to losing.

"Thank you for saving my life, Carol," Joan said in a voice softer than the one Carol was used to hearing. "The doctor said if you and Sergeant Padgett hadn't gotten there when you did, I would never have made it. I was so drugged I would have either drowned or bled to death."

"Hey, what are friends for?" Carol said, quickly brushing tears from the corners of her eyes. She refused to imagine what would have been the certain outcome if she had waited until Tuesday to check on her friend.

Although Joan was still very weak, she was alive, and she would recover from this ordeal. There'd be plenty of time for them to revisit what had happened. Right now, though, she didn't want to say anything that would cause Joan to recall yesterday's horror.

Joan, however, had a different idea.

"My cousin Michael was murdered by the man who did this to me," she said, raising her wrists slightly off the bed.

"I'm so sorry, Joan."

Without hesitation, Joan began to tell Carol about the man she had believed was her cousin. He had knocked on the farmhouse door Monday afternoon around four thirty. Joan hadn't expected to see him until the next morning. She was delighted when he introduced himself on her front porch.

"He seemed so happy to see me," Joan said, shaking her head wistfully. "I invited him in and apologized for not being able to have dinner with him."

Carol simply nodded and listened, knowing Joan had heard nothing of the mayor's murder, Jeff's arrest, or her own abduction. Out of concern for her condition, the police had postponed asking Joan any questions.

"I didn't have much time before I had to start getting ready to leave for Jeff's. I fixed us both a drink, and we sat at the kitchen table. He asked about my parents, and I told him they were over in Rome with the pastor of St. Gabe's and some other parishioners. I described my plans for remodeling the house and told him a little about my editing work. He seemed just as nice as all those times we talked on the phone."

"What happened that made him change, Joan?" Carol said, curiosity getting the better of her.

Joan put her head back on the pillow and closed her eyes, recalling the scene.

This was exactly what Carol had feared would happen if she started asking questions. Foolishly, she had asked anyway.

"I'm so sorry," Carol said, leaning forward and taking her friend's right hand. "Please don't think about any of it now. We'll talk about it later. When can you go home?"

Joan opened her eyes and smiled appreciatively.

"I should be discharged on Saturday. The doctor said I just need to let my body rest and recuperate."

Carol rose to leave, hiding her own exhaustion.

"Then rest and recuperation must start immediately, my friend. I'll call you tomorrow and come back to see you tomorrow evening. Tonight, get some sleep."

CHAPTER 91

"Yeah. Get some sleep," Joan repeated after Carol left. "Easier said than done."

The fatigue was still there, but the deep drowsiness was gone. How long would it take to fall asleep when she turned off the light? She put her head back on the pillow. Immediately, involuntarily, she relived the previous night.

* * *

They were sitting at her kitchen table. He seemed sincerely interested in hearing about their family back in St. Louis.

About five fifteen, she said she had to go upstairs and get ready for the dinner party at the city manager's home. She told him about meeting Jeff Ryan in the bakery, their impromptu date, and his invitation to join in celebrating the success of Bethany's festival.

On hearing Jeff's name, the man she had welcomed as a long-absent cousin snapped his fingers and said he had left something in his car. When he came back in the house with a leather carry-on bag, he was visibly enraged.

"What's wrong, Michael?" She rose from the table, anticipating she might have to defend herself.

It was too late. He pulled a small handgun from the back of his belt, aimed it at her, and told her to sit down. She was so startled by the change in his behavior that at first she was more puzzled than scared.

"What did I say to make you angry?"

He laughed. A sardonic, humorless laugh.

"You are a stupid bitch; do you know that, Miss Sizemore?"

His words slapped her across the face. This wasn't her cousin. Who was he? What was he doing here?

"There are two kinds of women in the world. You are of the kind easily duped by bull-shitters like your City Manager Jeff Ryan. So ignorantly innocent, you can't tell when you are being whoremongered. You are too stupid to live."

She tried to straighten up in the chair without seeming to move. This was a dangerous man whose raw fury was directed not at her but at some woman he imagined her to be.

Should she pretend to agree with him? Argue with him? Was there any way she could defuse his rage?

She took a stab. "Where's my cousin Michael?"

"Shut up! Don't you want to know the second kind of woman?" he asked, moving closer to her.

She could see perspiration popping out on his forehead and upper lip. The edges of his trimmed hair were wet with sweat, turning it a darker brown.

"The second kind of woman is like my dear, dead wife Amanda. The kind who seem to be innocent." He paused. "But aren't.

"Eventually, they wind up whoring with bull-shitters like your cousin Michael. When they find each other, it makes no difference who they are pledged to or what they have promised. They'll sneak and connive until they are together." He paused and smiled. "They wanted to live together. I made sure they died apart."

"You killed my cousin?"

"Who do you think that skeleton was, Miss Sizemore?"

* * *

Tears ran down her cheeks as she lay in the hushed, sterile hospital room, a world away from the peaceful drone of cicadas and the smell of freshly mown grass.

"Eternal rest grant unto him, O Lord. And let perpetual light shine upon him. May his soul, and the souls of all the faithful departed, rest in peace," she prayed.

CHAPTER 92

Opening Tuesday afternoon's edition of the *Bugle* had been like opening Pandora's Box.

The town's beloved mayor had been brutally murdered, shot in the head at close range, bravely taking the bullet for his friend Jeff Ryan.

The once-respected city manager had resigned and was awaiting arraignment on two felony charges, including abetting murder by hiding Michael Sizemore's body in the old Sizemore barn two years earlier.

The *Bugle*'s city editor had been abducted and had narrowly escaped being killed by the same gunman who shot the mayor and crushed Michael Sizemore's brainstem with a baseball bat.

The killer, known by several aliases, was still at large, fleeing on foot, or by car, or hiding somewhere.

His last known contact was with a man who had stopped to assist him on State Highway 163, near Prairie City, early Tuesday morning. Gil Stanton, fifty-two, of Des Moines, was barely alive when troopers from the Iowa State Patrol arrived at the scene.

Before he died from loss of blood as the result of a gunshot wound to the stomach, Stanton told police that a man with his left arm in a sling had fired at him without a word and taken off in a dark sports car, headed west.

CHAPTER 93

Carol arrived on the *Bugle*'s parking lot at 7:00 a.m. on Wednesday, just as Charlie Vogler was letting himself in the side door. He waited and welcomed his city editor with a hug and a happy grin.

Upstairs in the newsroom, everything looked the same as it had on Monday. But it didn't feel the same to Carol. Two days before, she had sat at her word processor writing a happy wrap-up of an old-fashioned street fair. Today, her topics would be a city manager accused of two felonies, a city government in shambles, and a cold-blooded killer on the loose.

"How naive we were!" she said to no one.

"Naive! Who's naive?" Charlie's voice echoed behind her.

She swiveled her chair to face him. "Charlie, you startled me!"

"Relax, Carol," he said softly. "I didn't mean to scare you. When you say something, don't I usually say something back?"

He walked over to her desk, grabbing a straight-back chair as he went. He turned it around with one hand and flopped down on the seat, his legs straddling the back of the chair.

"It's really good to have you back in one piece," he said. "I can't describe what this place was like yesterday. Besides all we had to do, I thought the guys were going to lose their minds thinking about what might have happened to you. We were all slap-happy by the time we got the paper out. And by the way, we couldn't have done it nearly as well without your help."

"I'm just glad I was able to do something besides sit around waiting for a ride home," Carol said.

In their second phone conversation Tuesday morning, Charlie and Carol had decided she should stay in Prairie City and report by phone from the farmhouse until the *Bugle* went to press.

Knowing she would be there awhile, Carol had accepted the offer of a shower, dry clothes, and breakfast from Emily and Andy Dakins, the couple who had given her refuge when she knocked on their door before dawn.

After devouring coffee, scrambled eggs, ham, and buttered toast, Carol had answered questions from a couple of state troopers regarding the events of the previous night and early morning. In return, they told her about the gunshot fatality on Highway 163 and what they were doing to find the man they now referred to as Frank Mitchell. Carol then called Ron Davidson at the *Bugle* to give him that information for his article on the manhunt.

Then she had scribbled out an account of her abduction and escape, retelling Frank Mitchell's story of revenge in just the broadest strokes since she wasn't sure which details were true and which might be the products of a killer's megalomania. She had dictated the story to Bob Hartman over the phone.

"Well, well, well, if it isn't our city editor, safely returned!" Bob boomed as he entered the newsroom.

There were dark circles under his eyes, but his face bore a smile as he approached Carol's desk and just barely refrained from hugging her.

"You doing okay? What time did you get back to town?"

She'd only been absent from the newsroom one day, yet it seemed she had just returned from a long foreign tour of duty. Carol told him about being chauffeured from Prairie City, meeting Jack Padgett at her apartment, and visiting Joan in the hospital.

"How is she doing?" Hartman asked, morosely shaking his head as he had done more than a hundred times since five o'clock yesterday morning.

"She's weak but otherwise seems okay. The doctor told her she can go home Saturday."

"Does she know how close she came to dying?"

Carol nodded, steadfastly refusing to revisit her own graphic memories of Joan's ordeal. Today, tomorrow, and in more days to come, she would be reporting on the swirl of disaster that arose from the dust of Michael Sizemore. Thinking about it was something that could wait till later.

CHAPTER 94

Unlike Bob Hartman, Ron Davidson and Tom Matthews were not shy about giving Carol elated hugs when they arrived in the newsroom. But, true to form, Tom couldn't resist tempering his affection with a little teasing.

"I was so relieved to know you were safe," he said wryly. "I was able to watch the entire All-Star game without any distractions."

The reference to yesterday's nationally televised baseball game, which under normal circumstances she too would have watched, only accentuated Carol's feeling of having just dropped in from another country.

Charlie suggested she take the afternoon off and get some rest, but she refused, preferring the company in the newsroom to the quiet of her apartment.

Jeff Ryan's arraignment was slated for 3:00 p.m. Carol didn't expect any real news to come from his courthouse appearance, since everyone who read Tuesday's newspaper already knew that the city manager planned to plead not guilty to the felony charges. Charlie had quoted Ryan saying as much in the article about his arrest.

"Under the circumstances," Ryan had said at the police station, "I can't stay on as city manager. I'm not resigning because I'm guilty of anything but because Bethany needs a full-time city manager, and my time is going to be taken up defending myself. I'm confident that when a jury learns everything, if this case even goes that far, they'll understand why Mayor Jason Eberle and I did what we did, and I'll be judged innocent."

Carol wanted to know exactly what more there was to "understand" about Ryan's and Eberle's actions the day Michael Sizemore was murdered.

After returning from lunch with Tom and Ron, she asked Charlie to tell her again about the statement Ryan had made in his room at the Hawkeye Hotel. "Jeff said they 'panicked'?"

"Yeah," Charlie answered. "Ryan said he and the mayor were afraid Eugene Montgomery would stick around town. If they went to the police right away, he would read about it in the paper and find a way to kill them. Their plan, presumably, was to wait long enough to make sure Montgomery had gone back to Des Moines."

"Did Ryan say how long they planned to wait? A week? A month? Four years?"

"No, he didn't say. That's where Ryan seemed to want to hang all the blame on Jason Eberle. He said, 'Whenever *I* brought it up, *Jason* didn't want to deal with it.'"

Carol doodled in her notebook as they talked. During his monologue in the car on the way to Des Moines, Frank Mitchell had told her that Eberle and Ryan were willing to do whatever he told them to do. But Mitchell hadn't told her what made him so confident about their silence. She shook her head.

"Something's not right, Charlie. The longer they waited to tell the police about Sizemore's murder, the harder it became to tell the truth. I can understand that. But at the start, they were innocent bystanders. What made them so willing to become accomplices?"

"That's what *you* still have to find out, ol' girl," Charlie said.

She walked over to the state editor's desk.

"Bob, imagine for a moment that you're an upstanding member of the community, an honest man. You come upon a murder that you had absolutely nothing to do with. The murderer tells you to dispose of the body and not tell anyone, and then he takes off. What would you do?"

Bob Hartman leaned back in his cushioned swivel chair and clasped his hands over his head.

"You mean *after* I picked myself up off the floor?"

"Yes, after that, of course."

He squinted as he mulled the hypothetical. "Seriously, I'd go to the police. Not without fear, mind you. I'd tell the police what happened, describe the killer and his car, and ask for a round-the-clock bodyguard till the guy was locked up."

"That's what I thought an honest, upstanding citizen like you would do. Anybody would be afraid of retribution, but for two city officials to hide a murder for two years is a little . . . ."

Bob had gone to work filling his pipe. He pressed the tobacco down into the briar's bowl.

"Remember what I said about motive, Carol? Money, power, sexual jealousy, revenge . . . . If Frank Mitchell can be believed, *his* motive for murder was to avenge the infidelity of his wife and her lover. But you've got to find Eberle and Ryan's motive for cooperating."

CHAPTER 95

Carol had a few minutes to spare before leaving for the courthouse, so she decided to make the call. A woman answered on the second ring and handed the phone off as soon as the reporter identified herself.

"I thought you might be calling," James McFarland said.

"Have you seen your brother-in-law, Mr. McFarland?"

"No, but if I do, I'll kill him."

Carol could hear McFarland's wife making scared, worried noises in the background, trying to shush and soothe her husband at the same time.

"You know the state patrol is looking for him. Have you talked with them yet?" Carol asked.

"What's the point of talking to them? If he comes here, I shoot him. Then I call the Des Moines police and tell them they can pick up his dead ass. If he doesn't come here, I can't help them. They should know how to track down the sonuvabitch bastard better than me."

In spite of herself, Carol had to smile at the man's fierce logic.

"You and your family could be in serious danger, Mr. McFarland. I just spent several hours with Frank Mitchell. In the last two days, he's murdered two people in cold blood, almost killed a friend of mine, and would have killed me if I hadn't been able to get away. He's on the run, and he's desperate. He might come to you thinking you'll help him."

"You don't have to tell me what a murderer he is. He killed my sister Amanda and made it look like she took her own life. We'll just see who's in serious danger if he shows up here."

"I know about your sister's murder, and I'm very sorry. How did you find out her death wasn't a suicide?"

She heard a deep sigh on the other end of the phone and guessed McFarland was debating with himself about whether or not to say any more to a reporter. She stayed silent, checking her watch, hoping he would keep going. It was twenty minutes to three. It would take her less than five minutes to get over to the courthouse.

"After you called me last week, I decided it was time for me to do some investigating of my own," he said.

Then, for the next several minutes without pause, James McFarland poured out the story of his visit to 403 San Gabriel Drive. It seemed to make no difference that Carol was a reporter. At that moment, a listening ear on the other end of the line was enough to remove the cork.

CHAPTER 96

The arraignment was an unremarkable event, except for the fact that Jeff Ryan was the only city manager in Bethany's history ever to have been brought before a judge on criminal charges.

Charlie could deal with that civic failure on the editorial page if he cared to.

Tomorrow's page-one story would report only that Ryan had pleaded not guilty to the two crimes with which he had been charged. It would include the news that Ryan was released on his own recognizance and that Judge Clay Ferguson, one of Iowa's senior judges, had scheduled the start of the trial for Wednesday, August 22, at the Lee County Courthouse in Fort Madison. Neither the city manager nor his attorney had had any comment for the press.

After the four-minute proceeding for Ryan, most of the spectators left the courtroom. The rest of the court's time had been taken up with several small claims cases.

It was a little before five when Carol left the courtroom. She had promised Joan when they talked by phone that morning that she would bring two carry-out dinners to the hospital at six thirty. Rather than drive home and come back downtown again, Carol decided to go back to the newspaper and work on some articles for tomorrow's edition.

She arrived at the *Bugle* just as Tommy Goodwin, manager of the advertising department, was exiting the building through the front door.

"What are you doing here, Carol? After what you've been through, I should think you'd be home getting some rest."

"I've got a little time to kill before I visit a friend in the hospital. What better place to spend it than at the *Bugle* right?"

"There ya go!" he said with a laugh, holding the door open for her. "I'll leave you to lock it up then. Have a nice evening."

"You, too, Tommy," she said, closing the door and turning the deadbolt.

The first floor of the *Bugle* was still bright from the late afternoon sun, but with the fluorescent lights turned off and the presses and typesetting machines silent, Carol had the feeling she was intruding on the building's well-earned peace and quiet.

She went upstairs to the newsroom, intending to get some of the news from the courthouse written by 6:10. Then she would pick up two fried chicken dinners at HoJo's and visit Joan in the hospital.

"Advantage Number Fourteen to living in a small town: Nothing is more than five minutes away," she said out loud as she sat down at her computer screen.

The Jeff Ryan article would be a clear-cut report on what had happened in the courtroom plus the obligatory background information, which she knew by heart.

Breaking news is always the easy part, Carol mused, as she finished the lead and started recapping the events that led up to the arraignment. In the next several days, she would have to write a longer, more difficult article about how two popular public servants had become ensnared in a toxic plot of revenge and why they decided to ignore the law.

"You're working late, Carol."

Startled, she spun around in her chair. Standing in the doorway between the newsroom and the advertising department was Frank Mitchell. He was dressed in a deliveryman's uniform—khaki slacks, ball cap, and jacket with the name "Greg" stitched in red lettering above the breast pocket.

Carol sprang to her feet. "How did you get in here?"

Mitchell showed the humorless smile she had first seen two nights earlier in her kitchen.

"You have a problem with surprise entrances, don't you, Carol? Maybe one day, if you had more days coming, you might figure out how to lock your windows *and* hang onto your keys.

"What are you talking about? I've got my keys!"

"Oh, no you don't," he said, swinging a blue plastic key ring around on his right index finger

It was the key ring Charlie had given her on her first day of work, which held a key to the *Bugle*'s side door and one for the alarm switch. She winced, instantly realizing her mistake. When the state trooper had delivered her purse a little before nine last night, she had looked inside and seen her wallet and the keys to her car and apartment on the sterling silver key chain that was a gift from her mother. She had assumed everything else was still in place. Since Charlie had held the side door open for her this morning, she'd had no need to dig her office keys out of her purse.

"Why did you come back here?" she asked him. "You could be a thousand miles away by now."

"That would be nice for you. But I don't discourage so easily. There is still unfinished business for me here. I can't start my new life until all of the old is finished. It's taking me a little longer than I expected, but believe me, I *will* finish it."

"What do you plan to do?"

"I've got to take care of my three remaining friends in Bethany. I thought I'd start with you. Then visit Miss Sizemore in the hospital. And finally, *former* City Manager Ryan."

"You won't get away with this. The police are looking for you everywhere."

"Oh, yes. We do have to factor in the astute tracking powers of the Bethany police don't we?" he said, giving her the slippery, sarcastic smile she detested. "The fact is, Carol, I've managed to come back to the scene of the crime unnoticed, and I'll be able to leave the same way. My little yellow Acme Auto Parts truck blends right into this backwater."

He moved toward Carol's desk, putting the key ring in his pants pocket and pulling the .38 Charter Arms revolver from where it had been hidden under his jacket.

"Sit down," he ordered, waving his gun hand toward her chair.

She glanced at his left arm. He held it gingerly at his side, but a casual observer wouldn't know he was wounded. Keeping himself positioned between Carol and the newsroom doorway, Mitchell leaned over and looked at her desk calendar.

"Aha. 'Six thirty, Joan,'" he said, reading the note she had scribbled in the square for Wednesday, July 25. "It's time to call your sick friend and tell her you won't be able to visit this evening."

He pushed Carol's Rolodex in front of her.

"Find the number for Bethany Memorial Hospital and dial it," he said, putting the receiver to her ear. "Be sure to make up a really good excuse."

When he heard the hospital operator speak, he handed her the phone.

"Hello. Would you please ring Joan Sizemore's room?" she asked.

"Hi, Joan," she said in the most normal voice she could summon. "I'm really sorry about this, but I'm not going to be able to get over there tonight. I've got a lot of articles to finish here at the office." She listened. "Me, too. But the Cards' game will keep you entertained tonight. I'll get over there tomorrow for sure . . . . Have a good night's sleep."

"Good," Mitchell said as she hung up the phone.

CHAPTER 97

Joan tried to be cool when she heard Carol's reason for canceling, but she couldn't shake the disappointment. She was counting on her friend to help her get through this depressing time of lying in a hospital bed doing nothing but remembering.

For Carol to excuse herself by saying she had articles to write and to not even apologize for failing to bring her some real food for dinner was completely unlike her.

"Oh, grow up!" Joan chided herself.

She was reaching for the bedside call bell to request a dinner tray when a uniformed Jack Padgett knocked on her partially open door.

"May I come in?"

"One of my heroes! Of course you may come in, Sergeant Padgett!" she said, trying to sound cheerful.

After Joan thanked him for saving her life and he wished her a fast recovery, Padgett explained his visit.

"I think you know we need to ask you some questions about what happened Monday night. If you feel up to it, Officer Wilson and I would like to stop by tomorrow afternoon. Would that be okay?"

"Sure, I guess so," Joan said, wanting to help but not eager to talk about the experience.

"Thanks. Our shift starts at three o'clock. We'll come by at quarter after." He hesitated a moment. "And there's one other thing. I don't want to alarm you, but I think you should know that the man who tried to kill you is still at large. We've got area police departments, sheriffs' offices, and the state patrols in Iowa, Missouri, and Illinois all on the lookout for him. Our best guess is he's fled the area. But we can't take that for granted. We're keeping a close watch on the hospital grounds while you're in here."

"You think he knows I'm alive?"

"If he has read a newspaper or listened to the radio, he knows."

Since her admission to the hospital less than forty-eight hours ago, Joan hadn't seen or heard any news. Suddenly, it dawned on her the imposter's attempt on her life was news.

"This has been in the paper, hasn't it?"

Padgett nodded. He hated to be the one to break more bad news, but Joan would learn it all soon, no matter what. He decided to give her an abbreviated version of the other crimes her attacker had perpetrated.

Joan listened without a word. She was shocked and saddened to hear about Mayor Eberle's murder and Jeff Ryan's arrest. But the news of Carol's abduction was impossible to believe. She had just seen her last night, right here in this room, and Carol had said nothing about it.

"Why would she have kept that to herself?" she asked the police sergeant.

"Miss Sizemore," Padgett said, "Carol and I found you on the verge of death Monday night. There was no way she was going to come in here the next day and tell you her troubles. I hated having to tell you *tonight*."

Joan absorbed what Padgett said. Her next thought sizzled through her like an electric shock.

"I . . . I think Carol may be in danger right now!"

"What makes you say that?" Padgett asked.

"It seems silly, but this morning she promised to bring over carry-out dinners this evening. Right before you got here, she called and said she wouldn't be able to make it because she was still working. She *never* stays at the paper past four o'clock. And she didn't even mention the fact that we planned to have dinner together. It's not like her to break a promise so lightly."

"Well, there's been a lot going on in Bethany the past two days," Padgett said. "She probably does have more work than usual. How did she sound?"

Joan paused and thought about the brief conversation. "She sounded okay, but *what* she said was strange. After telling me she wouldn't be coming, she said I could listen to the Cardinals' game on the radio for entertainment. She knows I never listen to baseball games."

Padgett frowned. "There is no baseball game tonight," he said. "This is the All-Star break."

He said goodbye and was gone.

CHAPTER 98

"They do call this the 'morgue,' don't they?" Mitchell said with a chuckle, as he directed Carol to sit down at the table in the little room and locked the door. This would be the perfect place to end her life. It was windowless, and with the door closed, there was no chance anyone outside the building could hear a shot from the small revolver. He could take his time performing one of his last acts of revenge. He had proven, after all, to be a master of patience.

* * *

He sat waiting midway down the row of stools in front of Foley's polished mahogany bar and studied his reflection in the mirrored back wall. Clean-shaven, angular face. Neatly trimmed brown hair parted on the left. Brown eyes. Long-sleeved, light blue shirt, wrinkle-free, open at the neck. Nothing hard to look at. Nothing memorable. Natural camouflage for someone whose job is to observe, unnoticed.

Fred Whitlock would be here soon. Whitlock would be followed by whatever state-paid parasites or political cronies were on his agenda today.

He tapped his right index finger on the ice cubes in his club soda. Waiting.

Eureka!

Walking into Foley's and seating himself at the end of the bar closest to the door was the man he had been waiting for, the man he had seen in the café in Ottumwa, the man who was having an affair with his wife, the man he would soon bludgeon to death. Michael Sizemore.

Casually putting his right hand up to shield his face and pretending to survey the selection of liquors and liqueurs on the bar back, he took the measure of his enemy in the mirror.

The tall, tanned, trim Sizemore wore a white dress shirt under a brown suit jacket that fit perfectly across athletic shoulders. A few gray hairs were beginning to displace dark ones at his temples. Sizemore ordered Smirnoff on the rocks and coolly pulled a five-dollar bill out of a money clip and slid it under an ashtray.

He saw in Sizemore's reflection the face of a man who assumes he is everyone's superior. No surprise there. The world was full of Sizemore's ilk. Affluent and arrogant, attaching to other men's wives and girlfriends for sport and pleasure, born with radar for women whose innocence is a saccharine facade.

He watched, morbidly fascinated, as Sizemore sipped his vodka.

Suddenly, Sizemore rose to his feet and turned to face the door. He greeted Fred Whitlock with a smile and an outstretched hand. Sizemore picked up his drink and followed Whitlock to a table for four in sight of the bar.

They always band together, he thought, as he watched their reflections. Just then, two more men walked though Foley's doors. The tall one was about Sizemore's age; the shorter was in his mid-fifties. Both wore suits and ties. They headed straight for Whitlock's table.

"Jason! Jeff! Good to see you again!" Sizemore said, shaking their hands.

He smiled at himself in the mirror. The wait is over.

* * *

"We got interrupted last time, but that won't happen again, Miss Hagan," Mitchell said, taking off the khaki uniform cap and running his fingers through his trimmed brown hair. "I've got a little while before I begin my late shift as an orderly at Bethany Memorial. Got any more questions for me?"

CHAPTER 99

It was a little after six when Sergeant Jack Padgett parked his patrol car in front of Carol's Maverick on Main. He figured Carol had entered the building through the front door; he hoped she had left it unlocked. No such luck.

The *Bugle*'s large plate-glass window allowed Padgett to survey the unlit first floor and confirm it was unoccupied. If he knocked loudly on the door, Carol probably would be able to hear it up in the newsroom. But if Carol's reference to a nonexistent baseball game had been a furtive call for help, he might put her in more peril by announcing his presence.

Padgett had a hard time believing Frank Mitchell would be so foolish as to return to Bethany while everyone was looking for him. Still, Carol's account of Mitchell's behavior during the abduction told him they weren't pursuing a rational man.

There were no other cars in front of the building, so he checked the *Bugle*'s side parking lot. Vacant.

Turning back to scan Main more carefully, he noticed a yellow panel truck parked across the street, about a half block west. It was labeled "Acme Auto Parts." Padgett recognized the company name, but there were no Acme Auto Parts stores in Bethany. What was an out-of-town truck doing downtown after hours?

"Check out Iowa license 9-4853, issued in Wapello County," Padgett told the police dispatcher over the patrol car radio.

Within a few minutes, Padgett learned the truck was part of a fleet belonging to an Acme Auto Parts store in Ottumwa and not reported stolen.

Padgett peered into the storefronts near where the truck was parked. All the shops were closed. Where would the driver of an out-of-town truck be after 6:00 p.m. on a Wednesday night? If he was eating dinner, why wasn't he parked in front of the Brass Kettle or the Keg & Grill?

Once again, he called the dispatcher.

"Tell Officer Wilson to get over here to the *Bugle*, no siren or lights, and tell him to wait in his car. Call Charlie Vogler, too. Ask him to get down here fast and bring a key to the front door."

CHAPTER 100

Her survival, Carol was sure, was no longer in her own hands. She had escaped this man once. There was no way she would be lucky enough to do it again. The first time he held her captive, she had had a slim measure of control behind the wheel of a car. Now, seated in a chair by the library table, with Mitchell standing in front of the locked door with a gun pointed at her, she had not a crumb of control. Her only chance to contact the rational world had been the phone call to Joan. She had blown that chance.

Why in God's name did she ever think Joan would be able to decode a silly clue about an unscheduled baseball game? Heck, Joan was such a stranger to baseball it was hard to believe she was really a St. Louisan!

Why was she thinking about baseball? She must be losing her mind. She was minutes away from being shot to death and she had no serious thoughts.

What was Mitchell waiting for? Why didn't he just shoot her? Hadn't he seen the movies where the longer the bad guy waits to shoot, the more time the good guys have to stop him?

Time. That was what she needed. That was her only hope. She had to give somebody time to figure out that she needed help.

"I do have another question," she said. "What kind of business deals were Jason Eberle and Jeff Ryan doing with Whitlock and Sizemore?"

CHAPTER 101

Padgett walked east on Main toward the Brass Kettle Café and K.C.'s Keg & Grill. In the few minutes it would take Charlie Vogler to arrive at the newspaper, Padgett hoped to find an Ottumwa truck driver having a bite to eat.

In both establishments, his nose was greeted with the pungent odors of beer and overheated grease. His inquiries were greeted with shrugs and silence.

Padgett, feeling soggy in the lingering heat of the evening, pushed his hat back and wiped his forehead with a pocket handkerchief, then headed back to the *Bugle*.

A feeling of dread was rising in his gut. Over the last two days a seemingly invisible murderer had eluded law enforcement agents in three states.

When he had accompanied Carol on Monday night, he had found Joan Sizemore near death; he never suspected she was the victim of a murder attempt. Police were on the scene of the mayor's murder minutes after it happened, yet they failed to track the killer/kidnapper to Carol's apartment, barely three blocks from where Jason Eberle had been shot. State police and highway patrols couldn't find the wounded fugitive who had slaughtered an innocent motorist, even after the gunman abandoned his car in broad daylight.

This guy, Frank Mitchell or Eugene Montgomery or whoever the hell he was, seemed illusory. Yet the violence he left behind was real. And now he could be preparing to strike again, on Main Street.

Would he be able to do anything to stop it this time?

He saw Officer Matt Wilson and Charlie Vogler in front of the newspaper, watching him walk toward them, awaiting his explanation.

Quickly the sergeant told them why he had sped from the hospital to the *Bugle* and why he had called for them.

"Charlie, I hope I come off looking like a dope and that Carol's simply working in the newsroom. But we've got to get up there fast and find out for sure. I need you to give us the layout of the second floor."

The managing editor's congenial smile was gone. His skin had turned clammy when he heard Padgett suggest that Carol's abductor might have returned for her. He took a ring of keys from his pocket, selected the key for the front door, slid it off the ring, and handed it to Padgett. He took a notebook from his back pocket and drew a diagram of the second floor.

"The advertising department is an open space at the top of the stairs. There are restrooms just to the left, and those doors, of course, are always closed," Charlie said, trying to sound calm. "We always leave the doors to both the newsroom and the library open. The darkroom stays open, too, unless Kenny's in there. He's not working tonight.

"These doors all should be open," he said, pointing in turn to his sketches of the newsroom, darkroom, and morgue.

"Do you know how to operate a police car radio?" Padgett asked.

Charlie nodded.

"Good. Wilson and I are going in now," he said, looking intently at the managing editor. "Give us a few minutes to survey the second floor. If we're not back down in five, use my radio and ask the dispatcher to send another cruiser, no lights or siren. If Mitchell's up there, I think me and Wilson can handle him. The backup's only in case he makes a run for it. Wait for us out here."

CHAPTER 102

Standing inside the front door of the *Bugle*, the two policemen listened for the sounds of Carol tapping on a keyboard or talking on the phone. They heard nothing but their own shallow breathing. Padgett motioned that he would go up first, scout things out, and signal for Wilson to follow.

Crouching low at the top of the stairs, the police sergeant studied the space. The center of the advertising department had five outsized desks. The surfaces of the desks could be tilted upward when layout artists were pasting up ads. Around the room were wide cabinets with shallow drawers containing illustrations of every type of product ever advertised in a newspaper. With no dividing walls in the space, Padgett was relieved the room's heavy furnishings could provide cover if needed.

Beyond the main room, Padgett saw the newsroom door standing open. He couldn't see much beyond the doorway, but he heard no sounds from within except for the muffled clicking of the UPI and AP teletype machines.

The door to the darkroom also was open; the interior was still.

The door to the clippings library—the morgue—was closed.

Listening intently, Padgett could hear a faint voice coming from the library. His muscles tensed. If he and Wilson tried to enter that room and surprise the gunman, he might start shooting at anything in his path. Their only option was to lure him out of the room.

The droning from behind the closed door was a monologue, rather than a conversation. The speaker sounded calm, but Padgett had no idea how long that calm would last. They had to act quickly.

He had formed a plan even before signaling Wilson to join him. Mutely mouthing words and gesturing, Padgett directed the patrolman to enter the women's restroom. Then he positioned himself directly across from the restroom door, low to the floor, behind one of the large desks. He wiped his sweaty palms on his uniform trousers and drew his Smith & Wesson from its holster, willing his hand to stay steady.

Whoever walked out of this building alive would do so on the strength or weakness of his plan. In less than a minute, the suspect would hear a familiar, innocuous noise. If Padgett's instincts were right, the gunman would assume that some unlucky newspaper employee had arrived on the scene. The police officer hoped the gunman would emerge from the library alone to deal with the unarmed and harmless worker.

Padgett checked his watch.

Five . . . four . . . three . . . two . . . one . . .

CHAPTER 103

Frank Mitchell reflexively turned his head toward the door when he heard the flushing sound, and then looked back at Carol.

"Who is that?" he said. "Who would be coming here now?"

"I have no idea."

"Well, we'll have to find out, now, won't we?"

He motioned Carol up from the chair and got behind her, holding the revolver close to her back.

"Listen, bitch," he hissed in her ear. "You and I are going to deal with this very quickly. I will never take the gun off your back, so don't think you can run. I want you to unlock the door, and walk out in front of me but don't block my view; you understand? Stay right with me. I'll tell you when to move. Don't say a word unless I tell you to. Got that?"

Carol nodded, pulled back the slide bolt above the doorknob, and opened the door. The gun's muzzle grazed her blouse at the center of her back, just above her waistline. Her body shielded his, but he was tall enough to see over her head into the large room. Rays of evening sun angled through the tall windows of the second floor, casting a soft light. Nothing looked any different than it had when Mitchell had first entered.

He wondered why there were no more sounds. When someone uses the toilet, they flush, wash their hands, and leave the restroom. Yet he heard no water running, heard no one moving. Why would someone who came to work after hours not turn on a light, put something down on a desk, or make some noise other than flush a toilet?

Mitchell realized he was being decoyed. The someone in the bathroom was waiting in ambush. He smiled. Once again, he would outmaneuver the enemy.

He kept Carol in front of him and guided her with his gun hand toward the restroom doors. "Women" was the one closest to the morgue. He knew this was the one the ambusher would have chosen. In one continuous motion, Mitchell grabbed Carol's right arm with his left hand, shoving her back and to his side. He raised the revolver to chest level, kicked the door open, and fired two shots, shattering glass.

"Carol, down!" Jack Padgett shouted, as he rose from the floor, aimed his police revolver and pulled the trigger.

Carol immediately dropped to the floor. Mitchell's body fell forward, blood gushing from a hole near his Adam's apple where the .38-caliber bullet had exited.

Carol jumped up, spattered with blood.

"Are you okay?" Padgett asked, moving swiftly across the room.

She nodded and steadied herself against the edge of one of the large desks.

"Wilson, are you okay?" he said in a louder voice, the revolver still drawn.

Wilson walked out of the restroom, his gun in hand. "If a few bruised ribs from a door slamming into my chest are 'okay,' then I'm okay."

Padgett kicked the weapon away from the gunman and leaned down to check his left wrist for a pulse, just to make sure.

Frank Mitchell's dead eyes were wide open, revealing his final emotion: surprise.

CHAPTER 104

Carol's ears were ringing from the gunfire that had exploded near her head moments earlier. She had wiped Mitchell's blood from her face and arms with a damp paper towel, but still wore a spray of red speckles on her white blouse and light blue skirt.

When she walked through the *Bugle*'s front door onto Main Street, she saw a small, curious crowd gathered in front of the building, drawn by the sight of two Bethany police cars and an ambulance with lights flashing.

The heat and humidity engulfed Carol as it always did when she stepped out of the air-conditioned newspaper building and onto the sidewalk. This time, though, the heavy July air was not an encumbrance but a welcome embrace.

Not ten minutes before, she had been sure she was going to die, isolated in the chilly, windowless morgue. She'd had no profound thoughts. She just knew she loved her life and wanted more of it. Exactly as it was.

She felt a hand softly touch her shoulder. She turned and saw

Charlie, his eyes moist and his face filled with relief.

"Carol, are you okay?"

"I'm way better than okay, Charlie. I'm alive."

CHAPTER 105

Denny Hagan reached over and refilled his sister's wine glass with Burgundy. His two boys were on their way to bed, thanks to his wife, and the only noise left in the backyard was the crickets' chirping. The sweet aroma of barbecued pork steaks lingered on the screened-in porch where Carol and her brother relaxed on the last Saturday evening of July.

"Thanks for letting me invite myself to dinner," she said.

"You know you're welcome any time you're in town."

At Charlie's insistence, Carol had left Bethany for St. Louis as soon as her last article was down the chute.

"Go see your family, Carol, ol' girl," he had said.

After the events of the previous Wednesday evening, the managing editor had become a tad protective, and Carol hadn't argued.

The news of Mayor Eberle's death, Jeff Ryan's felony charges, the attempted murder of Joan Sizemore, Carol's narrow escapes, and Frank Mitchell's bloody end all had been reported in the *Bugle*.

The more complex saga of corruption, callous masquerades, and the cover-up of murder had yet to be written. Carol faced a week of finding sources and asking questions when she got back to the newsroom on Monday.

But tonight she had something else on her mind,

Uncovering secrets in Bethany had stirred up the questions she had had as a girl about her father near the end of his life. He had been ill, of course, but there was something more than that. Something had changed him in a way that seemed worse than illness. Her brother knew what it was.

She looked over at Denny's profile as he blew cigarette smoke away from the table and was surprised once again at how much he resembled her father. Being with Denny always made her both miss her father more and feel closer to him.

She recalled the evening of her twelfth birthday, sitting around another supper table. She had asked her brother why their father was unhappy in the months before he died and had received no answer.

Now, she asked again.

"What happened to Dad that last year?"

Denny Hagan looked at his sister straight on with an open expression that promised she'd hear the truth, like it or not.

"That last year was a long time ago. What specifically do you want to know?"

"I want to know what made him so sad. He was always happy and then, all of a sudden, he wasn't. Did it have something to do with that policeman who went to jail?"

"Not something. It had *everything* to do with that policeman who went to jail," Denny said.

"Was he innocent?"

Denny's face, illuminated by three short candles in the center of the table, was shaded with sadness. It was the same expression Carol had seen on her father's face the day he went to court in his police uniform.

"He was guilty," Denny said. "Officer Jake McCarthy stole money while he was on the job. He took it from crooks, but it was still stealing."

"I remember the day two plainclothesmen came to see Dad," Carol said. "They were asking about someone named Jake. Dad told them he was sure Jake hadn't done anything wrong. If the guy was guilty, why did Dad defend him?"

Denny took the last swallow of beer from a red plastic cup, knitted his hands together, and stretched his arms above his head.

"When Dad talked to the IA guys, he thought they were trying to pin the theft on McCarthy before they had all the facts. Dad didn't believe McCarthy would ever take money, so of course, he defended him."

"You guys need anything out there?" Denny's wife said through the pass-through.

"Another Busch would be good, hon," he said. "And would you mind grabbing me another pack of cigarettes off the dresser?"

"What did Jake McCarthy actually do?" Carol asked.

Her brother slid his chair back, crossed his legs, and began a story filled with infamous and familiar Italian and Irish names and inside information only a cop, or the worshipful son of a cop, would remember from sixteen years before.

The incident had taken place at an old Hall Street warehouse the Detroit Mafia used as a clearinghouse for the cash from their bookie joints in North St. Louis and across the river in East St. Louis. The Fifth District officers who planned the raid had chosen their best cops to storm the warehouse. They arrested three high-profile racketeers, plus an assortment of thugs, and seized about a hundred fifty thousand dollars. Officer Jake McCarthy had pulled the assignment of transporting the confiscated cash downtown. Somewhere between Hall Street and headquarters, McCarthy put his hand in the kitty and pulled out ten thousand for himself.

While Denny talked, his wife rejoined them on the porch, carrying beer and cigarettes. Her cheerful expression clouded over when she heard the conversation. She poured herself another glass of Burgundy.

"So one of the good guys was really a dirty cop," Carol said.

"There was more to it than that. Dad had personally recommended McCarthy for the assignment. He couldn't believe somebody he handpicked would be such an idiot. He had put his reputation on the line and was ready to go to the mat for McCarthy."

"When did Dad learn the truth?"

"After the internal affairs guys came to our house that day, Dad went to visit McCarthy at his house," Denny said. "McCarthy introduced Dad to his wife and to his eight-year-old daughter. The little girl had muscular dystrophy, and the doctor said she would get progressively weaker and be confined to a wheelchair or a bed for the rest of her life.

"McCarthy told Dad in private that the medical bills, on top of house payments and other stuff, were drowning him in debt and that he had taken the cash out of desperation. McCarthy said he knew right away it was a mistake, but since he had already lied about it, he figured he would lose his job if he came clean."

Carol felt anger rising toward the man she had never met.

"What the heck did McCarthy think Dad would do when he found out the truth? *Lie* for him?"

Denny lit another cigarette and stared into the yard for a long moment, as though waiting for the darkness to eclipse his bitterness.

"Dad told me that the only thing he could do was hope he wouldn't be called to testify," Denny said. "No such luck. All of the officers had to testify, and, of course, Dad told the truth. His testimony helped send McCarthy to jail."

Denny's inflection made it sound as though the story had come to an end. But Carol knew better. Hanging in the air was an unspoken epilogue. She didn't want to ask, but she needed to hear the whole truth.

"Did internal affairs go after Dad for not saying right away that McCarthy had taken the money?"

Denny blew air through his lips in a silent whistle and brushed his hands through his short, sandy blond hair.

"They called him in the day after the trial was over and questioned him about his association with McCarthy and when he had learned of the theft," Denny said in a heavy, even voice. "Dad told them exactly what had happened.

"A couple of days later, IA called him in again," Denny said. "They told him they believed that he hadn't been involved with the theft itself. They said he was a good cop and they wanted to give him a break, but they couldn't overlook the fact that he failed to come forward with what he knew about an ongoing investigation. He got a three-day suspension and a letter of reprimand in his file."

The three of them sat in pensive silence, staring at candles whose molten white wax was forming misshapen blobs on the checkered vinyl tablecloth.

Carol wished she could ignore the impact of what her brother had just told her, but she couldn't.

"That ended any chance Dad had for promotion, didn't it?" she said.

Denny nodded.

"Is that why you gave up on the police academy?"

He nodded again.

Carol recalled images of her brother sitting with her father at the kitchen table, drinking coffee in the late afternoon or after dinner, when everyone else had scattered. The father telling police stories and the son asking questions, wanting to know every detail of their shared passion.

She realized it must have been during those kitchen table sessions, in the summer and fall of 1957, that Andrew Hagan told his son this story, piece by piece. By the time he finished, her father knew he was seriously ill.

When her father died in the winter of '57, Carol had felt sorry for herself, absorbing only what a ten-year-old is able to understand of death. This evening, she felt a deeper sorrow for her father and her brother.

Her father had run out of time to redeem his mistake. Her brother was left with a lifetime to live with it.

CHAPTER 106

"Hey, Carol, you need a refill?" Joan asked as she pushed open the screen door, wine bottle in hand.

"No, thanks. Not yet. Will you be much longer?"

"Give me three minutes and I'll be there!" Joan said over her shoulder as she closed the door and went back inside.

The sun was beginning its descent as Carol relaxed on the front porch of the Sizemore farmhouse, a half glass of Chablis on the wicker table in front of her, and waited while Joan checked on their celebratory dinner of chicken Kiev.

Carol had spent the last week putting all the pieces of the skeleton puzzle together; the resulting article had been published in yesterday's *Bethany Daily Bugle*. And today, Saturday, August 4, it had been sent across Iowa and beyond, via the AP newswire.

Frank Mitchell had made his last contribution to the story that evening in the *Bugle*'s morgue, when Carol, stalling for time, had asked him about Eberle's and Ryan's business deals.

The killer boastfully told her how he had discovered Highway Commissioner Fred Whitlock's cross-country real estate scam while looking for a doorway into Michael Sizemore's life. He had used his discovery of the commissioner's abuse of power to coerce his way into the cozy quartet of Whitlock, Sizemore, Jason Eberle, and Jeff Ryan.

Mitchell had complained that he was deprived of the bonus pleasure of destroying Whitlock's fiefdom when the contractor succumbed to a heart attack.

Carol later had talked by phone with Nona Reynolds, the Los Angeles neighbor who unwittingly exposed Mitchell's masquerade when she told James McFarland it was "Martin Sizemore" in the photo with Amanda. Carol figured that Mitchell had stolen the identity of Michael Sizemore and created the identity of Martin Sizemore during the last week of June 1971.

"Michael Sizemore" was the role Mitchell assumed in written correspondence with the Sizemore family, or when he was on the phone with people who didn't know the real Michael's voice, or in person with people who didn't know what the real Michael looked like.

"Martin Sizemore" was the loyal cousin Frank Mitchell had fabricated so he could perpetrate his fraud in California—carrying on the Sizemore real estate business for his poor cousin Michael who was trying to recover from the tragic loss of his fiancée.

When Carol had asked Jeff Ryan to talk about his and Mayor Eberle's association with Fred Whitlock and Michael Sizemore, Ryan declared it was none of her business.

Acting on a hunch, Carol had compiled a list of Iowa's mayors and recruited help from her friend Erica Landers in Santa Monica. With the list in front of her, Erica was able to match eleven of those names with names that appeared on the deeds of sale that also bore the names Eberle, Whitlock, or Ryan in the period between 1969 and 1971.

Ten of the eleven mayors had refused to take Carol's phone calls. The only one who was willing to talk had terminal cancer. He said he wanted to clear his conscience about what he called his "unethical" conduct.

The FBI had begun an investigation of the transactions to determine whether the LA real estate purchases by Iowa officials were unethical or illegal. Carol simply reported on how the scheme had worked: For several years, Michael Sizemore had served as a real estate broker for a group of wealthy Californians, some whose wealth came from questionable sources. For various reasons, not the least of which was the need to launder money, the investors often preferred distance and anonymity in their land investments.

Fred Whitlock had been able to steer Sizemore's buyers to parcels of land in Iowa that were under confidential consideration for major development. In exchange, the California investors, with Sizemore as their conduit, had provided Whitlock and his cadre of Iowa politicos information about California properties that were going to appreciate in value over a period of years.

When Carol told Jeff Ryan that she had learned enough from her own investigation and from the dying mayor's confession to implicate both him and Eberle in the land scheme, Ryan had agreed to talk.

"Fred Whitlock described Michael Sizemore as a visionary," Ryan had told Carol. "Whitlock told us that by investing in their syndicate, we would receive a forty-to-fifty percent return on our money in five to seven years.

"Jason and I were both blown over by how simple it seemed. Then, when Fred introduced us to Sizemore in Des Moines, we were convinced. The way they explained it, Sizemore had found a way to take advantage of friends in high places without harming anyone. His clients in California got a low-profile place to put their money, and we got a very profitable long-term investment."

"Why did they limit their invitations to public officials?" Carol had asked.

"Whitlock only had access to the land information because he was on the highway commission. He believed that by recruiting men like himself, who also had reputations and offices to protect, he could guarantee the secrecy of the deals. And he was right.

"Whitlock treated Jason and me like we were close friends. When we heard that only guys like us were investing, we felt we were part of an exclusive club. But since he swore us all to secrecy, we never knew who the others were. Whitlock was protected because we all honored the promise of confidentiality."

When Carol asked how Frank Mitchell had gained entry into the club, Jeff Ryan had insisted he didn't know.

"Hell, we didn't even know his real name. But he knew who we were and how we had invested," Ryan had said. "He bought into a couple of our deals in Los Angeles right after he joined us. Jason and I thought he was a pain in the ass from the beginning. We had no idea who he really was or what he was up to."

Carol vividly remembered her last conversation with Frank Mitchell in the *Bugle*'s morgue. When she asked him about his relationship with Bethany's mayor and city manager, his icy response had given her chills.

"It was child's play to ensnare Eberle and Ryan as my accomplices," Mitchell had said. "Men who are seduced by the promise of easy money are the same ones who cover their asses out of cowardice or pride. Once they walked into the trap, I knew they were mine for the rest of their lives."

Despite the warmth of the August evening, Carol again felt a chill. Eberle and Ryan had tried to convince themselves they weren't doing anything wrong because what they were doing was no different than what other "good" men were doing. They couldn't imagine that their smug hypocrisy would be a route to violence and death.

Sitting on the porch of this ordinary farmhouse on a dusty rural road in the middle of America, Carol took little pleasure in the story she had just written. She felt vindicated, yes. And proud of her work. She hadn't caved in to authority or given in to self-doubt. She had simply dug beneath the official version of events and found the truth.

No happy ending. Just a good job.

About the Author

After three years of teaching high school students, Catherine Soete realized that putting ideas on paper was, for her, a truer calling than instructing teenagers how to do so. The University of Missouri's Journalism School opened the door to writing as a career, and she is forever grateful. She lives in St. Louis, Missouri, with her partner Amy and their furry kids, Romeo, Charlie, and Sofi. *Grave Secrets* is her first novel.

CPSIA information can be obtained at www.ICGtesting.com
Printed in the USA
BVOW02s1223110715

408371BV00001B/35/P